This book is for Cecilie.

I warned you before and I will probably warn you again…beware the Wendigo.
Also, eat lots of raw spinach because it's good for you.

Under Satan's Umbrella:

A Compilation of Twisted Tales

By

Steve Goldsmith

PublishAmerica
Baltimore

ISBN: 1-4137-9356-8
PUBLISHED BY PUBLISHAMERICA, LLLP
www.publishamerica.com
Baltimore

Printed in the United States of America

Contents

~*Boy in the Dark*~

Six-year-old Billy was asleep in bed. He was asleep but he wouldn't be for long. His eyes flickered as he rolled over onto his back, a hiss of breath leaving his mouth.

Then he heard the creak from beneath his bed.

His blue eyes sprang open. He could hear a scratching under his mattress.

Billy dived under his covers and held his breath, listening, listening.

His body shivered, his heart raced.

Stop being a baby, there is nothing under my bed, he told himself.

He gulped and lifted the covers enough to peek out, then feeling brave, pushed his whole head out. He saw the plastic wizard toy on his bedside table. It was six inches tall, had a grey beard, and wore blue robes. The wise wizard held a magic staff.

Billy stretched an arm out, reaching, reaching, the night's coldness wrapping around his skin. As he stretched, the sleeve of his Harry Potter pyjamas slipped away from his wrist as if the sleeve were too frightened to venture out into the room's darkness. Billy's arm was exposed, goose bumps sprouted. He grabbed the wizard and snatched it back under the covers with him, holding it tight.

Composing himself, he crawled to the edge of the bed. He had to check what that creak had been.

'Protect me,' he whispered to the wizard.

He leaned on his forearms, stretched his neck to the bed's edge, and then slowly, slowly, slowly hung his head down beyond the mattress. His blonde hair flopped, hanging limp. The blood rushed to his head. His eyes lowered below the wooden frame of his bed and he stared into the dark.

He could see the long shadows that were moon-beamed through the thin curtains and onto the carpet. The moon's light reached part way under his bed. He could see the arm of his Teddy bear. He watched it. He thought he could see Teddy's eyes. They were looking at him. *But they couldn't be*, he thought. *Teddy has closed eyes. He's supposed to be a sleeping Teddy, eyes sown shut.*

As Billy blinked, he was sure Teddy blinked also. His head began to heat as he watched. He suddenly pulled himself back up into his bed, breathing hard. He wanted to scream; he had to scream but he could find no voice. He remembered he had the wizard in his hand. He relaxed.

'Teddy's eyes weren't open, were they?' he asked the wizard.

He had to check.

He lowered himself again. He waited a few seconds for his eyes to adapt. Teddy's eyes *were* shut. He breathed out, relieved.

Falling back onto his pillow, Billy shut his eyes to sleep some more. He stretched and the tips of his toes peeped out the bottom of the covers. He pulled them in, feeling the cold, but as he did, he felt the cramp in his tummy. He needed to pee.

He tensed his stomach muscles—trying to fight off the need, lifting his legs slowly, not wanting to make any sudden movements, scrunching into a ball. The need to pee remained.

He turned his head towards his bedside clock. Where there should have been red digital glowing numbers, was just blackness. Billy stared at the clock for a few seconds then remembered the power cut. Just before he had gone to bed, he had been sitting watching TV with his mummy and daddy, and then the screen had flashed off. The lights also, making it all dark. Mummy had found a torch so she could see to tuck Billy into bed.

Still scrunched up, he began to rock, the way his mummy rocked his baby brother to sleep. Baby Harry. Harry had been born disabled. He hadn't any arms. Billy didn't know why exactly, but Mummy had explained that we should have faith in God's decisions. Billy wished God would take away his pee. His room was very dark; the shadowy shapes of his scattered toys seemed to move whenever he took his eyes from them.

Billy pushed his small fingers inside the trousers of his pyjamas, and he held his willy. He squeezed it gently to soothe the ache. He was a big boy now and he didn't want to be wetting himself. Not at aged six. The rhythm of the squeezing seemed to help but the pee remained. His tummy felt inflated, ready to explode. He would have to go to the bathroom.

As he slipped the wise wizard into his shirt pocket, he remembered last Christmas. He had already opened some of his presents before he saw a smaller one. It was smaller but it had a purple ribbon around it.

'What's this, Mummy?'

'Open it and you'll find out,' she said, smiling, holding baby Harry to her chest.

Billy shook the present and listened. It rattled a bit. He twisted his lips in thought then shook again.

'Open it, Bill,' his daddy said, dropping a chocolate into his mouth then chasing it down with the sherry Father Christmas had left with the crumbs from the mince pies.

Billy quickly tore at the wrapping paper, tossing it aside.

'*Oh, wow!*'

'It's the one from the adverts!' his mummy said, excited by her son's beaming smile. Billy had all but forgotten about his other presents, opening the pack to get at the wizard.

'Look. Now you've done it,' his dad had said to his mum. 'We'll never get that wizard away from him.'

Billy's mum sighed, playfully punching her husband's arm. Billy's dad gulped down the remainder of the sherry from the glass.

'And you aren't setting a very good example, are you? Drinking at...' she checked her watch, 'seven in the morning!'

'It's Christmas!' he replied, shrugging his shoulders. Billy was over by the Christmas tree now, making the wizard climb the branches and swing on the decorations.

'Show your brother, Billy,' his mummy said. Billy leaped up and ran over to Mummy, holding the wizard in front of Harry's slightly unfocused eyes. His little brother blinked, and then dribbled as he smiled.

A cold chill awoke Billy from his memories. He swung his legs round and over the edge of the bed—for a moment his searching toes could not find the floor. Then they touched down on the soft carpet. Billy sighed. He quickly stood and took a step away from the bed, turning his head back and staring to the underneath darkness. Just in case.

Billy now faced the door. His eyes were adjusting to the lack of light and he could see the toys nearest to him. One was a yellow truck lying in the position he had crashed it the previous day, the other was a mechanical monkey. With batteries in, it moved its arms and made monkey noises.

Something tapped on the window. Billy spun his head round. The moon was shining bright through the thin curtains. The branches of the giant, ancient tree swayed in the wind—its black limbs poking at the glass.

Again holding his willy, gently squeezing, he took a step forwards, keeping well clear of the monkey, gazing down at his bare feet as he placed each foot. After a few steps, he glanced up to the door. It seemed as if it was moving away from him.

The moon cast black shadows across the carpet. Billy lifted a foot, and then withdrew it, swaying on one foot as one of the long, arm-like shadows twitched directly beneath where he was to have placed his foot. The shadows were infesting the area of his floor, lifeless, and then whenever he moved, they wriggled like a pit of snakes. He could almost see their red eyes and hissing tongues. The hairs pricked up over his neck.

As he put a hand to his heavy beating heart, he felt the wizard through his shirt pocket. He took the wizard from the pocket, gazed at the little bearded face, and then held it towards the shadow serpents as if it were a crucifix. It worked—the serpents were suddenly dead. Motionless.

'Don't be scared,' he whispered. 'They're all dead.'

He stepped forwards, still holding the wizard at the end of an outstretched arm—his protection against the shadow serpents jerking into life again. They did too, but not until after he had passed. Glancing back, he watched as they twisted, span and hissed angrily at him having gone by safely. He took several deep breaths then glanced to the door.

'Not far now,' he said.

Then he saw the dark figure in the corner of the room. He waited for the goose bumps to assemble, and then swallowed. His mind was numb—then it raced with the possibilities of who the dark figure could be. He rubbed his eyes and looked again. The figure remained. He blinked hard twice. Still there. Gazed to his feet then up again. Still there. Glanced to his little toy wizard. But the dark figure remained in the corner of the room.

He drew air through his nose then gently released it from his mouth as he took a step forwards. Suddenly the figure was clear. *Real.* He took another step forwards, and another…another…

'Who are you?' Billy asked.

The dark figure did not respond.

Billy raised the little wizard and took another step forward. Then another step…

He stopped dead, heart pounding as the shape moved; simultaneously wind rattled the outside guttering. Billy had been an inch away from wetting himself, but he held it off with his squeezing fingers.

He looked up to the dark shadow of a monster, and gulped. If it were not for the shadow serpents on his floor, he would have run back to bed by now and hidden beneath his covers. He gazed to his inviting moonlit doused bed—the covers folded back and beckoning him to return to their warmth, to abandon his thoughts of peeing.

A creak from the corner of the room caught his attention. Billy's head twisted round violently, just in time to see movement in the darkness— followed by another creak and then his wardrobe door started to open, as if in slow motion. Billy gasped, ignoring the shadow serpents, running to his bedroom door, but expecting to feel their teeth sinking into his bare ankles, to hear their hisses.

At the door, panting, he turned and saw that the dark figure had moved, perhaps he'd hidden inside the wardrobe. As he stared to the black void inside the wardrobe, he could have sworn he saw a set of green eyes!

Billy pulled his bedroom door open, slipped out and shut it behind him, leaving his hand on the knob to stop anything trying to follow.

Six-year-old Billy was standing in the hallway. To his right was his parents' room. Should he wake them? That's what he would normally do, but he knew Daddy had a job interview the next day and the last time he had one of those and been woken, he'd complained to Mummy about not getting enough sleep. Billy heard his daddy telling his mummy that if he'd gotten his sleep, he would've gotten that job.

Billy turned his head and gazed along the hallway towards the white bathroom door. It was open just a crack. He breathed deep, still rhythmically squeezing his willy, hoping he could hold the pee long enough to reach the toilet. It was not far now, but the top of the stairs lay just beside the bathroom door, and from where he stood it looked like a black pit…from which anything might emerge.

Billy pressed his ear against the wood of his own door and listened. At first nothing, but then what he thought sounded like giggling. Or was it the gutters rattling again? He wasn't sure. As a floorboard creaked just beyond the door, Billy did now leap away, holding on to the railing, beyond which was the drop down the stairs. Billy closed his eyes and took deep breaths. He knew he couldn't hold the pee much longer, but he also knew he couldn't go back into his room tonight.

He raised the little toy wizard and started the journey to the bathroom. He took slow thoughtful steps, his ears alert for the slightest of sounds. He knew the creaks were his own feet, but he wasn't so sure about the other noise; it sounded like whispering ghosts trapped in the attic.

He reached the top of the stairs, and took a quick look down. Beyond the shadows at the bottom, he could clearly see the front door of the house. The letterbox suddenly opened and shut, as if chattering. It was like the mouth of a monster he wanted to lip-read. The letterbox continued to open and shut, open and shut, as if taunting him. Billy spun round and stepped over to the bathroom door, peering in through the crack between door and wall. He blinked, trying to penetrate the darkness.

Then he heard the movement behind the door to his left. His baby brother's bedroom. Billy listened, sure that he'd heard a footstep or two—but Harry was a baby, he couldn't walk.

Then he heard a sob, and another. He looked from the bathroom door to his brother's door. His bladder sent him a pain to remind him why he had gotten out of his bed in the first place. But he had to make sure Harry was okay. It sounded as if he were crying. Billy pushed his brother's bedroom door open and stepped in. He paused, paralysed by confusion.

'Daddy,' he said. His daddy was standing over the cot, pressing down on a pillow where his brother's head should have been. His daddy gently lifted the pillow, and gazed at Billy. His daddy was crying now, crying hard—Billy could tell there were tears rushing down his cheeks. His face a distortion of shadow, but he knew his daddy was scared just like he was.

'Daddy, whatya doing?' Billy asked.

His daddy did not reply. He backed away from the cot, holding his face in his hands and slumped to the floor, still weeping.

'*Mummy!*' Billy shouted as he looked from his daddy to his motionless baby brother. '*Mummy—quick!*'

Billy heard footsteps and his mummy's voice of concern.

'What is it, Billy? Are you having nightmares again?'

She stepped into Harry's bedroom, shining the torch over to where his daddy was slumped on the floor.

'*Oh, my God!*' she yelled, running over to Harry and picking him up.

'*Oh, thank God!*' she cried, holding baby Harry closely to her chest. She told Billy to follow her as she dashed from the room. She seemed so scared too—everyone was scared. It was not just him. It was his whole family. Billy now felt the hot pee trickling down his leg.

His mummy, carrying Harry, ran down the stairs. Billy followed her into the garden and then to the car.

'What about Daddy?'

She did not answer. Instead, she started the engine.

Billy watched their home disappear behind them as he clutched on to the wizard.

* * *

Chief Inspector Collins glanced down to his pad of notes.

1. Trevor Hemmingway had never wanted the second child. The first had been a heavy enough burden on his relationship with his wife, Sally, and financially, a second child just was not viable.

2. After the birth, he had been shocked, even repulsed by the disabled child. He had sunk into a heavy depression, frightened to go near the baby—freaked out by Harry as if he were an alien creature.

3. He had recently been fired from his job, was taking anti-depressants, and he had been drinking heavily for months.

Inspector Collins tapped a pencil against his chin as he pondered the information. It was out of his hands now, but to him, it seemed as clear as day.

* * *

Billy shared a room with his baby brother, Harry, in their new house. His mummy had said he didn't have to, because the house had another bedroom if he wanted it. Nevertheless, Billy stayed with his brother, for he wanted to protect him when he awoke at night and it was dark.

Daddy no longer lived with them. He was staying at the prison until he got better, Mummy had told him.

Billy was no longer afraid of whomever it was that tapped on the window, or of whatever it was that lurked beneath his bed. The shadow people who seemed to appear in dark corners during the night, also failed to frighten him.

The little wizard sat on the bedside table, watching, protecting, as Billy and Harry slept.

~*Fanatical About Mary Chambers*~

She comes down the stairs with the cigarette between two fingers. She is beautiful, dressed in a long dark dress, her hair tied in a bun. She reaches the foot of the stairs and confronts her husband.

'Where is it?' she asks. 'I know you have it. *Give it to me!*'

Her husband nods gently, a smile appears on his face, his eyes slowly rise from the toes of his shiny, black shoes. He wears a tuxedo; his hair is dark, slicked back.

'Oh, you'll get it alright!' he sneers as he reaches for the gun that is not so well concealed beneath his jacket. An explosion goes off. Husband falls to the floor, eyes wide, panting, hand to his chest. Camera pans to the smoking gun she holds, then tilts up to show her wicked smile.

'Thank you,' she says, leaning down and taking the document from her husband's pocket. She strides to the already open door, slamming it behind her. Music plays, screen to black and the credits roll.

This was the end of *Unholy Water*, one of my favourite Mary Chambers films: the brilliant British screen actress of the forties and fifties. She always seemed to get the tough bitch roles. At the start of her films, she is just another weak female lead, but she finds the inner strength and determination to fight back and by the close of each movie, she is on top—as she is in *Unholy Water*.

I'm not just a fan in the usual sense of the word, but more in its unabbreviated sense. Fanatic, that really would be a better way of describing my love for Mary Chambers.

I first saw one of her films when I was only seven years old. It was shown early one morning—a re-run, some sixty years after the original release. I was not discouraged despite the film being in black and white. Her beauty mesmerized me; her high cheekbones, slim face, shoulder

15

length blonde hair and wide eyes from which she would seductively glance.

Since that first time I saw her I have been hooked. In fact, it has taken over my life more than I could have ever imagined. I have tried to find girlfriends who act like her, who look like her, speak like her, who are everything she was. Firstly, this has meant I have struggled to find girls to date; secondly, my relationships haven't tended to last all that long.

Mary Chambers' characters (as I have said) are bitches. Once or twice I have found girls that are just as bitchy: one left me for a friend, getting pregnant behind my back whilst I was away for a weekend watching the football. A real bitch that one.

In another of my favourite of her films: *Newspaper Boy*, she convinces her husband to go away on a hunting trip with friends; whilst away she organizes a meticulous plan to frame him as the murderer of their newspaper boy. The husband knows the police will think he is responsible when they find the body. Then Mary Chambers' character murders her husband, but makes it look like suicide. She has killed both of them and gets away with her husband's fortune.

In another of her films: *Backdrop*, she hangs her stepsister at the close; I paid five hundred pounds at an auction for the rope used in that film. Worth every penny.

My collection of memorabilia is quite extensive now: clothes she wore, scripts, cigarette holders, and even some love letters she had sent a boyfriend. They set me back a couple of thousand pounds. However, it is only money—people spend money on loved ones all the time, this seems no different to me. You cannot tell me I do not know what love is because I do. *True love.* Sure, Mary Chambers isn't my girlfriend, hell, she's been dead for ten years—but not dead to me, memories don't die, at least not until you're old and senile.

My house is like a Mary Chambers museum and I am sure she would appreciate my keeping her memory alive. Recently, as funds have been a little tight, rent needing paying, I have not been able to attend the auctions, and when I have, I've been out-bid. I find it difficult watching items that should be mine, sold to people who probably know very little about her and cannot possibly love her more than I do.

Two months ago, I was sitting at the back of the auction hall. I was waiting to see, in real life, the dress Mary Chambers had worn in *Unholy Water.*

The bidding was between an elderly man in black, with a receding hairline, and a middle-aged ginger-haired woman in a green dress.

'Two thousand pounds anyone, any bidders?' the auctioneer asked.

The woman raised her hand.

'Very good. Two thousand to the lady in the green. Anyone for two thousand one hundred?'

The elderly man raised his hand.

'Two thousand two hundred,' the auctioneer said excitedly.

I looked to the purple dress—I hadn't known it would be purple as it featured in a black and white film, but it was so wonderful; I could imagine her now, walking down those stairs to confront her husband.

Without thinking, my hand shot up.

'Young man with the blue sweater,' the auctioneer said. 'Two thousand three hundred.'

I sat shaking. I didn't have *that* sort of money; in fact, I was close to that amount in debt. I swallowed hard. I didn't know what had happened. Impulse, I guess. The elderly man glanced to me with a smirk and then raised a hand.

'Two thousand four hundred. Would the man in the blue sweater like to go any higher?'

I chewed on a fingernail, ran my hand through my hair—the dress was so beautiful, I just had to have it, had to. I put my hand up.

Shit, shit, shit, shit. I don't have that sort of money!

I had no say in the end, as the green dress wearing woman bid higher, followed by another bid from the old guy. He eventually bought the dress for a staggering three thousand six hundred pounds. As he exited the hall, he winked at me. I could have punched his brains out there and then. The bastard, he knew, somehow he knew how much I loved Mary Chambers and he had decided to buy it just to torture me.

That night I waited outside his house, peering up over his garden wall. I could see him in the kitchen, washing up some plates. He lived in a small cottage just outside town—I had followed him there. I was going to have that dress. I would wait until he went to sleep then I would sneak in and take it. Easy.

The final light in the house blinked out and the cottage and the garden were enshrouded in darkness. The only light came from the moon, which sent long shadows of the house over to where I waited. After another ten minutes, I made my move.

Tiptoeing across the garden, keeping low, and around to the back of the house. I gazed in through a window and into a lounge. Empty. Dark. There was a small television set and a sofa, bookshelves on the far wall. I moved along to the next window. I could see the dining room—my eyes sprung open cat-like on seeing the purple dress hanging on a hook, encased in a protective bag.

I wiped the sweat from my forehead and checked the back door that was next to me. Locked, of course, these old people do nothing but worry about today's youth, probably paranoid to death with the thought that some psychopath might try to break in. Silly old bastard.

I remembered the film *Break-In*, Mary Chambers was nominated for an Oscar for that role. I recalled a scene where she had to break into her mother's home to find her recently deceased father's will. She was to replace it with a will that was a little more generous to her needs. I smiled. That was a great film. She had used a hairpin to pick the lock.

Damn, I should have thought of that earlier.

I searched my pockets: a pen, identity card, mints. No good. Sighing, crouched low, I gazed over to the window. Without hope, I tried lifting the window, stunned, as it rose under pressure. The stupid idiot had locked his doors, probably with the best locking system in the world, but had not bolted the window. I climbed through, and onto the dining room carpet. This would be easier than I had ever imagined. The dress was just across the room, illuminated by the moon. I tiptoed across, and took the plastic sheathed dress in my hands.

'What a treasure to add to my collection!' I whispered.

The dining room light flashed on and I met eyes with the old man. For a few seconds time froze as we stared at one another.

He reacted first, spinning on his heels and dashing from the room; I set chase, sprinting after his shadow through the house's darkness, banging my hip against something and screaming in pain. The roar of pain triggered his voice box and he yelled, '*Leave me alone, please, take the dress!*'

I followed him into his bedroom; he leaped onto his bed and grabbed the telephone. My jaw dropped.

'*Nooo!*'

I dived upon him, snapping his fingers away from the buttons—he struggled beneath me, begging me not to hurt him, twisting round to face me, and then thrusting his head forward to bite my nose like some deadly snake.

I wrenched the phone from his grasp and brought it crashing down against his face—blood shot into mine, blinding me for a second; I blinked and watched as his eyes rolled back into his head, then rolled down again, unfocused. His eyes readjusted and he stared at me, terror-filled. I brought the phone down again, and again and again, each blow accompanied by a hollow thud and splattering of blood, my final blow grazed off his nose and scraped the skin from his cheek. He was motionless. I stood with a blood-dripping phone in my hand raised above my head and ready for one final blow should the elderly man try again to refocus his vision. As my heartbeat calmed, I realized *his* heart had stopped altogether. He was dead.

I don't remember much after that; I recall putting the phone back on the hook, and just staring at the man I had killed. It was not like the Mary Chambers films at all. Whenever she killed someone she walked away head held high, sometimes lighting a cigarette. And the blood, so much blood everywhere, such a mess. And it was *red*, so much red liquid. In Mary Chambers' films, the blood was never red. She never made a colour movie.

The following morning I awoke at home; the purple dress was across my bed, on the purple fabric there were bloody handprints.

I am a murderer. I cannot take it back; I can never take it back. My love and my obsession for Mary Chambers had forced me to kill.

I wish I could have known Mary while she was alive; I would do anything to be with her. Her spirit will always live on as far as I'm concerned, somewhere, anyway—maybe through her granddaughter. I have been following her for a few weeks. In fact, I'm inside her house now, waiting in the closet. I knew she wouldn't have let me in, but I hope she will listen to me, as I just want to tell her how much I adore her grandmother.

She walks into her bedroom, over to her dressing table. She, I think, is taking off her make-up, and then she climbs into bed and switches off the lamp. The room is black; I wait until my eyes have adjusted then I open the closet door. She is asleep, her head lying softly on the white pillow. She is beautiful, not as beautiful as her grandmother is, but beautiful nevertheless. She does resemble Mary Chambers. I stand over her and just observe. The blanket above her chest rises and falls, a gentle wheezing breath leaves her mouth.

I pull the gun from my pocket and point it towards her forehead.

'Wake up,' I say. '*Wake up!*'

She opens her eyes and stares at the gun. Her mouth opens—she is about to scream.

'*Don't!*' I say. 'Don't say a word then I won't hurt you.'

She is visibly shaking. Her mouth quivers, her eyes unblinking.

'Who are you?' she asks.

'I'm a…a friend of your grandmother, Mary Chambers,' I say, shyly. I can't think of anything else to say.

'What do you want?' she asks, agitated. She's panicking—I need to calm her nerves before she does something stupid. My finger is trembling over the trigger.

'My money is in the cabinet,' she says. 'Jewellery over there,' she says, pointing to the dressing table.

'I loved your grandmother.'

She stares at me—the moon escapes a cloud and shines upon her face.

'She was a wonderful lady,' I say.

'Yes, she was,' she replies, shifting herself into a sitting position. She moves slowly and cautiously—she doesn't want me to panic and blow her brains out.

As she sits, the light brings out her jaw-line and her high cheekbones. I gasp.

'You look so much like her,' I say.

She shifts uncomfortably. I see her swallow hard.

'No, not really,' she says. 'I'll turn the light on—I look nothing like her really,' she says.

'*No!*' I say as she reaches for the lamp. 'Leave the light off, I like it better this way; no colour, don't like colour—better this way, dark and light, black and white, it was always better this way.'

She does not answer. She's right though; she has a resemblance to her grandmother, a little that is all, in the daylight the similarities diminish to nearly nothing. Her hair is brown, dyed pink at the front.

I lift the black bin bag from my feet and undo the knot.

'Put these on,' I say, passing her the purple dress and blonde wig.

She looks as if she will panic again; she begins to cry, tears roll down her delicate cheeks.

'That was your grandmother's dress,' I say, moving the gun a little closer to her head. 'I won't hurt you, I promise, just do as I say, Mary.'

She begins to cry. 'I'm not Mary. I'm not my grandmother.'

'Put it on,' I insist, angry.

She slips the dress over her nightgown and then reluctantly pulls the wig over her head. Her eyes fidget, darting everywhere except to me.

'Look at me,' I demand.

She glances up shyly.

'You're beautiful,' I tell her. She's just as she was in the films, as she was in *Unholy Water*, and all the others. I begin to sob; I can't believe this is happening to me. I wipe the tears from my cheeks with the back of my hand. I step forwards, lowering myself over her; she spreads her legs and allows me to lie upon her. We kiss passionately, she runs her fingers through my hair, over my back and across my buttocks, encouraging me to take off my belt and release my bulge.

'I love you *so much*, Mary…*So, so much.*'

'I love you too,' she replies. The words fill my body with heat, with love.

I feel a thud on my head. I blink and fall from the bed, dizzy. As I stand, Mary faces me. The purple dress torn, stained with the elderly man's blood. I cannot see Mary's face, shadow covers her, but her hair glistens from the moon behind. She has struck me with something hard.

Then as I stare upon her, someone grabs me from behind; I can feel the hand around my throat, squeezing, I twist round and fall onto my back. Suddenly, Mary stands over me, so beautiful, she grabs the hand in which I hold the gun and forces it toward my mouth.

'No, please, don't, I love you, Mary!'

The gun barrel presses against my lips, trying to penetrate, only for my teeth to block.

'Mary, please don't hurt me—I'm a massive fan!'

The gun slips into my mouth, my finger trembling on the trigger, her hand squeezing, crushing my hand, her slender fingers around mine, and looking at me through her eyelashes. She smiles.

'I love you,' I say, the gun impairing my speech.

Stephanie Chambers watches. On her knees in bed, shivering, holding the glass ornament she has hit the intruder with—she is still trying to scream but cannot find a voice. The intruder sits on her floor, holding the gun in his own mouth, talking, muttering something, then the gun fires— a shower of brain and fragments of skull catapult across the bedroom, blood streaking over the floor and the window glass.

Stephanie gazes down at the headless mess of the intruder on the carpet. She lifts the phone to dial for the police. What she cannot understand is why the intruder has just taken his own life. And why had he been begging her grandmother not to hurt him?

Just for a fraction of a second, Stephanie could have sworn she saw her grandmother in the corner of her bedroom.

"Which service please?" says the voice from down the phone.

~*The Wishing Urn*~

I pushed open the glass door of the brothel and walked towards the counter, where I was met by the smirk of an elderly man whose creased blue shirt needed as much attention from an iron as his wrinkled face.

I walked across the dark lobby, turning my head, noticing the girls that lounged about on pink sofas in the gloom. They giggled behind their hands.

'How can I help you?' the man behind the counter asked.

I leaned on the counter and peered back over my shoulder. One of the girls, wearing stockings but nothing more, had shoved a vibrator in her mouth. It buzzed and hummed as she ran her lips up and down its pulsing.

'Are you after a whore? I can offer you the best girls in town and they are dirt cheap,' the old man said.

'No, I'm not interested in your girls,' I replied. 'I have a wife.'

The wrinkled man scratched at his chin. He eyed me carefully. Up and down. 'That's too bad,' he said, running a hand back through his thinning white hair as his hooked nose twitched. His smile displayed yellow teeth.

'I dreamt of this place…I dreamt of those girls, I dreamt of *you*. All of it, I dreamt it all.' I paused to take breath. 'I dreamt of the Wishing Urn.'

The brothel owner rubbed his face, disturbing his cavernous cheeks. He must have been in his early hundreds.

'I see,' he said, nodding. He gazed over to the girls. 'Can you give us a minute!' he demanded, waving a dismissive hand. I turned to watch as the whores disappointedly rose to their feet and began to walk away; one of them—a blonde—hopped on her only leg, trying to apply her lipstick; the oldest whore, whose hair was grey, scratched viscously at a dark patch on her head. I wondered if it were an infestation of head lice. The one-legged whore was the last out, and then the door shut.

The room of gloom was silent. The brothel owner gazed vacantly towards the door the whores had gone through. Then he crouched down and pulled out the golden urn.

He placed it upon the counter.

'That's what I dreamed of,' I said, looking up from the urn to the brothel owner. His nose twitched, his mouth lifted on one side as if somebody hiding in his nostril had tugged at an invisible fishing hook.

I leaned forward to touch the urn; the man snatched it away from my eager fingers.

'*No!* If you have dreamt of this place, you must also have dreamt the rules?'

I sighed. 'Yes,' I said. 'An eye for an eye.'

The ancient man smirked. 'Or in this case, an eye for a wish!' he said, chuckling. His breath entered my nostrils and caused a wave of nausea to grip my body. The stench reminded me of when my Aunt Poppy had a tooth infection. The dentist had removed nine decaying teeth that day.

'It's only by sacrificing an eye that the urn will grant you a wish,' he continued.

'Only one? I thought it was three wishes?'

'No, my boy, that's only in fairytales!'

'Very well.'

He took a small square card from behind the till and clutched on to a biro. It had a leak and black ink was dripping over his fingers. He seemed to neither notice nor care.

'Just a few details if you don't mind?'

'Of course.'

'Name?'

'Stuart Douglas.'

'Age?'

'Twenty-two.'

'You have a wife, what's her name?'

'Lara.'

The man's nose twitched as he scratched the scar by his nostril. 'And if anything should…go wrong, is she the person I should contact?'

'Yes.'

He took my phone number and address then stashed the card in a plastic container.

The brothel owner lifted an opening in the counter and beckoned me to follow. We went through a rainbow of hanging beads. Two of the whores were standing naked by the kettle.

'Be useful and make our guest a cup of tea!' he growled.

The brunette with the bigger tits flicked the switch. I smiled and followed the man into another room. There was a furnace. Around it, black candles were glowing.

After my cup of tea, it was time for the removal of my right eye.

'Roll up your sleeve.'

He pulled the cork off the end of the needle and gazed upon it in the light, then wielding it like a dagger, approached me. I felt the hot prick then dizziness came on immediately.

When I awoke, I saw him holding a pair of tongs ahead of him. In the black pincers was a small white orb. I realised it must be my eye. He held the tongs in the flames of the furnace. Beneath was the urn. The flames heated the eye, it popped and hissed, and then liquid began to drip down into the open urn. The flames seemed to be licking at his hand also, but they can't have been, as he didn't flinch. As the eye split and pussed, I felt a bolt of pain through my empty socket. The mushy eyeball slid away from the tongs and spilled down into the urn. The ancient man thrust a hand into the flames and lifted the golden urn.

I raised my hand to my face, and felt gently for where my eye had previously been. I prodded with a stiff finger; my hand began to tremble as I felt the sore crater. I swallowed then quickly took my hand away.

'Very good, you're awake!' the elderly man said as he placed the lid back on the urn. The black candles hissed then died. 'Don't worry about the soreness—it will go in time.'

Back out front, the elderly man placed the cooled urn before me. My mouth was dry, limbs were like jelly, and the eyeball-less socket itched madly.

'Only one wish,' he warned. 'And once you have wished, the wish can only be wished upon one further time. Understand?'

'I think so,' I said, gently scratching at my empty eye socket.

'So if your wish doesn't turn out as you would have liked, you will have only a single further wish to put it right—if you offer another eye, that is,' he said, pointing to my remaining eye, grinning. 'Is that clear?'

'Yes.'

'This isn't a fairytale—someone else can't wish for you to cancel your wish. As I say, wishes can only be wished over once, only changed once.'

'I had one guy that had used up both his wishes, sacrificing both his eyes. Poor blind bastard. I told him there was nothing he could do, that even if he found another eye he wouldn't be able to change what he had already wished. He ignored my advice and killed a tramp for his eyes. He demanded I let him wish again…and I did.'

'What happened?'

'Nothing! *Absolutely nothing!* A wish can only be corrected once, so be careful.'

I nodded firmly, steadying my breath.

'Go ahead,' the man said, his lips cutting up into the crags of his face. 'Choose well. Remember, there is always a price to pay, so do not be greedy. But of course, you know how it works.'

I exhaled a lung of air—wrapping my fingers around the golden urn. It was hot, but not too hot to hold. I closed my eye.

I want to be rich beyond my wildest dreams.

I let go of the urn.

'Thank you!' I said, blinking my eye as tears began to leak down my cheek.

'You're free to go.'

As I walked to the door, the old guy called, '*Good luck!*'

I ran along the snow-covered street, my feet crunching down, white mists leaving my mouth as my hot breaths met the cold air. I reached my front gate and stopped. Hands on knees, leaning forwards trying to catch my breath. My body trembled, heart racing. I slowly stepped up to the front door, took my key from my pocket and unlocked. I pushed at the door but it wouldn't budge. I pushed a little harder and this time it opened a crack and a fifty-pound note dropped out onto the doorstep.

'Yes! Yes!' I whispered, looking around to make sure no one knew of my newly acquired fortune. Now my wife and I could move to the Caribbean, start a family, be free of the financial restraints of this fucking world! We could buy a Ferrari and a yacht. And we could make babies without the nagging doubts over where the money to feed, clothe, and school them would come from.

I thrust my way into the house and shut the door behind me.

'*Oh, my God!*'

I tilted my head back, eye wide, my smile hurting my cheeks it raised so high. The room was jammed full of money—pyramids of the stuff.

I jumped into the crisp notes, rolled into the money; laughing, crying, weeping, laughing, and then my foot hit something hard.

'What was—?'

I looked down and my eye met those of my wife. She was lying on her back covered in money. Her eyes were glazed and open. Her mouth was stuffed full of fifty-pound notes. It didn't look as though she was breathing—how could she be with money thrust down her hugely inflated throat? Her stomach was also bloated. I knew if I were to cut her open, the money would spill with her guts.

'*NOOOOO!*' I screamed, dropping to my knees, desperately pulling the notes from her mouth, from her lifeless corpse. Every time I emptied her mouth, it refilled with more of the expensive paper that was climbing her throat as if it were a ladder. It was no use. She was dead. I had killed her with my greed.

I sat with head in hands, trying to think, trying to find a way out of this. I loved her so much; I could not live without her—not even with all these riches. I was taken back to when I had been at school, aged eleven. On the last day of term, the teacher brought in a selection pack of chocolate bars…we were allowed one bar each. I went back for a second and a third—two of the girls in the class in tears when the pack ran out before they had had their chocolate.

'Well, I hope you're proud of yourself!' Mr. Edwards shouted at me. I turned and saw my reflection in the window—chocolate dripping down my chin.

Holding my dead wife's hand, I wept hard, soaking the money around me. I was weeping because I had already thought of the solution to the situation. The act I would have to commit if I wanted things back as they had been. I fought my way into the kitchen, battling against the piles of money, and took the sharpest small knife I could find. I returned to my wife and gouged out her left eye. My right eye was missing. At least between us we would have a set.

With the eyeball wrapped in money, I ran as fast as I could to the brothel. As I pushed the glass door open, the girls began to giggle; varnished fingernails running seductively over legs; kisses blown from the sofa, trying to tempt me. I ignored them and walked straight over to the brothel owner who sat reclined in a deck chair with his eyes shut. One of his eyes shot open and focused upon me. He yawned then opened his other eye and gingerly stood up, stretching out the cricks in his aging body.

'You're back,' he said, sounding bored.

'*My god, it was horrible…the…the…*' I stopped. I didn't think I should say my wish had killed my wife…he might not accept her eyeball if he knew she hadn't given it willingly—that I had taken it without her consent. I breathed out to calm my nerves, wiping the sweat from my head.

'Please…I would like another wish.'

The brothel owner brushed his white wispy hair over his balding scalp and smirked. 'Of course, my boy, follow me—'

'No…I mean…I already have an eye,' I said. Swallowed. 'My wife's.'

I expected him to refuse the trade, but he was quite willing. He gazed at the eyeball under a lamp, nodding his head. 'Very pretty…yes, I like this one. '

He melted the eye into the urn and placed it before me. His stumpy, crooked fingers remained around it for a few seconds, then they released.

'Remember, my boy, there is always a price to pay,' he warned once again. 'I suggest you just ask for things to be put back how they were. This is your one and only chance to correct what has gone wrong.'

'Yes—*yes*,' I said, clutching on to the urn impatiently. I had planned to do just that. Put things back how they had been. Breathing deeply, closing my eye.

I wish for my wife to live again.

I dashed back down the road to my house. I pushed on the front door. The money still piled high. I took a deep breath, and then released it gently. Hand pressed over my thumping heart. I wondered if a man's heart had ever broken ribs from sheer pounding. Mine was giving it a go.

'Darling, are you home?'

Silence. I rubbed my moist head.

'Hello…Lara.'

'I'm here, honey.' I sighed mightily then gazed to the heavens. 'Thank you,' I whispered.

'Where are you?'

'Over here,' she said.

I rushed across the room. I still could not see my beloved wife.

'Down here.'

I gazed down to the ten-pound note her face was on. Where the Queen had once been, was now my wife's face. I fainted and did not regain consciousness for an hour.

'It's okay, at least we have each other,' she said to me as I held the note in front of my eye. I couldn't believe my wife was now just a face on a piece of expensive paper. A one-eyed face.

'But I have no more wishes! A wish cannot be wished upon twice,' I said slowly, remembering the ancient brothel owner's words. 'I'm so sorry, darling; I thought it would be okay. I didn't wish for anything too big, just a bit of money,' I said, closing my eye, trying to fight off another gush of tears.

After I had composed myself, I returned to the brothel to speak to the owner. As I entered, he looked up from whatever he was gazing at between his legs. He shook off and zipped up his fly, wiping his hand on his shirtsleeve.

'Has it not worked out, my boy?' he asked, his foul breath irritating my nostrils. I covered my nose, pretending to be rubbing at it, waiting for his breath to pass.

'How about a whore to cheer you up?' he said, pointing over to the pink sofas. I glanced over. That had not occurred to me until now. My wife had not a body. No body meant no sex. And no children. We finally had the money to afford kids, but in return, we had lost the womb.

'No,' I insisted, shaking my head. 'I have my wife with me,' I continued as I took her from my wallet and placed her on the counter. The brothel owner's head furrowed in surprise as he gazed at the ten-pound note on the desk.

'Hello,' my wife said—the brothel owner almost jumped out of his shoes.

'*What the hell am I to do?*' I asked, raising my hands to my face.

'I did warn you,' he responded. Then together we said, 'Every wish has a price.'

I began to cry. As my eyelid shut, a tear dropped and exploded onto the ten-pound note.

I looked up on hearing the cackled laughter of the whores. The brothel owner gazed in their direction, smirking, as he scratched at his nose. He pointed to my wife.

'Be careful!' he warned.

My tears had made the note damp. I dabbed up the wetness with my sleeve, lifted her to my face and kissed her gently. I slid her back into my wallet, and then slipped it safely into my pocket.

'How about an hour with Angela to lift your spirits?' he suggested, his lips twisting up at the corners, his yellow teeth on display, rotten breath exhaled.

Angela hopped up onto her only leg, pulling off her bra to show me her sagging tits. She began to laugh, as did the other whores and then the brothel owner started too. The laughs thudding against my skull as if attacked by a woodpecker—images of my wife lying on her back, glassy-eyed, mouth crammed with money, filtered into my mind's eye. I shook my head; the images exploded but the laughs of the brothel remained. The man's mouth was open so wide in hysterical laughter that I could see his black rotten teeth. I blinked, disbelieving my eye as I noticed the maggots crawling, burrowing in his gums—swimming in and out of the red flesh as if through water. One dropped onto his tongue then bounced up before falling out onto the floor by my foot. I stamped hard on it, turned and ran—as I sprinted, their laughs followed me into the street, only then terminated by the glass door snapping shut.

Walking through the thawing snow, I stopped at a stationery shop. I did not want the note to be wet or ripped. I might lose what remained of my wife forever.

I had the note laminated, sealed in transparent plastic, and I placed it back in my pocket.

On the journey back to my house, I saw a couple holding hands, laughing—close together, keeping each other warm on this cold winter's afternoon. They stopped and cuddled, and then the girl pressed her nose into the guy's neck. She kissed softly.

I took my wallet out—feeling the bitter cold wrapping around my fingers. I wanted to tell Lara how much I loved her. Tell her that we would make this work. Somehow it *would* work.

As I pulled the laminated ten-pound note from my wallet, I froze, paralysed at the sight of her sagging head, her gaping mouth, her bulging eye.

'*I…I…I…can't…breathe!*' she croaked.

I tore at the sides of the lamination, trying to pull it away, trying to free my wife.

'It's okay, darling, it's okay,' I whispered, frantically ripping at the note. It was of no use. The plastic sealed her tight. I supported the laminated note in the palm of my hand. My wife's head hung limply as the final breaths whistled through her teeth.

~Roadkill Supper~

A cutting morning breeze awoke Milligan Peak from his dreams. He blinked, then yawned, and then stretched, before sitting up and tasting the dry metallic tongue that lay in his mouth.

He had slept in a forest clearing and was now sitting on a camping mattress, legs hidden in his sleeping bag.

Milligan rolled his head and brushed the hair from his eyes. He gazed at the sun and figured it was about 8 a.m. Yawning, he reached for the kettle that rested above the extinguished campfire. The kettle was empty, he sighed, climbed from the sleeping bag and pulled his pants up over his hairy tanned legs and fastened the zipper. He pushed on his sandals then he leant down to start the fire. He placed some fresh kindling under the logs then lit a match, protected by the palm of his hand so the wind didn't blow it out. With the fire lit, he stretched his arms high in the air then made his way through the trees to the river and refilled the kettle.

With the kettle sloshing with water, he returned to his fire, placed it over the flames then took a cigarette from his jacket. He lit the cigarette, sucked and then exhaled smoke, smiling. This was the life, he thought. So what if he didn't have a house to live in, he didn't have a job, and he didn't have a wife or children—this really was the life to live. There were no worries, no pressure, no guilt—just pure being at one with nature. He flicked the ash of his cigarette and then inhaled again, enjoying the cool breeze on his face. He glanced to the sun. It was going to be a hot one today, he thought. Just then his stomach rumbled.

"Hungry are you?" he asked his stomach as he patted it. It groaned again. "I thought so…well let's see what we can do for you."

Milligan put the cigarette behind one ear, careful not to set his hair alight, then leant over to his cool-box, and flipped the lid.

"Mmmm," he said, withdrawing some empty beer cans, and a single can he hadn't yet drunk. The plastic bags he kept his meat in were empty, just the meat juices remained at the bottom of the cool-box.

He replaced the lid, retrieved the cigarette from behind his ear then puffed away.

"Looks like we gonna have to go hunting," Milligan said. He was a southern Englishman by birth, and had been trying hard to lose the accent since moving north, so to fit in with the northerners. However, nobody yet had mistaken him for one—most just looked at him and frowned, wondering why he was trying to adopt the northern accent.

The kettle began to whistle. He leaned over, took the kettle from the heat and poured into his cup, then added the coffee. He finished his smoke whilst drinking the coffee, and then pulled his shirt on and collected his knife and a trash bag. He put the fire out—he didn't know how long he would be—and ventured into the woodland, up the slope and through the long grass.

The sun was beating down and Milligan could feel the sweat spreading in the crevices of his body. He took a hanky from his pocket and wiped the sweat from his scalp and face.

"Jesus, it's hot!"

He carried on through the grass until he reached the highway. He looked one way then the other; the road stretched as far as his eyes could see in either direction. He could hear the trees creaking in the sun and the light breeze rustling the leaves, but apart from that, all was silent except for his own deep breaths...and the occasional grumble of his stomach.

As he stepped out onto the tarmac, he heard the distant sound of a truck. He gazed to his right, then left, then back to the right. He could see it approaching now, just a tiny dark speck on the horizon.

Milligan waited for the truck to near—there was no path along the road and he didn't want a truck knocking him down before breakfast. The truck approached, a big sonofabitch it was, eighteen-wheeler. Its engine roared as it devoured the highway, the sun reflecting off the windshield.

As it passed, the bearded driver waved and blew on the horn—Milligan returned the wave; he knew old Jessie, saw him quite often along the highway.

The wind from the speeding truck hit Milligan smack in the face. It was a welcome reprieve from the rays of the sizzling sun.

He watched the truck disappear in the distance and then he started down the road. He placed his feet, walking steadily along, listening to the sounds of life among the trees that bordered the far side of the road, feeling the sun's heat. As he walked, he occasionally kicked pebbles, all the time keeping his eyes peeled for oncoming trucks.

Then he found the mangled rodent on the road. He crouched down and stared at the little thing—looked like a mouse, but its insides crushed right out of it, intestines lying covered in blood on the tarmac. Little thing must have just popped under the weight of one of those trucks. Maybe old Jessie's truck had only just now done the deed. The mouse's tail twitched, blood pooled beneath.

"Poor little thing," Milligan said as he got to his feet. He thought it was too small to be worthy of breakfast, so he left it in peace. What he wanted, what he dreamed about, was a nice fat fox…that is what he fancied this sunny morning.

When he had been living the life of the ordinary man in a little house in Kent, he had taken for granted how much food cost. After moving north, he had gotten a steady job at the gas station, had a regular wage. But all those grocery trips added up and he must have spent thousands on food, and what for? What was the point?

Along this stretch of road, he could find as much food as he needed. And he thought his new form of "shopping" was beneficial for several reasons. First, he was reducing the workload for the people paid to scrape up roadkill. Second, he was helping to reduce the amount of animals slaughtered for food: His ration was no longer necessary because he was eating animals that had already died. Saves money, saves animals. Makes sense.

Yep, that's right, I'm pretty smart when I wanna be, he thought, smiling.

He continued his walk, glancing up at the sun. He hoped he wouldn't have to walk too far—it was bloody hot, and he fancied getting back, cooking himself a nice fox, having a coffee and smoke and then a swim in the river. Yes, sir, that's what he would do. He smiled, thinking about all those "normal" people getting ready for work at the local store or fast-food joint. Those people stuck behind a computer screen in an office.

Back in Kent, he had worked for an insurance firm, it paid well but he had been fed up of sitting in an office with a bunch of snobs. The move north was something he had always dreamed of doing…A more relaxed lifestyle.

He had worked at the gas station for a year even though the career prospects were non-existent. But he had been happy, living the easy life, he thought. But now he had taken freedom to a new level, Total Freedom, he called it, living off the land, being at one with nature.

He nodded defiantly against the "normal folk," as he walked on, rubbing at the back of his neck where he was a little sun burned. Another truck started an approach. The rumble of the heavy vehicle entered his ears. It was Steve Brooks' truck. Milligan waved. Ginger-haired Steve gave him the thumbs-up as he went by.

Milligan wiped at his dry mouth. If he had known it would take this long to find breakfast, he would have brought some water. He had his beer at least. He took it from his pocket and pulled the ring. The foam bubbled out, so he sucked it away then took several long gulps. He wiped the moisture from his chin, burped, and then continued his search for food, glancing over his shoulder, considering settling for that squashed mouse. But that would mean he would have to come out again later for supper. No, he would push on, he thought.

He was approaching a hot spot for roadkill; without fail, there was some lifeless animal there every day. He squinted to try to see and sure enough, something stained the road. He frowned as he neared, scratching his head. He stood over the patch of blood. Where was the roadkill?

He looked both ways along the road.

"They never scrape them up this early," he said, as his stomach grumbled. He chewed on his lower lip and thought about it some more— shaking his head, releasing a breath of air, which he quickly replaced with a mouthful of beer. He continued his trek, putting more yards of hot tarmac between himself and his camp, and the next stretch of road was a gradual rise as well. He had rarely come this far in search of food. But at least there was some tree cover; the shade brought relief from the sun's rays and he was tempted to rest, but his stomach insisted he should carry on at least until he had found breakfast. He could then rest before heading back. He reluctantly agreed to his stomach's demands.

To his annoyance, he then saw another bloody patch—further evidence of there having been a recent roadkill. As with the last, there was no dead animal marking the spot. Milligan gazed at the spilled blood.

"Jesus, what the hell is going on?" he wondered. "Why would anyone take the roadkill this early?"

Milligan was desperately hungry by now so he pressed on. He tried to list all the names of people he knew that might have done this. Some kind of practical joke? Maybe it had been his former boss Jake Gummer from the gas station. When he had resigned three months ago, he had told Jake he wanted his "Total Freedom" and would be living off the land from then on. Jake had driven past one morning last month, swerved over towards where Milligan was collecting the dead cat. He wasn't trying to hit him, just to scare him, and it did the trick. Milligan had dived from the road down the embankment, thinking his ex-boss had gone crazy.

Yeah, maybe it was Jake, he thought. *The sonofabitch knows I need the roadkill for food—maybe he took them so I can't eat. If it is him…I'm gonna shovel fox shit down his fucking throat!*

Milligan, not one to be defeated, pressed on for another kilometer until he came across another roadkill site. Again, the dead animal missing, but blood marked the spot as clearly as chalk outlines the dead.

Milligan could feel his heart racing—this was starting to piss him off now.

"*I'll tear their fucking heads off!*" he yelled. Some birds shot out of the surrounding branches. "What the hell is going on?"

Milligan marched on. He panted hard, his cheeks flushed and red, his hair disheveled and ridden with sweat, his neck beginning to peel under the scorching sunbeams. His armpits were dripping, the sweat clogging and making him very uncomfortable.

He reached the next spot. There was only a little blood. There was though what looked like some fragments of bone and some fur. He crouched down and touched the blood—it was wet, fresher than the last. It hadn't had time to dry or soak away. He glanced up and around…into the trees. Was somebody watching him?

He continued, heavy breathing, weak-limbed, wiping the dripping sweat from his brow. He thought about stopping, taking a break in the shade—but he couldn't, that was like admitting defeat, he was getting closer, he knew it, not far now, just keep going.

The next roadkill bloodstain was again missing the animal.

Milligan shook his head, bemused. He stared into the surrounding trees. He could hear birds, and then he heard an animal rustling in the undergrowth. He stood and tried to decide his next move…then he saw the trail of crimson drips heading across the road and into the forest. He stared hard upon the bloody trail, started to follow, oblivious to all around him. It was only as the truck's horn blurted that he realized he had walked right out in front of it. He jumped back and the truck narrowly missed crushing him. He checked the road both ways. It was clear. He followed the trail to the far side, and then opened the branches to gaze into the dark undergrowth. The density of the trees made it difficult to make anything out, so he ventured in, palming branches aside as he delved deeper.

After twenty yards he stopped. He heard another truck whiz by behind him. Milligan took some deep gulps of air as he restored his energy. He had walked many kilometers with only a can of beer to keep him hydrated, and he was now feeling the affects. What he would give for a nice cold glass of water!

He continued, crouching so to crawl through some prickly bushes, before coming out into an opening. The greens of the undergrowth interweaved above his head, forming a ceiling. Milligan found he couldn't quite stand straight, but the protection from the sun was a welcome one.

Milligan looked around, thinking he'd heard a rustle.

"Is anybody there?" he asked. "Jake? Is that you? You playing some kinda prank on me? I already told you I can't work another goddam day at the gas station. Come on now, stop fucking about and show yourself."

Silence followed Milligan's speech. Goose bumps began to sprout over his arms and he had a tingling sensation running along the bottom of his neck. Although the opening in which he found himself was shaded and cool, he felt cramped and claustrophobia began to set.

I'll go back to camp, he thought, *make myself that fishing rod I've been promising to make*. Fishing would be a whole lot easier than walking God knows how many kilometers in search of roadkill.

He had made his mind up, but before he'd had the chance to turn, he heard scurrying, and then cracking sticks, and then disturbed leaves, and then heavy footfall—and all around him, as if approaching from all directions.

"Jesus! What the hell is that? Who's there?" he cried out, fear spreading. He swallowed hard then turned to run. He charged into the undergrowth, thrashing his way through—the branches tearing at his skin, entangling him. He had to keep running as he could hear a chorus of chaotic movement right behind. Something was chasing him!

Milligan frantically fought his way through the branches, ignoring the pain as one split his lip; another poked him in the eye. He had to escape; he had to return to the road.

Then the sun hit him full in the face and suddenly his feet were on tarmac. He staggered out into the road and turned, exhausted, gazing back into the undergrowth—all that in the second before the blaring horn, the screech of brakes and the impact that sent Milligan careening through the air. He landed and several of his bones snapped. He looked up, blinking stupidly in the direction of the truck. It had stopped in a sideways position blocking the road. The driver ran over to Milligan, took one look and vomited onto the hot tarmac.

"Help me!" Milligan wailed as pain erupted throughout his body. The driver hesitated, and then said he would go for help. Milligan slumped down into semi-consciousness, but was alert enough to notice the wheels of the truck rolling by, and to hear the driver shout, "I'll be back soon!"

Milligan didn't know how long he'd been there when he again opened his eyes. He knew it was still extremely hot, that he was still in the road, and that he must still be alive to have figured out the aforementioned. Nevertheless, he regretted opening his eyes as with it went his last drop of sanity, he thought. He blinked hard, trying to erase the sight. Heading towards him, having emerged from the undergrowth, were a dozen or more animals. There was a limping fox—something had torn open its stomach, and as it limped, its internal organs slithered out in splashes of blood. But what should have been a death warrant injury, seemed not to dissuade the fox from closing. There was a badger with a crushed head, so flattened that its brain couldn't possibly have still functioned. It fixed Milligan with the gaze of its one good eye, approaching with a grin upon its face.

Then there was a deer; it walked on its front kneecaps as a vehicle had evidently shattered the bones of its lower legs. There were rodents, squirrels, rabbits, and even a goat. All of which were in some way disfigured, bloodied or mangled. All of which should have been dead or on Death's doorstep. None of them should have been emerging from the undergrowth and crossing the busy highway to reach him.

Milligan did all he could think of doing. He screamed. He did so at the top of his lungs, yelling for someone to help him, for God to save him, all the time the roadkill animals neared, panting eagerly, grinning like demented clowns.

But it was no use. Nobody could hear his cries. He was alone.

In realizing this, he turned onto his stomach, fighting the agony he suffered and began to crawl. He had gotten only a yard when he felt teeth sinking into his legs, claws ripping at his flesh. In a daze, just before losing consciousness permanently, he met eyes with the fox. For the final minute that he lived, Milligan was convinced that the fox had actually winked at him.

~*The Lump in the Road*~

It's hard to describe the emotions I experience when phoned about a serious road accident. I think the first is of fright—when the voice at the other end of the line tells me of the crash. This revelation—which even after fifteen years working Motorway Safety and Maintenance—never fails to send goose bumps over my skin and never fails to cause a churning in the pit of my stomach. Then the visions: horrible, awful pictures in my mind's eye that more than once have led me to question my sanity. The worst aspect of all is that my imagination often cannot produce visions as crazy, terrifying as those that I'm destined to see.

The next emotion, as I place the receiver down, is shock. A few seconds where I wonder whether I have dreamt the phone call. I think about the families and friends of those involved in the accident. I don't know them; hell, I don't even know the names of the victims…I often never do—except for occasional photographs and biographical details published in the local newspapers. Nevertheless, I feel for them, I really do.

Then arrives the realisation that I'm employed to assist in the aftermath. This recognition usually kicks in on the drive to an accident; drives I often can't remember afterwards. This is the stage that my heart pounds as if ready to detonate—the stage where icy shivers run down my spine.

The fourth stage is of resilience. When I've seen the crash site and a colleague and I climb from the car and walk over to help the police and the medics. Often it's to keep sick voyeurs away or moving bits of wreckage from the road. Our real work, however, starts after the injured arrive at hospital and after the police have finished their questioning.

The fifth stage is the feeling of responsibility. During this phase, I repeatedly think of my job title: *Motorway Safety and Maintenance*. I think about it as I lie in bed trying to sleep, and the next morning whilst eating my breakfast. Only when I'm back at work and certain *I am* doing my job properly, do I feel like I can move on.

My fears the day after an accident are to whether it could have been avoided. And in my position, most importantly, was it something that I should have prevented? Has the road been maintained as well as it could be? This is the key question I must ask myself. *If* after close scrutiny I find the road is in perfect working order, I'm able to cope with the tragedy— it's not easy but I have to, and I accept loss of life as part of my job description.

Then came the fateful day of January 14. It had been a quiet day for myself (now's a good time to introduce myself, I'm Owen Davies) and my colleague on duty that evening, Tom Henson.

The phone rang, and as normal when I'm in the office, I answered. It was an accident on the A21. I made a note on the pad I keep beside the phone.

"Tom, there's been a four-car crash. Get your jacket." Tom's just a kid. Twenty-two years old; has a nineteen-year-old wife and a baby just born. The poor bastard has seen more mangled bodies in two years than anybody should have to see in a lifetime. He's a tough kid. A great kid. I can rely on him without fear; I *never* have to worry about how he'll react when witnessing a nasty smash. What he does is keeps all his feelings under lock and key. I'm sure his stomach churns and knots as mine does, but he keeps it hidden. I don't know, perhaps his grief pours out after he's gotten home and put the kid to bed. How he handles it, isn't important, that he does, *is*.

We travelled out to this particular crash on January 14, as we have done together the past two years—in silence. Tom has a habit of rubbing the bridge of his nose when he's tense; this is the only sign that it's not just another routine maintenance check.

The flashing lights is the first evidence we're close, then my mind takes in snapshots of what has happened. On this occasion, I see a crumpled BMW on the central motorway verge. I see a small hatchback car on its roof down a bank; I see sideways-parked police cars.

"There's a woman trapped under the car," Tom said. His eyes are like those of a hawk. My eyes are not as good as my ears so I hear her before

I see her.

"Please get me out of here! I can't move, I can't move," she muttered through tears. "I can't feel my legs!"

We watched as the experts did their stuff, trying to cut her out. Halfway through the process her body juddered violently and she begun to shriek. She reacted as if the cutting equipment had sliced her in two. She became motionless and there was a noticeable calm to the medical people trying to assist her. They exchanged glances and shook heads. The cutter was now taking more time over the operation—it looked to me as if she'd died. I found out later she had suffered a massive and fatal heart attack.

I escorted Tom away; I can't help trying to protect him, or is it me I'm protecting?

There was a woman holding a rag to her head, trying to stunt the bleeding. She was talking to the police.

"I don't know what *it* was…we were just…well, changing lanes and this…*this thing.…*"

"What thing?" the police officer asked.

"I don't know," the aggrieved woman said, taking the rag from her head and staring at the wet blood that stained it. The gash on her forehead spurted and blood ran down her cheek.

"It was *something* in the road."

"What kind of something, Ms. Croft?"

"*I don't know…*I already told you, *I don't know!*"

One of the medics arrived, and escorted her away. The policeman doing the questioning looked down to his feet, then turned and walked away.

Tom had left my side and was clearing some dangerous debris from the other side of the road. The cars over there were still moving, though at a slower pace than normal, mainly because drivers were slowing to see the crash wreckage. Our side of the road was at a complete standstill. A hundred yards away a jammed queue of cars led up the hill towards a bend in the road. Many of the drivers had gotten out of their cars and tried to see what was happening. The police stood guard to prevent them getting any nearer.

Why anyone should want to see a crash site I will never understand. I couldn't help noticing the amount of blood spilled. Drops, pools, and streams of it were everywhere. I could see the medics carrying another body from the car down the grass bank. Blood saturated the white sheet that covered her.

As I stood taking deep breaths, I felt unsteady on my legs. I instantly glanced to the road as if it were the tarmac's fault and not my legs for being so weak. I watched some blood soak away as if by magic. I stared hard, surprised by the road's absorption. I crouched and ran my finger over the area. It was totally dry—though I could see no crack that the pool of blood could have escaped down.

"Owen, can you give me a hand?" Tom called, as he attempted to bend the rail between the lanes of traffic back into position.

We spent most of that night at the scene, helping to clear up and then to get the traffic moving again, though slowly and only in a single lane.

The following afternoon, after only a couple of hours of sleep, wearing heavy bags under my eyes, and suffering a soreness and stinging to my tired eyes, I virtually sleepwalked over to the kettle to make Tom and I coffee. Then the big boss, Lance Witherspoon, entered the office.

"Owen, can I speak with the two of you?"

"Of course, sir," I said, running a hand through my uncombed hair before entering the office. Mr. Witherspoon sat down, leaning back, bringing his hands together as if in prayer by his chin. He breathed deeply, the sound emphasised as the air hit the tips of his fingers. He's in his late fifties and always wears the same damn tight fitting grey suit. His trousers are too short and his grey socks always exposed. The same grey socks he probably wore at school forty years earlier.

"Owen, I've been on the phone to the head of the police department. He claims several witnesses, including the one survivor of the eight involved in the crash, say the car in front suddenly swerved as if trying to avoid something. The car lost control and crashed, leading to the other three cars crashing and several others only narrowly avoided the collision. The girl that survived—a Ms. Croft—claims the reason the first car swerved was a lump in the road."

My heart really banged hard. *A lump in the road*, I knew from my boss's tone of voice and from the anger that glistened in his eyes, was something for which I would be held directly responsible. I hated the man from that moment; I knew he was worried only about his own reputation. He had lost all concern—if he ever had any—for those involved in the accident.

"Sir, we only laid new tarmac on that stretch of road six months ago," I said.

"So why does Ms. Croft—and others—claim there to be a lump in the road, *Owen?*" he said, virtually spitting my name as he might a piece of food that had been stuck between his teeth overnight.

"What others, sir?" I asked.

"There have been calls ever since the accident made the newspapers. Many claimed they had noticed the bump and thought it very dangerous. Now that a serious accident has taken place, apparently caused by the poor maintenance of the road," he said, allowing his eyes to drift from me to Tom and back to me, "these people have felt obliged to step forwards. Come out of the woodwork," he said, uncrossing his legs and crossing them the other way. He brought his hands away from his face and pointed a finger at me.

"What are *you* going to do about this?" he asked. His face had reddened; the office lights highlighted the glistening beads of sweat on his forehand. "Your job is to maintain the road on which the accident occurred. If there is a problem—a fault...*God help you.*" He smiled, stood and left the office. I had to fight the urge to grab his arm, swing him round and knock his teeth out. *Yes,* he had a good point; and *yes,* it was my responsibility. But it was just as much his as it was mine...in fact, more his responsibility—he was the boss, this was *his* operation.

Evidently, he wanted to pass all blame onto my shoulders. Perhaps he thought he could save his own career by jeopardizing mine. I now know that to be the case.

I calmed down as Tom handed me my jacket.

"Come on, Owen. We know we laid that tarmac right. Let's go and give ourselves peace of mind."

He always had a calming influence over me. He smiled faintly as I took the proffered jacket. In that smile, Tom confirmed that we were in this mess together; that he would stick by my side until the bitter end. If I thought I could convince him otherwise, I would have done so.

We drove to the stretch of road on which the accident happened.

We headed up and down that piece of motorway several times until certain there wasn't a fault with the road. We tried each lane and neither saw nor felt any unevenness. What was obvious, however, was how steep the road was just before where the crash had taken place. Too steep in my opinion and on a long bend as well, it would be very easy to lose concentration and to gain in speed without being aware of doing so; this combined with the dazzling streetlights that you head down towards at night, could have contributed to the accident.

Alternatively, perhaps tiredness explained the driver seeing something in the road. I remember on one occasion, driving through vast tiredness despite my wife telling me not to, I was convinced I could see foxes in the road—running away from my approaching car. Only in rubbing my eyes and looking again did I realise they were only traffic cones. It is amazing what tricks tiredness can have on your eyes and imagination.

"Mr. Witherspoon, it's Owen Davies," I said, phoning my boss once we had arrived back at the office. "We've had a thorough search of the road and can find no problems with it. It's perfectly smooth," I said.

"Well, how do you explain the reports of a dangerous lump?" he asked.

I shrugged. Then said, "I can't," realising over a phone line he couldn't see my shrug. And I really couldn't explain the sightings. Maybe one could be put down to tiredness or drugs or imagination, but not several sightings.

The only other possible explanation was *there had been* something in the road, perhaps something as inconspicuous as a car mat. Something that would blend with the road enough to make people blame the road itself—yet enough to cause the jumping sensation people had claimed. Mr. Witherspoon thought I was taking the piss. I don't blame him—it didn't seem likely a car mat would cause drivers to swerve across the road.

"Well you had better be right; otherwise there will be hell to pay!"

I had to hope and pray that was the end of it…but of course, it was not. There was a report of another crash that very night, I knew come morning I would be out of a job.

Tom sat loyally by my side on that journey, rubbing at the bridge of his nose more vigorously than normal; I think he knew I would soon be out of a job. I found myself thinking of my wife, Jane. I should say my deceased wife, as she lost her life five years earlier in Italy.

"You should pull over and take a rest. There's no rush," she had said that fateful night, rubbing at my thigh. "I saw a services sign just ten minutes ago. Why don't you stop for a break?"

"I'm fine," I had said to her. "I really want to put some miles in. We're behind schedule; I don't want to dash about Rome like headless chickens."

That was the last thing I ever said directly to her. A couple of minutes later I was on the inside lane as a truck moved from the slip road and onto the motorway. I misjudged how much time I had to move across, thinking I could accelerate through before the truck pulled out. I moved into the blind spot, where he couldn't and didn't see me in his mirrors. He struck the side of us—the many tons of truck causing us to career across the road. For a moment, I thought I had regained control, and then the steering wheel just twisted violently from my grasp as if a ghost had suddenly yanked at it. We hit the central reservation—the bonnet smashed inwards, compacted. I opened my eyes, shocked I had avoided serious injury. I first noticed the truck had stopped a little ahead of us. The driver was running over. Then I turned to Jane; her head snapped back at an impossible angle. The headrest had broken off from the force of my wife's head hitting it.

As Tom and I arrived at the crash site, it was all too familiar. Car parts scattered about, blood staining the road, and a witness claiming she was in the car behind the one that had lost control.

"The car just swerved...trying to avoid that bump in the road," she said, pointing vaguely in its direction along the motorway. I followed the line of her arm. If there had been a lump, there wasn't now. She seemed dazed by this. "Definitely saw it," she insisted. "It was *massive*...like a wave or something." She raised her hand parallel with her armpits. "I *swear* to you, it was *this high!* Like a giant wave...I swear to God it was."

The medics took her away; one of them whispered, "She's got a concussion."

A week later, now redundant, I returned to the fateful place. I approached through the trees that bordered the motorway. I set up a video camera and drank from a thermos of coffee. I had to know what was happening; I had to know about this lump people continued to blame for the accidents that had cost me my job, and far more importantly, had apparently caused people to lose their lives.

I had sat for about an hour when I heard the rustle in the trees. I expected it to be the police.

"Son, don't you realise it's dangerous to sit beside a fast road?"

"Yes, Officer, I know, I have worked on this motorway for fifteen years."

However, it was not the police...I wish it had been. In fact, it was not anything human. I stared as the dark shape slowly stepped through the shadows. It walked upright on two legs and had what appeared to be freakishly long arms. It could have been some giant ape—totally black in the darkness of night. It stood between two trees, and though I could see no features: no sign of eyes or a mouth, I knew it observed me as I did it. After a minute, *It* turned ninety degrees, brushed aside the branches that hindered its progress, and continued its journey. I think it must have been nine feet tall.

I watched, as the thing made its way to the edge of the motorway, crouching out of the headlights of oncoming cars. I was stunned into paralysis, yet tingling with excitement to see what the strange creature would do. There was a stream of three or four cars and then a long, dark stretch of road. I thought the thing would make a dash but instead just waited for the cars to pass. There were no car lights in sight—it was 2 a.m.

And then the black creature, the ape-like-thing, yet with no apparent facial features or hair, stepped out into the road, then carefully, again human-like, lowered itself and lay on its side across the far lane of the motorway. I was stunned. It blended immediately with the tarmac. Except for the lump that it formed, it was invisible. Then I saw the car lights approaching, I stood, mouth open, ready to shout. I could see what was about to happen; the mystery was solved, yet a far greater mystery unearthed.

As the car edged ever closer, the lump sank into the tarmac. With only metres to spare, the lump disappeared and the car passed safely. I stood staring at the tarmac for another hour. A million thoughts buzzed around my mind, but I couldn't catch any of them to help fathom what I'd just witnessed.

I have spent a week at home; frightened to switch the TV on or read the newspaper in case there has been another accident…especially now I'm certain I know the cause. The only factor that stops me speaking of my sighting is the certainty they will lock me up and throw away the key. They would throw away the key if I told my story.

God, what should I do? My mind is blank. The only person I could involve is Tom, and I really don't want to implicate him unless I have to.

What I know is something unnatural…supernatural, is responsible for the accidents. I don't think *It* intentionally hurts people…*It* is just there, for whatever reason, and couldn't help the accidents it has caused.

I gaze at myself in the mirror. I notice the crow's feet stretching from the corners of my eyes, the extra frown lines on my forehead, even yellowness to my teeth I have not noticed before. Through my hair as I tip my head forward, I can see the glare of the bathroom light.

You're getting old. Old is what you are…and crazy. What the hell do you think you saw out there? I ask myself, eyes locked with those of my reflection. *What did you see? You not going to answer me, huh? No comment from monsieur reflection? Jesus, maybe I am crazy after all.*

I saw a thing, I tell myself. *A huge dark shape that might have been an ape…or maybe a bear. Only it had no features, it made very little noise…and of course, it melted into the road. It was your imagination, Owen, you said yourself it was dark and had no features…it was just a shadow. But shadows don't brush branches aside and they don't stop beside the goddamn road and wait for the traffic to clear so they can go and fucking well merge with the tarmac!*

Just the same, however convinced I am of my sanity, I have to know for sure. I have to involve Tom. I'll call him now.

Jesus. It's hard to write this account again…but I suppose I must. Tom and I headed down to the section of motorway via a country road and then walked the final half-mile as I had previously. I hadn't told Tom exactly what we were doing, just that I wanted to show him something. I don't think he even considered questioning me. I asked a favour and he had obliged.

After a couple of hours, I thought we should pack it in—the thing didn't appear to be ready to show itself for a second time. Then of course, *It* came, as it had before from the undergrowth; emerging through a rustle of trees. I looked to Tom to make sure he was watching as I was. His eyes trained on the beast. I raised a hand to tell Tom it was okay. He nodded. The beast didn't wait around and made straight for the road, only taking a quick glimpse right to check whether a car approached. The road was clear so the thing lay flat on the road. It had gotten down as if on one knee and then rested weight on an elbow, before lying on its side. I kept gazing from the incredible thing to Tom, just to make sure he still watched.

Then the two beams of light appeared, approaching at least a hundred miles an hour, I should guess. The thing lifted its head; the bulk of its form only partially melted or absorbed, or whatever it is the beast does into the road. It seemed transfixed for a moment as animals are sometimes when caught in the beams of car lights.

The next few seconds are a blur. I remember the screech of tyres and the headlights suddenly upon Tom and I like a stage spotlight. Then the car losing control and smashing into the railing. Fire erupted, smoke billowed—the noise deafening. I stood, mouth agape, feeling violently sick. This worsened by noticing Tom had taken a whack from a piece of debris and his face was a mess of blood. I ran to his aid.

"*Jesus, Tom!* Are you okay?"

"I'm okay," he called, presumably over the ringing in his ears if he was experiencing the same as me. I insisted he moved his hands so I could assess the damage. He had a nasty cut around his left eye, a semi circular gash. He was lucky to escape with his eyes intact.

They closed the motorway and the following day they started the process of relaying the road. Tom and I watched for a while before heading off for lunch at a café. From there I went home, whilst he returned to work. Only fifteen minutes after parting, he called me on my mobile.

"Owen, it's Tom. Get yourself down to the accident spot."

"What's happened?"

"No time to explain. *Just come now!*"

It was the first time I had ever heard him raise his voice. It was the first time he had demanded something of me. When I arrived, I knew I was dreaming…only I wasn't. I wish I had been. The area of road where our mysterious friend had twice appeared bubbled like boiling oil in a cauldron. A circle of people stared in amazement.

"The hot tar was laid down, then just started bubbling and swishing about like that!" a guy with tar-stained overalls told everyone. He wiped his forehead and blew out his cheeks.

The road had come to life…when I saw the bulbous growth emerging I stood and held my breath while others screamed, and some ran. It was this thing of course, stretching, trying to emerge from the road as it must have done on previous occasions. I expected *It* to do just that and then perhaps make for the trees. It seemed a mammoth task for the thing and it struggled. With its upper body and head above the road surface, its long arms outstretched as if reaching for the sky, it appeared to have lost momentum and been paralysed. The thing was stuck solid like a statue in the dried tar.

"This is one of the most amazing specimens we have ever found," the science geek with glasses and an inability to keep saliva in his mouth said later that day. "We'll cut it out, fossilised, and take it for experiments," he said, grinning like a loony.

"You can't do that," I said. "I'm telling you, there's nothing underneath all that tar…it's not an animal. It's not anything from this world," I said weakly. I could see my words were not helping. There was nothing that I could do. They would treat it like a dinosaur fossil no matter how hard I tried to dissuade them.

It was several days before the scientists tried to excavate the thing. I had toyed with the idea of observing the process, but then chose not to. I knew *It* was not anything natural. I thought it better to keep my distance.

I had been driving when I heard a news report about a disaster at the crash site, the site at which the strange apparition in tarmac had emerged. I followed close behind a police car to see for myself what had happened.

I knew they should have left it be, I knew it. Damn idiots meddling with something they know nothing about!

Now, I had seen many crash sites in my time: I'm talking exploded skulls; brains turned to mush and spilled over the road; decapitation—yet nothing prepared me for what my "passive" beast had done. The thing that I thought had not intentionally caused the accidents.

There had been about a dozen people working on the excavation, they were now all dead. It took little imagination to figure how the thing had killed them. The corpses were in couplets, paired off, their heads smashed together so to form one hideous mess of skull and brain parts. In pairs like this they lay across the road; the scene silent except for a light breeze.

I wondered where *It* had gone. I turned on my heels and gazed as far as my sight would allow, without obstruction, in each direction. There was no sign of the thing. I then looked directly up to the sky.

"There's another one down the bank," one of the police officers said. I sighed and walked over to look. It was Tom. His body ripped in half. His head and torso at the foot of the grass bank, his legs and waist tangled in the branches of the overhanging tree.

I vomited into the grass, cursing the day I was ever born. My decision-making had cost my beautiful wife her life, and now Tom had met the same fate.

I turned with the intention of throwing myself in front of the first car that approached. I almost did too, only Tom's voice in the back of my head prevented me from doing so. He said, "Get the sonofabitch that did this, Owen. Make sure you get him for me, you hear?"

I closed my eyes tightly and told my friend that I would. And I will…even if it takes until my dying day.

~Waiting to be Filled~

Below a tree that swayed in the wind was a freshly dug pit—a rectangular hole that yearned to be filled. So far, only a single beetle had entered, and plenty of room remained. The grave waited patiently…it would not be kept waiting for long…

"Let go of my arm, Terry!"

Terry forcefully led Davina through the forest as she continued to yell.

"I've told you once already…shut the hell up otherwise I'll slit your throat, bitch!"

Wolf sniggered. "Yeah that's right, bitch, shut the hell up!" He had acquired the name Wolf because of his unusually long and sharp teeth. Nobody had known how hairy his back was at that point.

"Just keep the noise down, will you?" Terry said, grinning with lips that were thin and chipped. His face sunburned; his shaven head designed to hide his large bald patch.

"Where are we going?" Davina asked, feeling Terry's fingers digging into her wrist, it felt as if all the skin had worn away, just exposed red raw flesh beneath. "Why do you have to hold me so tight? I'm not gonna run!"

Wolf theatrically laughed. "Yeah, good one, bitch!"

"Stop calling me that."

"Will you two fuckheads stop bickering?" Terry said, pushing the branches out of his face. He had started work at the garage that morning expecting it to be just another day. He was under the bonnet of the Toyota when Davina had come into the workshop. She would often come in around eleven with sandwiches and coffee for him, only this time she hadn't. She had come to end their stormy two-year relationship and tell him she had found someone else. That someone was Lance Jenkins, the faggot executive who always wore a shirt and tie even when he was not trying to offload the pile-a-shit health products he sold. He had set up his own little business and was making a fortune.

Terry had not taken the news of the break-up so well, throwing the monkey-wrench across the shop and smashing a mirror. Davina had agreed to meet him after work to discuss the situation. And they had...briefly. She had said she had been seeing Lance for a month now, and *yes,* she had slept with him. Terry had nodded, digesting the information.

"That's just fine and dandy," he had said then slugged the bitch, catching her clean on the jaw, blood spilled from her gob as you only ever see in gruelling boxing matches. She had wept—he had kicked her a few times, then phoned Wolf...and now here they were...on a nice little nature walk.

"Terry, where are you taking me? This has gone far enough—I'm sorry things didn't work out, I really am! But please, let me go, I won't speak a word of any of this," Davina said in as calm and soothing a voice as she could find.

"You're a whore, Davina, and now you must take your medicine...I think it'll make you better, darling." He grinned.

"Oh fuck you then if you can't be reasonable!"

Wolf grabbed her long strawberry blonde hair and tugged hard. "Go on, Terry, slit her goddamn throat—*she's a whore!"*

"Now, now, Wolf...you know that wasn't the idea, don't you?"

Wolf shrugged. Terry nodded. Wolf let go of her hair. Davina's head sprung up and she rubbed at the back of her neck.

They followed the track until they emerged into a clearing.

"Now...Davina, you must promise not to scream or yell, right? If you do, I'll slit your throat, got it?"

Davina swallowed. Terry's glazed blinkless eyes reminded her of just about every psychopath she had ever seen on TV. She knew he had a violent temper; she had been on the receiving end of his fists more than once. Nevertheless, he wasn't all bad; as long as she did as he said, she should be okay.

She nodded. "I won't make any noise."

"Gag the bitch!" Wolf said.

"No, that won't be necessary," Terry said. He stared at Wolf who stood wide-eyed, unable to control his clown-like grin, the saliva dripping from his mouth. He was bouncing on the spot, like a kid about to receive his Christmas presents. And his dick was bulging through his pants. The sick, satanic bastard always got a hard-on, especially before payback.

Terry pointed to the mud slope and they carefully made their way down, he still held Davina's wrist. At the bottom awaited the pit he and Wolf had dug earlier in the day. Davina saw the hole and resisted Terry's momentum, stopping dead.

"What is that?" she asked. Suddenly her imagination's videotape was playing films of all the burials she had been to and seen. The coffin lowered into the ground, the weeping from those dressed in black. The eerie silence. The atmosphere of death hanging in the air.

"Are you gonna get in or am I gonna throw you in?" Terry asked.

"Terry, please, this is stupid…we need to talk about this, about us!"

Terry smiled, shook his head. "Honey, the time for talking is over. It's time you learnt a lesson. You never screw around behind my back. *Never.* Now, *get in the fucking hole!*"

She shook her head—her breaths heavy, her chest heaving. Her brain heated fast and she feared she might faint. The smell in the air was of fresh grass, corn and flowers. It was suddenly sickly to her senses; making her feel nauseous just as bleach would when she was doing her cleaning job in the mornings. She thought of Lance, they were supposed to be having dinner tonight. But now this. The crazy son of a bitch was going to bury her. She was going to die. Die. Die. *Be dead.*

"There's nothing to worry about, honey," Terry said. "I already told you if you take your medicine, like a good little whore, then you'll live. If you don't, Wolf over there is just itching to slit your throat and then fuck your dead, twitching body. Because you know, honey, he's a sick freak."

Davina had a lump in her throat; she was desperate to cry but didn't want to—they could cut her, rape her, even kill her, but she wouldn't give them the satisfaction of crying. She turned to Wolf, who was licking his lips, grinding his teeth, his hands trembling and expectant. She could see the huge erection he was groping at through his pants. She turned back to

Terry, sickened.

"*Jesus Christ!* Terry…you said you loved me—and now what…you're gonna let him stick that thing in me?" she said, wincing, fighting off those tears.

"I already said…if you get in that hole, like I told you, I'll put a leash on Wolf and we'll go get us some pussy in town, right?"

Davina closed her eyes and took some deep breaths. When she opened them Terry was standing only a few feet ahead of her, holding up the long piece of transparent tubing, grinning. It was like a hose, just not attached to a tap. He looked as if he were waiting for the call for "action" so they could tape a commercial.

"You'll need this," Terry said. "Otherwise you won't be able to breathe down there."

Her head slumped and she stared at her toes. She glanced out of the corner of her eyes and saw Wolf was jigging up and down, so eager, so excited, so very turned on…

She stepped over to Terry without making eye contact and took the piece of tube. She stood on the edge of the pit and gazed down. It was about one and a half metres deep. She stretched out the tube to measure the length. There was enough. Then she heard the tractor; her eyes sprang open and she gazed through the trees to the cornfield.

Over the sound of the faraway tractor, she heard Wolf's rasping voice.

"Can I do her, Terry—*can I?*"

"No…not if she does as she's told. And not a word, Davina…I'll fucking kill you if you even think of screaming! I swear on my dead mother's eyes that Wolf will fuck you senseless. *Get in the bloody hole!* Oh…you had better take your sweater off—it might get as hot as hell down there, maybe hotter."

She unbuttoned her sweater and hung it on a branch, before lowering herself into the grave, heart pounding. She lay on her back. Then she put the tube in her mouth and held it as high as her arms could reach. Terry and Wolf towered over. Terry took the end of the tube and held it above the pit while Wolf began to shovel the soil. Terry stood casually, one hand on hip. He was gazing towards the cornfield; obviously keeping his eyes on the tractor should it come too close. Davina wondered if she should shout for help—not yet, it was too far away, the farmer would never hear. But if it came close, real close, maybe she should. She looked up to Wolf as he was vigorously shovelling soil, sweat dripping down his face, his facial bristles glowing in the afternoon sun—his unkempt head of curly dirty blonde hair, greasy and sweat ridden, his hairy arms bulging with exertion.

"It's going to be okay, honey," Terry said, again that PR smile.

Wolf continued to toss soil upon her body; she gazed up at the overhanging branches, watching the birds jumping about. A squirrel ran along a branch, chewed on what might have been a nut, then carried on into the green leaves and disappeared. Apart from birdsong, she was also aware of Wolf's grunts of effort as he shovelled, and the thuds as the soil landed on her. And still that humming tractor. Would it come this way? Would it be too late? Would Terry really kill her for leaving him, for having an affair with Lance?

Then the first shovel of soil slapped her in the face, getting in her eyes—it stung like hell. She turned her head, hindered by the tube sticking from her mouth, brushing the soil away as best she could. The plastic tube would soon offer her only means of breathing, she could not do without it.

She took one last look at the blue sky and the glow of the sun, which were visible through the branches. Then she closed her eyes, wondering if she would ever see daylight again.

She knew her head was all but buried, she could feel the soil covering her face; it prevented her from taking breath through her nostrils. Though it was swelteringly hot, and she could not move her arms or legs any longer, she did still have the tube wedged in her mouth. Davina sucked the fresh air. Whilst she had the tube, she also retained hope.

Wolf stopped to wipe the sweat from his brow, and to pull the shirt material away from his sticky armpits. "Jesus, Terry, this is hard work—pass me the water."

Terry handed him the water bottle and he took several long gulps, and then rubbed at his face. He picked up the shovel and continued to fill the pit. Terry took the bottle, had a sip, and then gazed down to the tube. He smiled.

"You're right, Wolf. It sure is hot." He lowered his mouth to the tube;

Davina's face submerged in soil, but he could feel her breaths leaving the tube.

"Maybe you need a drink, sweetheart? It sure is hot, must be like a furnace down below."

He moved the bottle to the end of the tube and tilted it so the water ran gently down.

Davina had been thinking, recalling those moments that had made her life worthwhile: The school prom when she had kissed Zack, the backpacking trip around Europe, the drunken night at Trafalgar Square. Then the water entered her mouth as she breathed in—choking, unprepared, spluttering…swallow, swallow, swallow her brain screamed, so she did, and continued to until the water stopped coming. She breathed hard, coughing again, feeling as if she had just returned to the surface after running out of air while deep-sea diving.

Terry sipped again from the bottle then put the lid on. He watched as Wolf finished his work as the appointed gravedigger. He tossed the shovel to one side and sat down on a log, panting, unbuttoning his shirt.

"Now what?" he asked.

"I guess let her sweat it out a while," Terry said.

"You not gonna kill her?"

Terry shrugged. "No, she was a shit fuck anyway. We'll go and find us some new bitches tonight."

Wolf grinned, nodding his head.

The sound of the tractor was much closer now, heading in their direction, following the track through the corn. Terry could see the red bodywork and the huge black tyres beyond the trees.

Wolf stood and walked over to the tube sticking out of the filled grave. He bent down and put his mouth around it, sucked hard and then blew powerfully.

Davina felt the air coming her way, it rushed into her mouth, tickled her throat and tasted old and rotten, like some kind of festering roadkill nobody had scraped up, which had been lying in the sun for days, getting further squashed each time a truck sped by.

Wolf sniggered, turned and saw Terry was undoing his fly. Wolf moved before Terry could shower him.

"I'll give her the medicine now…Chateau Urine," Terry said. He stuck his dick into the end of the tube, and then sighed, enjoying the release.

"Oh yeah, that's better," he said as the cramp left his bladder.

Davina was now taking slow, precise breaths—she was faint, her eyes tired below the weight of the soil. It was as if somebody were pressing their fingers into her eyelids, applying pressure to her eyeballs.

Then the fluid entered her mouth; she swallowed, once and twice, before realising it was urine she drank. But she had no choice—she had to just swallow, swallow, and swallow….

Terry groaned in satisfaction and shook off the drips. He looked down and saw that the tube was full of the yellow liquid. He waited for it to lower. His eyebrows met in the centre and his forehead creased when it did not.

Wolf was watching too. His laughs had stopped. "Jesus, I think you killed her—drowned her lungs with piss!"

Then the urine gradually lowered until it was all gone.

"Okay, let's get her out," Terry said, pointing to the shovel.

It was now that Terry thought that something was different. It was too quiet. Eerie. Then he realised it was because the tractor could no longer be heard. He glanced over and saw it had parked up not more than fifty yards away and he could hear the rustle of footsteps.

"*Jesus! Wolf!*" he called, waiting for his friend to look up, and then he pointed.

Terry flicked open his knife then went over behind a tree. He had his back against the tree and faced Wolf.

He mouthed instructions to him and waited. Wolf tossed the shovel into the undergrowth and stood ahead of the grave, trying to hide the tube.

The farmer came through the branches, a shotgun in his hands.

He saw Wolf, assessed the situation, and then continued up into the clearing.

"What you doing in there?" the burley, heavily bearded farmer asked. "This is private land—no one's allowed in here."

Wolf tried to control his body's shuddering. He watched as the farmer took a few more steps closer—only a couple of yards short of Terry, who waited with the knife in hand.

"I said what you doing up there?" the farmer demanded, cocking his gun.

"Just…just enjoying the forest," Wolf said, croaking, his throat so dry with anticipation, adrenaline pumping.

The farmer had noticed the strange demonic look to the stranger's eyes and sensed something was wrong. He noticed the pink sweater hanging on the branch—a girl's sweater.

"You here alone?" he asked.

Wolf's eyes darted to the grave, and then back to the farmer, sweat trickling down his neck. He licked his lips and tried to swallow saliva to moisten his throat.

"Yeah," he said, but it caught in his throat. "Yeah I'm alone."

"You see I thought I heard you talking to someone," the farmer said.

Wolf felt a moment's panic; his foot began to involuntary jiggle. His eyes darting from the grave to Terry, who stood pressed against the tree. Terry shook his head, mouthing: *Stop fucking looking at the grave, stop fucking looking at me!*

The farmer raised his gun. "Is that your sweater then?" he asked. "That pink one, that's yours, is it?"

Wolf shook his head, eyes wide, his whole body shaking, and then he quickly nodded. His body vibrated so violently that he thought it would explode.

The farmer started to walk forward, his eyes suddenly fixed on the tube. Then Terry jumped out, flashing the blade, slashing it towards the farmer's throat. The farmer blocked the assault with the barrel of the shotgun and they struggled. Wolf watched on as Terry tried desperately to out-strength the farmer who was twice his size. Then the gun fired, the blast accompanied by the spray of Terry's brains against the tree trunk, his body slumping to the ground. His so-called face no more than an explosion of mush as if a grenade had gone off in his mouth. The farmer wiped the blood and the brain fragments from his face, smearing the blood further over his cheeks. He raised the gun towards Wolf. Wolf turned and ran, striding through the trees, battering branches away, all the time hindered by the erection that remained like a pole of steel in his pants.

The farmer aimed at Wolf's back, but relented on shooting. He walked over to the tube and examined the area. He too was shivering—disbelieving that he had just blown someone's brains out. He noticed the shovel in the bushes and collected it. In putting his face close to the tube, he heard what sounded like a girl's sobs.

"*Christ almighty! If you can hear me…I'm gonna dig you out!*" he called then began to dig as fast as he could.

Davina swooned in and out of consciousness. She was floating aimlessly in blackness. What sounded like a loud explosion had brought her around. And there were vibrations around her—she wondered if it there might have been an earthquake or if some underground creature burrowed toward her.

Then she heard a voice, muffled and distorted, but a voice. It didn't sound like Terry's—and not Wolf's either.

The farmer dug lower, deeper, tossing soil all around, the tube becoming more and more exposed. With growing desperation, he rammed the shovelhead into the soil. For heaven's sake, don't let him be too late to save whoever it was down there!

Then with another powerful thrust, he heard a crack as the shovel struck something hard. He felt the vibrations right up to his elbows. A rock, perhaps? He stopped. He lifted the shovel. The head smeared in crimson coloured liquid. He stood staring at the shovelhead for some time, before placing it down and lowering to his knees. He used his hands to burrow, and then his fingertips were red, sticky and warm. He scraped away further and a pool of blood bubbled and spurted. He dug channels for the blood to drain away and found himself staring into a dark gash, a wide mouth sliced into the girl's throat by the shovelhead—all but decapitating her. There was no question that she was dead.

He removed the soil from her face so that he could take the tube from her mouth. He then closed her parted lips and prayed.

The farmer dropped Terry's faceless corpse into the grave, and then the breathing tube also. He returned to his tractor and started the journey back to his farmhouse.

Three days later, Davina was reported missing by her boyfriend Lance Jenkins. He openly admitted his love for her and revealed the affair in which they had been involved.

Wolf and Terry had also gone missing, but as Wolf's jeep was not in his drive, it was assumed the two of them had gone on one or their road trips. It appeared to Sheriff O'Driscoll that Davina might have changed her mind about Lance and returned to Terry. He thought that Davina, Terry and Wolf had gone away together. It seemed to add up. However, Sheriff O'Driscoll was willing to do the rounds, ask a few questions. It was his job after all.

He drove onto Joe's land, pulling up outside the farmhouse. Nobody answered the bell. The tractor was sitting alone in the cornfield. Sheriff O'Driscoll rubbed at his chin, calling out to the farmer. Nobody answered.

He went round to the barn and pushed the heavy doors open; the sun shone in and illuminated the dust that sprayed into the air. The sheriff took his hat off and stared up to the rope and then the wooden beam that held it. The farmer's body swung lifelessly in the noose.

~It Was My Shadow~

I have to tell someone what has happened to me...I just have to. But first of all I want to make it clear it *wasn't* me that committed those horrific crimes...it really wasn't me...*it was my shadow!*

It started six months ago. I was minding my own business. I had paid the gas bill and had just had lunch in town; ham and pineapple pizza I had, though that is irrelevant...I felt a little bloated, as you do after eating, so I went for a walk—a walk along the beach. It was a bright sunny day, the wind was light, and the sea lapped up the sand. In the distance I saw a seagull hovering, then swoop down, catching a piece of bread in its beak. I saw the little girl who had thrown the bread to the gull. She waved her arms about, waving and yelling in joy. The gull flew away up and beyond the cliffs. The girl for a moment looked disappointed, but soon overcame the loss remembering the sandcastle she had built.

As I got nearer, I was amazed at the incredible kingdom she had constructed, all with bucket and spade. There was one main castle; around it were several smaller ones with turrets, fences made from pieces of stick and even a seaweed garden with flowers in.

'What a beautiful castle,' I had said.

She glanced up with a wide smile stretching across her face. 'Thanks, mister,' she said, her confident, loud voice surprised me, as she can only have been six years old.

'You had better build a moat,' I suggested. 'The tide will be in soon and all your hard work will be ruined.'

She smiled. 'Yes, mister, I will...will you help me?'

I admit it had been many years since I last built a sandcastle, but on this occasion I felt compelled...and I'm not afraid to admit, quite excited by the prospect. The girl, whose name was Vicky, used her spade, whilst I used a branch that was strewn on the beach. When the moat was finished, Vicky grinned happily, but then looked almost disappointed seeing that the tide hadn't come in as I had predicted. It looked as if it would be at least another hour until the moat was tested. She said she couldn't stay for an hour, as her mum would worry. It was only at this point I realized that such a young girl shouldn't be out on her own anyway, despite crime being nonexistent in Harley village.

'Could I take you home later?' I said.

'No, mum says I shouldn't talk to strangers...I better go,' she said.

After all the hard work, I couldn't let our moat go to waste, so I suggested we collect water from the ocean then we could fill it ourselves. That wide smile returned, she grabbed the bucket and before I could speak she had run off down to the sea, and plunged the bucket in.

It was now the horrors started. I sat in the sun, closed my eyes and felt the heat on my forehead. As I opened my eyes, I saw my shadow cast over the little girl's sand kingdom. I looked up to the sun, then back down to the sandcastle and to where the girl was inspecting shells. Then a shadow moved...I looked around to see who stood behind me—no one—I gazed back and watched, paralyzed, as my shadow kicked to pieces the sand kingdom the girl had worked so hard upon! I rose to my feet, froze, I wanted to run for my life, yet I couldn't believe my own eyes—and the girl...I couldn't leave her! As she turned, she froze also...not from the sight of my wicked shadow, but at the sight of me standing over the sand city; she looked down and her jaw dropped, she began to sob, cry so hard. She dropped the bucket then ran away.

'Please, come back...it wasn't me...it was...uh...please it wasn't me!' I stopped and watched as Vicky vanished into the back of a house.

Suddenly fearful of her father coming at me with a shotgun—that is what I imagined—I ran from the scene and back to my home, where I lay on my bed trying to understand the incredible events that had taken place.

Though it was so real, on the following morning, waking, I had just about convinced myself it was some kind of dream or hallucination. It must have been.

A couple of weeks passed, everywhere I went, I would find myself watching my shadow, just in case...*just in case.* I had just had my lunch; lemon chicken and rice on this occasion, and I went for a stroll in the park; I had avoided my usual route along the beach ever since that first...first *incident.* I met a lady walking a dog.

'Fine day for a walk,' I said.

'Yes, isn't it?' she responded. I smiled and walked on. I reached the lake, stood with one leg up on a bench, and gazed out into the water at the swans. Just in front of me, an elderly man was breaking pieces from his sandwich and dropping them in; the ducks were racing for the soggy pieces of cheesy bread.

'Feeding the ducks?' I said somewhat stupidly.

'Yes,' he said. 'My wife thinks I'm at work, but I couldn't hack it so I quit—couldn't tell the wife though...you know what women are like!'

I smiled. He turned back to the ducks and threw his last piece of sandwich way out, it plopped into the water, and the ducks skated over the surface towards it.

'Go on, out you go!' the elderly man shouted.

Just then, out of the corner of my eye, I noticed my shadow! The sun was in front of me, burning down upon me, so my shadow, as I figured, should have been behind me—but it was not. My shadow strolled around and over to the elderly man. I was about to warn him, but...it was too late! He landed with a wailing splash, went under for a moment then came up spitting a mouthful of water and waving a fist at me.

'*Why the hell did you do that?!*' he screamed.

I said: 'It wasn't me, you have to believe me!' But of course, he didn't.

'*I'm no sexist!*' he roared.

I was baffled for an instant. Then replied: 'I didn't say you were!'

He began to climb from the lake; I went to help him, but he waved his angry fist at me again, so I just left as quickly as possible.

You might ask why I'm telling you all this information. Well, isn't it obvious? Surely you can see where this is leading. I'm getting there...just please be patient, I feel it's best I tell you the whole story. Then maybe...just maybe, you might believe me.

I paced at home, desperate, scared. What on earth could I do? I sat with my lamp behind me for hours on end, watching my shadow. It didn't move—it just remained where it was supposed to be, mimicking every move I made. Every now and then I would suddenly raise an arm or kick out a leg, just in case I caught my shadow off guard, just in case for a fraction of a second it lost concentration. Alas, it didn't! It mimicked and copied as if it were my…well, my own shadow. But I knew it wasn't, I didn't care if nobody would believe me, I had to do something, I have to tell my tale and try and convince you!

Moving on, the next incident happened one late evening. I was taking a stroll through town, as I regularly do before bed—just having a little exercise and stretching my limbs before sleep. I had completed my circuit through town and was about to return home for a mug of hot cocoa, when I was passing a line of people that waited for entry into some party or other. The men were dressed in tuxedos; the women were made-up, wearing long evening dresses. I smiled and nodded at them as I went by. *Then my damn shadow!* For a fraction of a second I noticed it advancing to one of the men—a man with a thick moustache and black hair. Before I could speak, my shadow had punched him in the face! The man cried out and collapsed on the floor with a bloody nose. I leant down to apologize—only bringing the guilt upon myself. The crowd of people drawn to the angry words of the moustached man, turned to look.

'*It was him, I saw it happen!*' shouted one blonde lady, pointing accusingly at me.

Everyone stared at me; they began to approach—I ran for my life and one or two people chased me for a while, but under such terror, I must have run fast enough to win an Olympic medal. I hid in the trees and waited…thought…sobbed. What the hell was I to do? I considered turning myself in at this point—I could try to explain the insane circumstances and just hope the authorities had a record of something similar; maybe this would have been my only chance. But I decided against it and returned home. I thought I was in the clear, I had avoided seeing anyone on my journey home, and I was just unlocking my door when I heard a call from behind.

'Hello, Malcolm.'

I turned and looked—it was Mrs. Mayfair, my neighbour.

'Please, get away from me…please!'

'What's wrong?' she asked.

'No time to explain—' I was right. Mid-sentence, I watched my shadow creep up behind her and pull the rope tightly around her throat, squeezing. For a second a tortured squawk came from her mouth, her eyes bulged, then she sagged and crashed down on the pavement! I stared at my shadow, and for the first time it seemed to be aware of me. Then it was gone, I turned then shrieked on seeing it behind me, I fell gasping. I gazed at my shadow but it was motionless! I moved my legs and watched as the shadow did the same. I could hear voices just around the corner— I went in my house, slamming and locking the door behind me, terrified. I ran into my room and hid under my bed!

I might have been in my room for days, I cannot remember—it is all just a blur…I think for a while I must have lost my mind as I have no memory. I was woken from my trance-like state by a knock at the door…pain fired through my heart and I was sure that I was in the process of having a heart attack. I screamed.

'*Please, help me—I'm dying—I'm dying!*' I shrieked. Two police officers smashed the door down and dragged me from under the bed. I shivered, so very frightened, praying for the peaceful release of death. They asked me if I knew anything of the murder of Mrs. Mayfair.

'*Yes, oh God!—Yes, I saw it—I was there, please lock me up, protect me—I'm afraid—It'll happen again if you don't help—please, for Christ's sake help me!*'

They started walking me out when the door slammed shut. I only remember seeing my shadow growing in a dark mass, towering over us by the door—then all went blank…black.

I awoke facing the two police officers. Joy took hold, then despair. Gags in their mouths stopped them from speaking. Tight rope prevented them from leaving their chairs. I was tied to a chair also. For hours nothing. Oh, God, I can see their eyes now—I cannot imagine…describe the terror in them. The flames of Hell were burning in their pupils—they must have seen the same fear and foreboding in mine. Then it returned! Oh, Jesus did it; I watched as it cut them with a razor, thin red lines cut into their faces. Then the ultimate horror…the muffled agonized shrills fill my head still…*I don't know if I can go on!*…It was too much…but I must finish my tale…*I must*…and pray that you believe me—as no one else will! If none I have told so far has stricken the fear of Satan himself into you, then surely the crime I next witnessed might.

My shadow pulled the cloth gags from their mouths and held tightly onto their noses, one at a time. The reason you may ask? The reason was so that they had to open their mouths to breathe—my shadow grasped their tongues and stretched them out beyond their teeth—and cut— sliced them clean off with a razor before tossing them into the centre of the room! The red muscles lay coated in blood and saliva—one twitched on the floor, sending an electric pain through my very soul. If only that was all, but he moved onto their eyes, *oh God!*—I watched as he gouged them out, gouged them from the sockets; only at this point did I think to shut my eyes, petrified, sickened. When I opened my eyes again the two eyeball-less corpses stared at me through their black empty voids. Blood had gushed down, stained and dried over their chins and down their shirts.

I noticed my bunch of keys on the floor and was able to topple over my chair…I landed with a bang. I got the keys in my hands and then scraped madly at the rope that bound me. It took hours of scraping; maybe days, but finally I was free—*free!* I ran aimlessly, trying to process any logic I could come by…then I knew I had only one choice—that's why I came here—why else would I hand myself in…surely, if I were guilty I would run away—not have turned myself in—*please believe me! Please you have to help me…please, oh, God, please save me from my shadow!*

They stared in through the one-way glass as Malcolm banged his hands against the other side, the mirror. Blood smeared around his mouth; his own blood spilled as he repeatedly bit into his own lips and gums—maybe in worry, maybe in self-mutilation, maybe in madness.

'What do you think, Doctor Haley?' the chief inspector asked.

Doctor Haley took his eyes from the sobbing man and looked to Chief Inspector Lyons. 'He is clearly insane…in fact, he is just about the maddest person I have ever seen…fancy trying to convince us his shadow caused all this tragedy!'

'Yes, I thought so,' said Lyons, 'but that's what insanity is, surely? A claim like this to a psychopathic madman, probably seems quite natural…why would he tell us such a tale, unless he thought there was chance we would believe him?'

Doctor Haley looked to Malcolm. Malcolm suddenly slumped to the ground and rolled into the centre of the prison cell. 'Jesus, what is he doing? Oh, look, he's trying to strangle himself—get someone in there to sedate him…quick before he kills himself!'

Two officers charged in to prevent the suicide, but they were too late. Malcolm lay lifeless on the ground with his fingers clasping his throat.

Doctor Haley and Chief Inspector Lyons watched through the glass.

'Poor bastard,' said Lyons.

'I disagree,' commented Doctor Haley. 'If I was as nuts as Malcolm, convinced my shadow was some kind of murdering demon…I would want to be dead too.'

They exchanged glances, turned the lights out and left the room. As they did, there was a slight movement by the stricken form of Malcolm, and then a shadow crept away.

Me had no choice but to do it, me didn't! Me's a shadow and nobodies must knowy bout me! No choice…you heard him telling on me, did you? Nobody must knowy bout me, nobody! Me's had to do it…had to! Me's a shadow me is!

~*The Veiled Lady*~

She watches from the window as the rains crash down over the forest. She waits as she always does for morning to arrive, for the sun to appear on the horizon. She has been following this routine for many years, isolated by her decisions.

Only this time something is different...she can see a figure emerging from the trees, heading towards the cottage in which she spends her days. Her forehead furrows in thought as the soaked man staggers towards her home, then stumbles, reaching for the door.

She pulls a shawl over her shoulders and brings the veil down over her face. It is the first person she has seen in the forest for over a year.

She opens the door and the man gazes up to her through streams of water that roll down his face. He mouths *thank god*, but no sound passes his lips.

The man dreams of a lady in a veil—she walks, almost floats, like a fairy across a garden plump with flowers. She clearly adores those flowers. The sun shines upon her, producing the illusion that she glows. Butterflies hover around her presence, drawn to her. Then she turns to him. She lifts the veil and as she does, dark clouds rumble over and it begins to rain— lightning strikes the trees, simultaneously illuminating the burnt and disfigured face she has concealed.

He wakes, panting; rubbing at his face, thankful it has all been a dream. But when he opens his eyes, he sees her; she sits in a rocking chair beside the fire, engrossed by her knitting.

He blinks and sits up, gazing to the burning logs in the fireplace, inhaling the woody smell. She wears a pale blue dress and matching coloured veil. He stares, uncertain, fearful of what might lie behind that veil. Is it the fairy-like lady, who attracts butterflies and loves flowers, or the disfigured monster that brings with it storm clouds and thunder? He swallows.

"You've slept nearly the whole day," she says, putting her knitting to one side and standing. The voice is angelic. His fears evaporate, he smiles.

"Thank you…thank you for bringing me in from that storm." He looks down to the clothes he wears and realizes they are not his. Underneath the blanket, which covers him on the sofa, he wears a beige shirt and a pair of red shorts. The idea of the lady having seen him naked causes him to blush.

"I hope you're hungry?" she says, taking a few steps closer. "Dinner will be ready soon…if you would like some?"

He nods. "Are you sure you have enough? I don't want to overstay my welcome."

"I wouldn't let you leave just yet, even if you wanted to," she says, standing before the fire, the glow of the flames projecting beams of light over her veil, revealing the soft looking skin and high cheekbones. "You have a temperature," she says, coming across the room fleet-footedly, leaning over him and bringing the thermometer into his vision. She moves her hand toward his mouth, then pauses, waiting for him to part his lips. He does so; his eyes fix on her pretty, delicate hands. He allows his eyes to drift to the veil and now she is so close he can again see her soft skin…but her eyes remain hidden.

"Your temperature is coming down," she says, her voice barely more than whisper, yet melodic. She has a voice that makes butterflies flutter in his stomach. He feels secure. Happy. At home.

She stands over him, assessing his health then walks away and out into the kitchen. He takes the opportunity to study the room—the fireplace makes it cosy. Bookshelves adorn one wall and a row of records another. He cannot see a television, which is a shame as the football is on that evening.

What is her name?

He, Martin Connor, had left Oakville Lodge three days earlier with the intention of hiking out to Goat Fell, but had evidently missed the turning and ended up some place deep in the forest. He had been completely lost, and without a compass, helpless. He hadn't worried too much at first, as he was certain of the route he'd come, though he had long since lost the footpath—his mind drifting off into the realms of the plays he wrote. His ex-girlfriend used to claim that when he was in the process of plotting a play he could walk off a cliff and not even notice until hitting the beach below. Losing the path should not have been as serious as walking off a cliff, but it had started to look that way, at least until he stumbled on the veiled lady and the cottage.

He hopes she might have a map to send him off in the right direction. *Do I really want to leave?*

When he had not found the original path, he had started to worry that he might be heading in the wrong direction. Then gasping for a drink—having finished his only small bottle—wiping sweat from his brow, he had gazed to the sun. He experienced a moment's déjà vu. He had looked to the sun at the start of his walk—it had been directly ahead, now it was over to his right, ninety degrees.

He followed the sun, thinking that must be the right thing to do, but he was still lost as darkness covered the forest, and no closer to finding his hotel. And the hunger began to set, as did the thirst after spending the best part of a day in the summer humidity without water. He was a city boy and had never taken the dangers of the Great Outdoors seriously. He would do from now on. At least he had found the cottage. *I'll ask the kind lady if she has a phone*, he thinks. He should phone work. He is supposed to be back at the bank today. He feels for his stubble, it is the most he has had since leaving college five years earlier.

As he is touching his facial hair, the veiled lady enters the room with a mug of something that steams. She hands it to him and he accepts.

"Thank you—smells lovely," he says.

"It's cocoa with coffee," she says. "I hope that's okay, I always have it when I'm unwell." He thinks he sees a smile rise beneath the veil. Should he ask about it?

"It really is kind of you to take care of me," he says. "I feel much better now."

She sits in the rocking chair beside the fire and begins to knit.

"The veil…if you don't mind me asking?" he says. She stops knitting, her entire body motionless. He regrets the comment immediately, wishing he could take it back. "I'm sorry, I shouldn't have asked. It's none of my business."

"That's okay; I just would prefer not to talk about it…not just now."

He smiles and nods. A slightly uncomfortable atmosphere fills the room, something for which he blames himself. "The food smells nice," he says, as a way to break the tension.

"Rabbit pie," she says.

He is unable to prevent an image of bunny rabbits sitting in a pie, entering his mind's eye. The cute little rabbits look around and wonder what is happening. Then the pastry lid comes down over their heads and before they can protest, the pie has slid into the oven and the door shut. Maximum heat.

"What's your name?" he asks.

"Annabel. And yours is Martin Connor," she says, smiling beneath the veil. "I'm sorry if you think I've been prying, but your clothes and your wallet were soaked through. I hung them to dry…I had to empty the contents of your wallet to help them dry out."

"No, that's good of you. Thank you. You really have treated me too well. Annabel…it's a lovely name. Do you…do you live here alone?"

Why did I ask that? Because it is an obvious question to ask, that's why.

She does not answer at first, releasing a sigh. "Yes, I live alone. I have done for close on ten years." She sounds sad. He thinks her isolation must be due to some terrible accident that has left her disfigured, hence the veil. "But I like it here…out in the forest. It's very beautiful especially this time of year," she says, suddenly more positive, as if the words are something she regularly repeats.

"It is a lovely home," he says. He yawns. "Sorry, suppose I'm still suffering from my walk in the forest. I can't wait to eat, it's been nearly three whole days since I have done," he says, smiling. His stomach grumbles loudly.

"It won't be long now," she assures him, and continues to knit.

"Do your family and friends get out here to see you often?" he asks.

She shakes her head. "I don't really have any friends," she says. "Well, except…oh, it doesn't matter."

Martin stands and stretches his arms above his head, yawns again, walks over to see her books. "Do you mind if I take a look?"

"No, go right ahead."

"What were you going to say before?" he asks, running a finger along the book spines. "We were talking about friends."

I'll be your friend, he thinks. *Is that all I want to be? There might be a monster beneath that veil…could a monster have such a perfect voice, a voice to send goose bumps over my skin?*

She exhales a long breath. "Come with me."

Martin follows her out into the back yard, which is a space of grass surrounded by trees. There is a fresh, woody scent to the air. There are no flowers.

Standing out in the sun—though he does not think she is aware—exposes her more than any light has done previously. He can clearly see the shape of her face through the veil, can even see the red of her lips and the white of her teeth as she smiles, and *(I think)* the glimmering greens of her eyes. He can only though see one side of her face, so presumes her affliction—whatever it might be—must be on the hidden side.

Then she does something that surprises him. She purses her lips together as if going to whistle, but instead, she makes a strange popping noise—as if she is trying to attract the attention of a cat, he thinks. When she opens a palm full of nuts, he assumes his guess is not far from the truth. He then notices several small orangey animal heads appear from the pine trees, then hears scampering, followed by one, then two, three, four, five and then close to a dozen squirrels running across the grass to where Annabel crouches with an open hand, feeding them individually as they queue to take food.

Martin watches in amazement, more at how the squirrels patiently queue for their share of nuts than anything else does. He can hear birdsong all around the cottage, and suddenly, especially with the angelic Annabel beside him, he cannot imagine a more heavenly location.

Annabel stands and smiles, and at this moment Martin has the strong urge to grab hold of her, fling off her veil and kiss her. To hell with any disfigurement, it would not matter—he could not care less. However, he cannot—though his heart wills him forward, his legs will not respond. His eyes fix on the auburn hair that has escaped the veil and rests over her shoulder.

"Martin," she says, softly. In his mind's eye, he imagines her stepping forward, lifting the veil and kissing him—imagines rolling about naked in the grass…

"Are you ready to eat?" she asks.

"Yeah, sure." As she enters the cottage, he sticks two fingers into the collar of his shirt to allow air inside. He could do with a cold shower, he thinks.

He follows her, the butterflies darting about his stomach—he feels so…so, he cannot describe it but fears he will not be able to eat a thing despite having gone so long without food. *God, am I in love with her? Is that what this feeling is?* He had been in love before, at least he thought he had been; he told his ex-girlfriend that he loved her, the one he'd spent two years of his life with, many times he'd told her and had firmly believed it. But what are the feelings he has for Annabel, for the cottage?

He thinks he might awake at any moment…the idea strikes him with fear. *God, no!* He speaks a silent prayer that it is real, that Annabel really does exist and she's this exquisite. *God, if only I can convince her to remove her veil, perhaps if I tell her that no disfigurement can make a difference.* And it cannot be so bad; he has seen most of her face. Probably no more than a slightly charmless birthmark, he thinks.

"After dinner I'll show you how to get back to Oakville Lodge," she says. He has heard the cliché about tugging at heartstrings many times, but at this moment, he cannot think of a better description of the pain he suffers. She is not supposed to say that, not in his dream world; she is supposed to ask him to stay awhile, and then they will fall madly in love and never be apart. *Take it back, please, say that you do not want me to leave!*

"Martin?"

"Yes." *Yes, darling,* he thinks

"It shouldn't be too difficult. There is a path beyond the garden—if you follow it, you will reach civilization. It's maybe fifteen miles, I'm afraid, but there's a clear path the whole way, you could then probably get a bus back to the lodge from there."

It might be a clear path but his mind will be crammed full with thoughts of her and this divine haven into which he has stepped. He will probably lose the path as he has done before, only this time he will not care; in fact, he can use it as an excuse to return to the cottage.

As they eat the rabbit pie, Martin watches Annabel. He suffers as he watches her carefully fork food beneath her veil to reach her mouth. On many occasions he wants to ask her why she must do so—is it necessary? Tell her she should reveal herself and not feel so self-conscious.

After finishing the meal, Martin helps clear the table, taking dishes over to the sink where Annabel has turned the taps on and is filling the washing-up bowl. Close behind her, he can smell the flowers around her, as if her aura contains their scent. *What flowers? There were none in the garden.* She turns suddenly as if sensing his presence. An awkward moment passes and Martin smiles, then feeling warmth spreading through his very soul, he moves toward her, hoping, praying she will not resist. He wraps his arms around her waist and they hug. He can feel her heart pounding; he can feel her breaths on his neck. However, he is too afraid to speak for fear of what she might say in response.

"Martin...we shouldn't," she finally says. He pulls away, but reaches for her hand and squeezes it in his. "Why not?"

She does not respond at first, just turns her head. "We just shouldn't."

"Don't you like me?" he asks. "I understand if that's the case...but then at least tell me, because I really like you and I need to hear you say it if you don't feel anything for me."

As a silence begins, Martin gazes out the window to three small apple trees, which stand ahead of the pines that surround the property.

"I do like you," she says, "that's why it's so hard."

"What's so hard, what do you mean?"

She opens her mouth as if about to speak, then closes. Martin takes a deep breath then reaches for the veil. Her hand meets his as he tries to lift; she resists at first then drops her hand. Martin brings the veil slowly up and then off...he steps back and leans on the fridge now her face has been uncovered. His eyes widen; he gently shakes his head. She drops her eyes, lowers her head as if trying to hide from his stare.

"What...why do you wear the veil?" he asks. "You're so incredibly beautiful!"

She is amazing. I can't believe it, he thinks. He tries thinking of a more attractive woman in the world and cannot. *And she likes me? That's crazy*, he thinks, suddenly feeling like the ugly duckling.

Annabel seems to notice his sudden lack of confidence, moves toward him, and holds him by the arms. "Martin, I do really like you."

The words are enough for him to regain his self belief and he leans forwards and kisses her on the lips; she doesn't at first respond, more as if she doesn't know how than because she doesn't want to. Is it possible she has never been kissed, that her self-imposed isolation has prevented her from such an experience?

She pulls away, then blushes; her auburn her glimmers in the rays of the sun passing through the window; her full red lips creating dimples in her cheeks as she smiles.

"Why the veil?" he asks. "I don't get it."

She chews on her lower lip as she thinks about her answer. "I've just had some bad luck in previous relationships. I guess I'm just afraid if I start something with you, it'll end the same way."

He is both disappointed and relieved by her words. She is not the angelic virgin he has taken her for, and she *has* had other relationships…but the only thing stopping her is fear.

"Well, I think we should at least try," he says. "Maybe we'll be different." He pauses to take breath, feeling claustrophobically hot. "I think I'm falling—"

She puts her hand over his mouth to stop him saying it. She shyly presses her face against his chest. "Just one thing you must promise me, Martin."

"What is it?"

"You must first promise not to ask why I need you to keep this promise."

Martin sighs. "Of course. What is it?"

"You must never—I mean absolutely *never* tell me you love me."

Martin looks down to her head, smelling her hair, feeling so warm and…*in love. I do love you though, it is insane I know, but I love you, Annabel!*

"I promise I won't ever say it."

Unexpectedly she raises her head and kisses him. The kiss continues, growing in passion, her hands slipping under his shirt and rubbing his back—then following her lead Martin pulls the zip of her dress down a little so he can run his own hands over the skin of her back.

They go upstairs; she leads the way, unbuttoning his shirt, slipping his belt off. He does not think their lovemaking will last long; he is already at bursting point. His body is a pincushion of orgasmic tingles.

Martin helps her out of her dress and even before it's off they roll on her bed; she shows great expertise as she pulls him inside her, then he lies back with his hands cupping her breasts; he teases her nipples while she slides up and down on him; her hair bounces on her shoulders. Each time she feels he's about to come, she slows her movements and kisses his chest, runs her fingers over his torso, nibbles his neck and ears. Then he is no longer on the verge of climax, and she begins to rotate her hips until that moment just before climax arrives again…and she stops, smiles. Finally, as Martin rolls so that he is now on top, he can no longer hold off from the fast approaching ecstasy.

Martin pulls away and lies on his back. He looks to Annabel; she is smiling, her eyes opening and closing tiredly. Then her eyes close and do not open again. She is asleep. Martin leans over, kisses her gently on the lips, on the nose, then on the forehead. And without thinking, he whispers. "*I love you.*"

He turns onto his side and cannot wait for morning; what promises to be their first of many mornings as lovers. He has no idea that he will never wake from his night's rest.

Annabel awakes to the sound of birdsong. She uses her forearm to block the sun's rays from her eyes. She smiles on seeing Martin in the bed next to her. She wonders if this one will be different to the others. She thinks she should leave him; she does not want to disturb him. Maybe she can cook him some scrambled eggs.

She then notices the sheet above his chest is not moving. Her heart freezes, she raises her hand to her mouth, trying to prevent a sob. She shakes him, she pushes at his lifeless corpse, she speaks to him, she slaps him hard and still he will not move. He is dead, like the others, he is dead.

"*You promised me!*" she yells. "*You promised me you wouldn't tell me you loved me!*"

Her eyes dart between his face and his chest as she tries to recall him speaking those fateful words. She cannot remember him saying them, but he must have otherwise this would not have happened—his heart would not have stopped as Trevor's did, as Paul's did, and how Sam's did.

She rests her face against his heart and listens. Nothing. Then she begins to weep, crying until she has no more tears.

Annabel walks out into the morning sun, trying to compose herself. She crouches and makes the noise with her pursed lips to attract the squirrels. Their little red heads pop out of the trees, and she hears their running feet. The squirrels queue patiently for their breakfast. One of them nibbles at the bag she holds.

"No, that's not for you," she says. She stands, brushes her hands off and goes to the apple trees. She plants an apple tree each time a man who loves her dies. Trevor's tree—the one marking his premature passing—is ten years old. Paul's is five years old, and Sam's only two. She smiles weakly.

"And now for you, Martin…a tree in your honour—so you may live forever."

She takes hold of the trowel and digs a hole. She drops the seeds in the hole, and then places Martin's heart in, before covering them over with soil. She has followed the same procedure for each of her dead lovers. She cries fresh tears; they moisten the soil.

She goes to Sam's apple tree and rubs her face against it. She then presses her ear over the bark so she can hear…so she can hear Sam's heartbeat. And she can, can hear it clearly, just as she had the night in her bedroom before his death. She glances to where she has just planted a tree for Martin. She cannot wait for it to grow.

~*Her*~

I was walking along the street, working off my fried breakfast, when I passed the car forecourt. A small dirty white building sat to one side; a glowing light bulb the only evidence that the place was open. There was a single row of cars with price boards on windshields.

I had been half-heartedly seeking a new car for some time but as I have no great interest in cars, I had kept putting off the day I parted with the Citroen I had owned for ten years. As I strolled by, I was wondering how a small business like this could make a profit. The lot looked ill kept and the cars were probably just as neglected. Then I saw a car sitting to one side, a little back from the others.

I stopped to look. I had never seen a car quite like it. It was a misty blue colour, had a low roof, shiny front bumper and two pairs of circular front lights. I walked around it, hoping to discover the make from the rear. There was no name or make apparent.

As I touched the paintwork, I realised just how shiny the car was. I could see my reflection—my eyes big and sad looking, my mouth wide across my cheeks. It reminded me of being a kid and going to the circus. Those mirrors that give the impression that you have been stretched or squashed.

It was then that the door of the white hut swung open and an Asian man stepped out wearing a dusty grey suit and cheap tie.

'Lovely, isn't she?' he said, stepping down onto the forecourt. He walked over, straightening his tie and smiling. He rubbed at his neck, wincing as if suffering some discomfort.

'This was my car until I got my new one,' he said, pointing over to the shiny Jaguar across the street. He was standing back from the car, as you might from someone with the flu—not wanting to inhale the germs. As he talked about the car, it seemed quite the opposite. He spoke so fondly about the car that I wondered if it might be the other way around. He stood away so not to risk giving his germs to the car.

I don't really know what happened next. We seemed to be talking for ages about the car, about all the journeys he had made in her, how well she ran, even his conquests in her.

'You really love her, don't you?'

He smiled, and then looked sad. 'I *loved* her,' he said. 'But we must move on in life,' he said, darkly. Were we really talking about a car? He rubbed again at his neck, massaging it with his fingers.

'Sore neck?' I asked.

He suddenly seemed uncomfortable, his eyes fidgety.

'Just a bit of an accident,' he said, producing a strained smile.

'Not a car accident I hope?' I asked, looking to the car he was trying to sell me.

'Oh no, nothing like that,' he said. A moment's pause passed whilst I waited for him to elaborate further on the neck injury. It seemed to be a subject he didn't wish to discuss.

'Lovely car, isn't she?' he said suddenly.

I had to agree with that. We talked further about the car and then without any real consideration (which was strange and so out of character, because I never make hasty decisions), I bought the car. He handed over the paperwork and the keys. As I tried to take the keys, he squeezed my hand with his and smiled. 'Please, you must treat her well,' he said.

'I will.'

'You'll know if she's happy,' he continued. 'She'll sing to you!'

I frowned. 'Sing?'

'Oh, you'll see! She'll sing when she's happy!' he said. 'And let it be known when she's not.' Then just as I thought tears were welling in the corners of his eyes, he said goodbye, turned abruptly and walked back over to his office.

I climbed into the car and sat. I could smell flowers. I couldn't see an air freshener but supposed there must have been one until recently.

It took a few seconds for the purchase of the car to sink in. An hour ago, I had left home for a walk and fresh air, and now: now I was the owner of a new car. German apparently. Mr. Bharat had said they were currently very popular in that part of the world.

I had actually made a spontaneous decision for once, bought an exciting car. Maybe not quite a sports car, but it wasn't far off.

My life couldn't really have been any more ordinary until that point. I had worked at the same school for the past twenty years, teaching the same classes. Whenever I was not at school, I seemed to be at home marking schoolwork, or trying to make improvements to the house I live in alone. But I like it that way; I like the peace and quiet. If I had wanted excitement, I would have been a firefighter or a pilot. But that just wasn't me. I liked being…well, I guess most people would have called me dull. That's why the decision to buy the car spontaneously was so completely out of character. But…I just had to buy her. It was a feeling I can't and will never be able to explain.

I planned just to drive around town before returning home. I taught at the local secondary school and had a heap of marking to do before Monday morning. However, once I had started to drive, I just didn't feel like stopping—that is until I needed to refill with petrol.

We drove out to the coast and along the sea road; the windows open, the wind sweeping back my hair, the salty air in my nostrils, gulls flying above, the sun shimmering in the blue sky. I felt young and free. I was enjoying the drive more than I could have ever imagined possible. Then she began to sing—like an opera singer on the low notes. A gentle humming. Not words as such, but sounds that would not have been out of place floating around Heaven's gates. I felt myself shiver with excitement, feeling refreshed.

Finally as the sky began to darken, I drove home, accompanied occasionally, by the sweet notes she made.

* * *

Whilst cooking my dinner, I felt the constant need to gaze out the window to the driveway and make sure she was okay—peering through the curtains to her sad blank lights. I felt as if I'd left a little puppy out in the cold. I fought off the urge to go and drive her—to warm her up. I had so much marking to do.

After dinner, I switched on the lamp in my study and began the foot high pile of marking. As I sipped coffee, my mind drifted to the car. I got to the stage that my concentration was so broken and my thoughts so strongly on the car that I wasn't sure whether the work I marked was correct or not. And I didn't really care. I started just ticking each question without much thought to the answers given. Then just turning to the back of the test papers and writing a quick note of encouragement that neither suggested my pupils had done well or poorly. I can't believe I did that. It was so incredibly unprofessional. So unlike me. But...the magic of the car had taken hold. I was at her mercy.

I shoved the papers to one side and quickly got to my feet and pulled the curtain back. I sighed on seeing her. I pondered the idea of another drive. It was not that late and if I was out no more than an hour, I could still finish the marking before bed. I picked up the key and went for a drive. The one hour turned into three; back out to the coast, her lights illuminating the white lines on the road, the moon hovering and shining above. She began to hum, to sing, that female operatic sound, melodic tones that filled my heart with love.

Then I saw the brake lights of the car ahead. We approached fast; she began to sing to me—as beautiful as birdsong on a spring morning. I let out a release of air, my body tingling. We had pulled alongside the car. The woman driving shouted something and waved an arm. We gave her a shove, a metallic crack as the cars clashed. The female driver's jaw dropped. I was a little surprised myself but now the song was loud in my ears—the scent of flowers in the air. I could feel a growing energy inside me; I felt my breaths harder to come by, sapped by the exertion, or physically drained by the sound of her song. The temperature of the car was rising, my whole body dripping in sweat as I panted, trying to stay focused on the road. The sound of her song grew louder as she reached for the loftier notes—almost a shriek, but of joy and passion, not of pain or fright. The sound that the world's greatest singers might have created if locked in a room together. Every sound was perfect, every note the craftsmanship of magic.

We made contact again, a crunch of grinding metal and a hollow thud. The woman was now in tears, her hands firmly grasped on the steering wheel—she mouthed silent words that I thought were probably an appeal to God to spare her life. Another nudge, this time her head banged into the glass, her spectacles dislodged and a line of blood trickled from a gash above her eye. I could barely breathe now, panting desperately, the smell of flowers in the air, the sweet climaxing notes of her music. Then the woman broke hard, swerved, and veered into the fence—crashing through and plunging down the slope the other side.

As the singing softened and as the car slowed, I began to re-catch my breath, wiping sweat from my brow, weak-limbed, exhausted. In the rearview mirror, I could see spirals of smoke rising into the illuminated sky; illuminated by the burning wreckage of the other car.

* * *

That night in bed, I dreamt of my car sitting in the middle of a field. On the roof, the decapitated head of the female driver we had smashed to oblivion. Blood leaked from her neck and spilled down the sides of my car—dripping down the windows and forming bloody pools around the tyres. Some of the blood seeped through the cracks on the bonnet and in onto the engine…and she began to hum, to sing. The car's lights flashed on and she accelerated away—the woman's head rolling off the roof backwards and into the bloodstained field.

As I lay awake in bed, wide-eyed, I could still hear her singing. I sipped at the glass of water by my bed and wondered if it had all been a dream. I felt a wave of guilt. I had been responsible for the crash. I had forced the woman from the road and killed her. Even if it hadn't been…*me*, no one would believe it was…*Her*.

I had started the day as a law-abiding citizen and now, *now*—I had killed an innocent woman. She probably had a family waiting for her to arrive home.

I looked through the window and saw my new car—*Her*—out in the drive. She hadn't even sustained a scratch from the earlier encounter with the car. The moon shone off her paintwork. I just had to go out there…see her.

We drove into the night; every so often, a car would pass and my heart would skip a beat. But we just carried on driving. There was a report about the earlier crash on the radio.

Then her song started—gently rising from the low notes until she was in full cry, releasing beautiful tunes into the car, the scent of flowers all around—waves of mesmeric music.

I knew the significance immediately. I saw the lights of the car ahead. I saw our next victim.

My foot pressed down on the accelerator and we gained speed. I felt the tingling sensations through my body—as if cold fingers were caressing me. I felt my heart pumping fast. I inhaled deep breaths as I tried to keep my concentration on driving—Her song so wonderfully refreshing and uplifting. As we approached the car, I couldn't help but grin in anticipation—knowing that her song would lead to a climax.

The man driving had a look of horror carved into his face as we gave him an initial nudge; he scrambled frantically, leaning onto the passenger seat and finding his phone. As we cracked the side of his car again, the windows shattered—the glass caving in on the driver; he screamed, dropping the phone and grabbing the steering wheel before he lost control.

With *Her* song loud in the air, we sped along the coastal road. Then as I looked up, I noticed the child strapped into the baby seat in the rear of his car. Guilt flooded my brain, suddenly the tingling sensations were sensations of icy fright, and the feeling of love was nausea, and her song no more satisfying than the wails of a dying woman. The baby looked innocently to me, big blue eyes leaking tears, its little face screwed in unhappiness as it sobbed.

I pressed down on the brake, and then tried to swerve away from the other car, but the brake was jammed—as was the steering wheel.

'*Damn you!*' I shouted; the other driver seemed to think I meant him, and he wept with his baby.

'*Stop it! Stop it!*' I screamed, stamping my foot on the brake, the song now disjointed and brain stinging. The simplistic beauty, the heavenly notes, replaced by sounds that might have resembled the death cries of a woman burned alive. I slammed my fist on the dashboard, stamped on the brake; the scent of flowers had gone rotten, smelling like sewage.

Sweating, aching all over and in despair, I stamped on the brake one final time, shrieking in anger as my foot hit the pedal and sent a bolt of electric pain through my body. But the brake hit the floor—the car screeched, skidded, and veered towards the fence. I closed my eyes and screamed as the cliff edge neared. Then the car stopped, the engine stalled. Silence.

I opened my eyes and saw that we had stopped on the side of the road—only yards from the sheer face and certain death. I breathed deep breaths. My mind a maze of tangled thoughts that seemed to materialize then lead into dead-ends. The other car disappeared into the distance…thankfully to safety.

Then the engine started and *She* began to wail uncontrollably. She shrieked; each note released sent streaks of pain through my skull, icy daggers into my heart. I grabbed my head in my hands, trying to cover my ears, trying scream as loud as I could so to cover the eruption of noise that blasted around the car—the seats violently shaking—the smell of rotting flesh all around.

I pushed open the door. As I tried to leap out, I felt the bite of the seatbelt against my neck. I groped desperately for the release button but it was jammed. I pressed on it repeatedly but it was no use. *She* had me now. She had me trapped…and I would feel her full rage!

The whole car vibrated as the engine wheezed, the lights flashing on and off, a volcano of hatred and betrayal exploding around me.

I scrambled about trying to free myself. I searched for something with which to cut the seatbelt. I opened the glove box—then before I could react, the arm shot out, the fingers clutching my throat and squeezing. I could feel her cold digits cutting deep. I pulled at the wrist, using all my strength to wrench it free, gazing all the time at the long slender female arm that had sprouted from the darkness at the back of the glove compartment—I pictured those chipped fingernails as they had come firing towards me.

'*I'm sorry!*' I gasped, but then I must have drifted into the realms of unconsciousness, as my memories end. When I awoke, I was still in the driver's seat, but the car now parked outside my house.

* * *

'It's a lovely car, isn't it?' the young businesswoman says. 'Why exactly are you selling it?'

I blow out my cheeks and smile. Luckily, I have prepared my answer to this very question. 'I think it's a reasonable price. To be perfectly honest, I have no choice but to sell. My wife, you see, she thinks we need something bigger so there's room for the kids.' I nod sadly. 'I wish I didn't have to let her go,' I say, rubbing my neck.

The woman smiles. 'Have you hurt your neck?' she asks.

'Yes, a little…I had an accident,' I say.

'Not a car accident I hope?' she says, concerned, looking to the misty blue car.

'*Oh no*, nothing like that…playing squash as a matter of fact,' I say. She seems to believe me.

'I'd like to buy it,' she says, smiling wide. 'I can't wait to take her out!'

I smile, remembering how excited I had once been about driving her. 'She's quite a ride,' I say, handing her the keys. 'She'll sing when she's happy.'

The woman frowns, thinking I'm mad. 'Did you say *sing*?'

~Wounded~

As I lay within the ditch, I could see the sun gradually setting—its blurred boundaries burn against the backdrop of a winter's blue sky. The bullet had sunk deep into my leg and I was losing blood rapidly. I had wrapped a piece of torn shirt around my leg to slow blood loss, but the wound was infected and needed urgent medical attention.

In the distance, I could still hear the gunfire; the sound of planes amongst the clouds, the dropping of bombs, and then the resulting explosions and every so often the noise of muffled faraway voices.

I had been stranded in the ditch for almost a day; since the previous night when under the cover of dark, the 4th Company had crossed enemy lines. All hell had broken out as the enemy ambushed us. It became every man for himself.

Above, the sun had lowered considerably; the sphere of fire was dull enough to gaze directly at. Then a stranger's face blotted the sun from the sky—the face of a middle-aged man, with pale blue eyes in the hollows of his sockets below his bush of grey hair and beside a pointed nose. He was a tall, thin and gaunt man with ashen face. He smiled at me.

The stranger pulled a rag and a bottle of blue liquid from his anorak; then after pouring a little liquid onto the rag, he turned to me and he pressed it over my mouth and nose. I struggled, but soon found myself drifting off into dream.

I awoke lying comfortably on a sofa. The man had given me a blanket and pillow—I could feel the house's warmth. I was in a large room with a radio on the mantelpiece. The flames burned fiercely in the fireplace. On the marble plinth in front of the fire were several large stone animal ornaments. There was a deer, a bear, a mousse and a buffalo. On the floor lay a tiger skin rug. There was also a huge window, like those of sliding French doors. There was no sign of the man who had brought me to his home.

Soon I felt sleepy and closed my eyes to rest.

In awaking, I found the man was tending to my leg wound. He was cleaning it with a sponge. In sensing me waking, he looked up, smiling.

'Who are you?' I asked.

His smile faded and he stared back at me. He didn't try to speak, just looked at me as if in deep thought. He raised his hand to his mouth and began to open and close it before shaking his head.

'You can't speak?' I asked. 'You're mute?'

He must have understood as he nodded his head and his agreeable smile rose high up his face. He looked back down to my wound and then reached to the floor and picked up a bandage, which he slowly began to wrap around my leg. When he had finished, he stood and walked away. I couldn't see where he had gone, but could hear the clatter of plates. Soon he returned with breakfast—a continental selection of breads and cheese, as well as strong black coffee and fresh fruit.

After eating, the man pulled on his grey anorak, wrapped a scarf around his neck and a woollen hat came down over his forehead, just above his eyes. He looked to me, noticing I was watching, and then pointed to the clock, moving his finger round as if it were one of the clock's hands. He stopped at six.

'You'll be back at six?' I said weakly. He nodded his head, opened the door—which let in a strong gust of icy wind—then shut it as he left. I watched through the wide window as he walked down the narrow stone path that led through a field of long grass and into the towering ferns that blocked views of the horizon. Within a couple of minutes, the stranger was lost in the thick line of trees.

The day was a lonely one. He had left some bread and cheese on the table next to a jug of water. From my position on the sofa I could do little more than look around his lounge. I noticed a bookshelf but doubted whether any of the books would be in English. Unsure of how serious my injuries were and whether standing would be possible, or even dangerous in my condition, I chose to stay put. I felt extremely weak, so probably would not have had the strength to walk even if I had wanted to.

The afternoon passed very slowly, I found myself watching the sun, as I had done the day I remained stranded in the bomb crater: killing time by watching time pass—watching the sun lower and the light fade. I waited for my nurse to return, hoping to ask him questions about who he was and how long it would be until I was well enough to leave.

The 4th Company had planned to push right through and reach the border by the evening, so the war may well have passed me by now. But if I could make contact, I hoped somebody would come to my aid. The thought suddenly occurred to me that the stranger might be holding me as prisoner and had left today to inform his people. What would I do if he returned with a group of enemy soldiers? There would be nothing that I could do.

At a little gone six, he arrived with a bag of fresh linen and bandages, which he showed me as he emptied the contents on the floor.

He prepared and cooked duck in a wine sauce for us. It was a much-needed meal and the best food I had tasted in the last three months. However, he had chosen to eat alone in the kitchen, leaving me with the tray of duck so I could take second and then third helpings.

That evening he sat reading a book in a chair beside the fire. I wanted to ask him questions but wasn't quite sure what to ask. He may have been friendly, neutral in this war, but I didn't want to give away too much information about the 4th Company or about myself.

'When will I be able to leave?' I asked cautiously.

The man placed his book down on his lap. His large nose pointed at me. He shrugged his shoulders, and then held up a single finger.

'One week?'

He nodded.

'Who are you?' I asked.

He gave a look of uncertainty—as if he didn't quite know how to answer the question. He didn't seem the most communicative—maybe it was the trouble of having to write the answers to my questions, as he was unable to voice them. Or it might have just been the language barrier.

He stood and walked to where I lay; he lifted my blanket and had a look at my leg wound. He smiled and then walked out into the kitchen. After a second, he returned with a small bowl of water and sponge, again beginning to clean the wound. I lay and watched the logs of the fire popping in the heat; the warmth of the room absorbed me and soon I found myself unable to keep my eyes open.

In the morning, after breakfast, I asked if he could turn the radio on before he left—he looked at me, perplexed. I pointed to the radio. He switched it on, twisted the knob and found the only station that wasn't crackling. Then with anorak in hand, he went through the door and walked down the pathway as he had the previous day and soon he was lost within the trees.

I followed the same routine as the day before, only now with the noise of the radio in the background, watching the clock's hands turning, the clouds drifting across the blue skies. What exactly would I do when I had recovered? I was convinced now that the mute man was neutral in this war, a good man and that he wouldn't hand me over. Nevertheless, I was isolated on enemy shores, and the idea of catching the 4th Company no longer seemed a viable option. I was also probably presumed dead, so nobody would be looking for me.

During the afternoon, I could again hear gunfire in the distance. It may have been a long way off, but the war wasn't over. In a way, it was comforting, as I knew 4th Company were still close, and there was a flicker of hope.

The mute came home, we ate, and afterwards he tended to my wounds. He dabbed the sponge on my leg and wrapped a clean bandage around it. It appeared to be getting better, some of the infection looked as if it were healing. The mute man leaned over my face; I thought he was going to take my temperature with the palm of his hand, but his fingers fell short of my forehead and came down upon my cheek. He ran his fingers softly down to touch my mouth. Before I could stop him, he leaned forward and kissed me on the lips. I shoved him, accidentally striking him in the face. He jumped back, holding his mouth in pain. His eyes welled with tears and he marched from the room. I couldn't believe what had just happened—the man had tried to kiss me; he *had* kissed me, taken advantage of me! Had I done something to encourage the kiss?

The mute returned, his lower lip quivering, he wore a face of defiance as he neared me—as if he used all his energy to hide how much my striking him had hurt. He moved a hand towards me. I raised my arm instinctively, but I thought his intentions were benign so I lowered my defence. He produced a small smile, which I assumed meant the misunderstanding had been forgotten. I could live with that. His hand neared my scalp, his fingers tensed and crooked, now shaped like a man with severe arthritis. The moment his fingers touched my head I felt a bolt of pain—as if fire had scythed into my brain, my whole body juddered once and twice, then I found I was breathless and the hallucinations started....

I could see my dear wife, Helen, cooking at the stove. She was peeling potatoes, but then there was a call from behind her. She turned and smiled as if to me from where I observed this vision. Then a man entered the kitchen and wrapped his arms around my wife and they kissed, passionately they kissed. He undid her apron and tossed it aside while she ripped his belt free.

I saw them naked, rolling about in bed; Helen screaming in an ecstasy I'd never before witnessed, digging her nails into his back, mouth wide, sweating profusely.

Suddenly I was again lying on the sofa in the mute's lounge. He towered over me, his eyes dark, shadows across his face; only the tip of his nose doused in the room's dim light. He turned and walked away; his footsteps ascended the stairs.

Then the fever started and would last for twenty-four hours. I trembled, panted, sweating all the time, having both hot and cold flushes. I thought I must have been experiencing the torment of a man in the final stages of a fatal poisoning. Only my final stages lasted for hours, my cold flesh encased by dread. And it was as if knives were stuck into my flesh and twisted, other blades burrowing deeper and grinding away at my bones, chipping at them like some phantom carving his initials. And my feet were agony, as if another phantom was standing pouring an endless flow of boiling water over them for every second and ever minute of those twenty-four hours without respite.

But as suddenly as the fever had begun, it cleared. I was startled, bracing myself for the onslaught of pain when the phantoms returned from their tea break. But it never came. Even more strange was that I felt a million dollars. It was as if the mystery fever had never been.

I noticed the moon, and when I checked the clock I realised my illness had lasted for almost exactly twenty-four hours. The mute brought me coffee and scrambled eggs, which I devoured so quickly he made me more.

But why had I seen those images? Premonitions? God, I hope not! I wasn't even asleep…it was after the mute had tried to kiss me, I remembered, he had touched my head with that crab-like hand and then the nightmares had started, like he had pressed a button and played the nightmare scenarios I keep locked away in the realms of my psyche.

I spent the evening thinking of my wife and my eleven-year-old daughter. Before this war had started, we had spent a week together in a little cottage in Cornwall. That week we were celebrating both my daughter's birthday and our fifteen-year wedding anniversary. It was a lovely holiday, the cottage was in the woods and there was the ocean at the foot of the garden. In the mornings, we would take nuts and bread out to feed the swans and squirrels. Then the letter arrived concerning my enlistment. Now, four months later, I was bed-ridden on foreign shores. How times had changed.

I was delighted the misunderstanding we had before my fever had apparently been forgotten and I was feeling more comfortable with my surroundings. We sat and talked, well I talked, and he listened—those pale blue eyes under heavy lids upon me, absorbing all I said. Occasionally he would rest a finger on his chin and run it up and down the groove.

The grandfather clock played its melody at quarter to eight and I was feeling tired. Ready to sleep. I had told the mute about myself that evening, about my home, my family and my time at war and hoped he would reciprocate by writing something about himself, at least his name, but when I suggested it, he became suddenly withdrawn and would pretend not to understand my questions. But I felt I was making progress and before I was well enough to leave, I thought he might have opened up a little more.

That night, despite my tiredness, I could not sleep. I lay listening to the radio, though I couldn't understand what was said, but a noise to cover the silence was a comfort in itself.

Apparently also unable to sleep, the mute brought us hot chocolate, dressed in his night robes. I sipped the drink.

'Thanks,' I said, smiling. He undid his robe and exposed his naked body to me. I choked, spat and placed the cup on the table, realising I would have to rebuff his advances once again. I thought the message I'd given him was perfectly clear; that we had advanced past the previous embarrassment. Obviously not.

I met eyes with him, hoping to speak rejection to his offer without seeming too harsh. I wondered if he saw it as his payment for his nursing me to health. In one sense, he had a point. He could easily have left me to die or handed me over to enemy soldiers.

'No, I'm sorry,' I said. 'I have a wife and child. No.'

I thought my speech would work and surely cement the fact that I wasn't interested—but he would not be dissuaded and advanced on me, forcing his groin toward my hands. I pushed him, trying to cover my anger. But it was *he* that was truly angry—his eyes burning with fury, his jaw muscles so tense I expected something in his face to pop. He grabbed my head in his claw-like hand and a streak of pain rattled my brain—I thrashed about, screaming, his fingers tight on my scalp...

I saw my daughter Lizzy; she was at the cottage in Cornwall, feeding the squirrels. Then *I* was in the hallucination, carrying a canister of petrol. I poured it over my daughter's head as she screamed. Then I struck and tossed a match towards her. In an instant flames shrouded her, singeing her hair, terrorising her clothes and began to blister her skin as she fell to the floor....

And I could smell the lemon scent of the shampoo we wash her hair with...

She was a human bonfire, waving her arms, screaming and weeping as she tried to smother the flames...

And I could see her playing with her dolls, looking up to me with a big, cheeky smile, the chocolate she had devoured smeared around her lips...

My beloved daughter's face melted, her teeth bared as her lips burned...

And I could hear Lizzy in her bedroom, singing 'Jingle Bells' to herself;

playing with the toys she had unwrapped that morning under the Christmas tree.

'Honey, dinner's ready.'

'Okay, Daddy, *coming*!'

And then I awoke and cried and sobbed, tormented, haunted by the images my mind had produced. I was crazy—this was the only explanation for these visions. Then I recalled the mute touching my head and knew that he was somehow to blame. He was responsible. I didn't understand but I knew. They were so real, so detailed unlike normal dreams. But they weren't dreams, they were something else, scenes the mute fired into my imagination with those bony fingers.

I again suffered from fever for the next day, unable to move, drenched in sweat, paralysed from doing anything but shivering helplessly, and trying to bite back the torturous stabbing and grating inflicted by my invisible phantoms.

When I had recovered that next evening, again feeling back to full health, my predicament became clear. If I rejected the mute's sexual advances, I would suffer more of the hallucinations and hellish fever.

And I began to believe he did not intend to set me free. I could stay and play his games, dance to his tune and…give him what he desired; or I could escape…at least try to anyway. But as if he had read my thought process, I found a thick metal chain manacled my ankle, leading to an iron hoop in the wall.

The mute walked into the room, realising I had woken, and handed me a tray of roast beef and potatoes. Unable to make eye contact with him, I took the tray. He wandered off and left me alone. I ate, chewing each piece of food a dozen times, as I thought through my options. As I was dabbing up the final pool of gravy with a piece of potato on the end of my fork, I realised my only chance for escape was during the day whilst the mute was out. I could reach the stone animal ornaments—the chain would stretch that far. Maybe I could smash the chains, or break the lock of the manacle with one of those animals. I could start as soon as the mute departed and work on it all day. The only problem was I had lost the previous day suffering from fever. As the mute collected my tray, the sickening truth hit home. I would have to submit to his demands. Only once, thankfully, but still that was once too many.

We sat in the lounge in silence, he reading his book, me sitting and counting the tiny holes on the ceiling. I could feel the cold bite of the manacle round my ankle. As midnight came and passed, I thought I might have gotten lucky—that beaten by my previous rejection, the mute had given up. I waited, praying that he would go up to bed. But he didn't. I heard his book snap shut. I waited a few seconds then turned my head, taking my vision from the ceiling. I found I couldn't meet his eyes at first but then forced myself. His eyes were upon me, dark, and mind penetrating. He rose and walked out toward the kitchen; I sighed, and then held my breath hoping he would make straight for the stairs. He stopped at the foot of them and leaned on the banister, I heard it creak.

Then my heart sank as he came over to me. He stood before me, loosened his belt, pulled it free and dropped it to the floor, the buckle chinked as it landed, his fingers swiftly made for his trouser zip and unfastened them, and they slid down his pale legs to his feet. I looked up to his gaunt face; his pale blue eyes fixed on mine. He thrust his hands into his pants, pulled them down to his knees, and stepped forward so his erect penis was before me. I stared up at him in horror—I couldn't do it. It was too much, I just couldn't. I pushed him away, retracting my hands as I shuddered.

'*Jesus, go away!*' I pleaded. '*I've done nothing to you!*'

But he would not relent. His face darkened and he moved his claw-hand towards me.

'*No, please stop!*' I said, swallowing hard. '*Not again, God, no more of those nightmares!*'

He paused, waiting for me to agree to the terms of our unspoken contract.

I nodded and slowly moved my hands towards him, trying not to break down in tears...

I wiped my hand, and then rolled over to hide my face. I could hear the mute slowly walking away from me, panting hard as he did. I didn't open my eyes again that evening—I couldn't bear to. I wished just to die—to fall asleep and to never wake. Then I remembered *why* I had done it.

Tomorrow. Tomorrow I would escape—somehow...I would escape and return to England to see my beloved wife and daughter.

That morning after the mute had gone, having my strength; I collected the largest, sturdiest stone ornament—the buffalo—and began pounding at the chain. The energy I exerted left me sweaty and weak and I needed water desperately. I had already drunk the last of the jug he had left for me.

The time flew, as it always does when it must not, and I became more and more desperate. It was just not working. I spent an hour trying to pick the lock with a clothes hanger but that proved just as fruitless. At five-thirty, I stopped hammering. It was useless. The stone buffalo had cracked and chipped all day and now had split in two...and the chain was only scraped and dented. I sobbed, having given up all hope. I used the half-hour before the mute's expected return to cool myself, relax, reduce my sweating and hide the broken ornament below the sofa. If he didn't suspect anything there was tomorrow. Always tomorrow.

We ate chicken that evening; I did my best to be positive. On several occasions he held my hand, and though I flinched, I allowed him to.

He approached me, dropping his trousers, closing his eyes and leaning his head back and bracing himself. I began to touch him; he held my hand tightly against his groin. I swallowed the nausea, repeating the silent mantra, I *must* have my strength, I *must* stay strong, I *will* escape, go to Helen, she would understand, she would still love me and it would all be okay, like it used to be before this damn war!

He made me open my eyes, and then my heart sank as he moved closer. I knew what he wanted from me as he touched his lips. There was no way I could do it. I waited for him to get within range. I forced a smile. He closed his eyes and I reached below the sofa for the stone buffalo— smashing it powerfully against his genitals, hoping to incapacitate him so I could follow up with a killer blow to his skull. He screamed an airy wheeze then crumbled to the ground—as if his bones had magically vanished, leaving an unsupported body to sag in a heap. I leaned over him and tried bringing the ornament upon his head but he had already rolled out of striking distance. He lay panting on the floor. I had struck some kind of revenge, but a revenge that could well cost me my life. A small price to pay. I lay back and awaited my punishment. He grabbed my head.

I didn't bother struggling. There seemed little point....

I could see the ocean. It was calm, serene. Helen, my wife, bobbed to the water's surface, eyes closed, gasping for air. In her arms, she held Lizzy.

'*Lizzy! Wake up! Wake up goddammit!*' Lizzy was stiff and dead.

Then the waves crashed over their heads and they were both submerged. I watched, praying they would again climb to the surface—only this time Lizzy would be alive. *And she was!*—albeit spitting and choking, but she *was* alive!

'*Daddy!*' she screamed, and then water splashed over her head. She spat: 'Daddy, where are you?'

But I could only watch as another wave swallowed her whole. Then the ocean was tranquil—the water wide, blue and empty. I wondered what could happen next. Then the bodies of my wife and daughter floated to the surface but now face down, lifeless, drifting with the tide...and I was forced to watch their journey for hours, days, as sharks tore flesh from their corpses, as birds picked at their remains...

I awoke in tears, which were stunted only by the outbreak of fever. It took its icy hold and I prayed that I would still have strength to escape when it had passed. My body shuddered; I mumbled and muttered, trying to fight the delirium. I opened my eyes and attempted to focus on the clock face. Time moved in a blur. What time was it? How long until the fever passed? How long until my mute tormentor returned?

Then the door swung wildly open, wind swept across the room and disturbed papers he had left out. The wicked man stared at me and smiled. Tonight he would not wait until after dinner. He would take advantage of me immediately, ravaged by fever, unable to defend myself. He thrust me down onto the tiger skin rug and stripped me of clothes; my trousers down to the iron manacle around my ankle. I was helpless—barely strong enough to raise an arm. He rolled me over onto my stomach. I couldn't see him, but heard him taking his trousers off behind me. The belt's buckle touched down softly on the floor. He undid the buttons of his shirt and the elastic stretched as he removed his pants. I felt him behind me. His shadow loomed close; I could see the dark outline of his head in the light from the fire. I tried to hold my breath to suffocate myself; I prayed for God to kill me.

I could smell his naked body upon me. He had lowered himself behind me when shouts penetrated the house and the door swung open once again, followed by screaming voices and gunfire. The man collapsed onto my back. An incredible lifeless weight. I turned my head. His neck was arched over my shoulder, his chin sagged by my cheek, from his mouth ran a stream of blood; his pale eyes stared blankly ahead.

I threw him off then lay naked on the tiger skin rug; my body wrangled with his fever. I looked up to see my friends from the 4th Company.

This tale does not however finish with a happy conclusion. Whilst I had been away, my wife had been engaged in an affair. I returned to discover her and my daughter had moved out from our home. It was over a year until I saw either of them again, and when I did, I was stunned to see that the new lover in Helen's life was the very same man I had seen her with in my first hallucination. A man I swear I had never seen before that strange nightmare.

The mute is dead. I saw his body buried with my own eyes. His powers though, which apparently passed through those bony fingers, will forever remain a mystery to me. And the memory of him has burned its mark upon my brain. I shall never sleep soundly again.

~The Flute Playing Tramp~

The tramp sat on the pavement leant back against the dirty wall. A patch of dust from where his head had been touching the stone building marked his hair. He had been sitting there with his legs crossed for two hours, sporadically playing his flute. A shoebox sat by his feet, waiting, hoping to be filled with contributions from those that passed. So far the box was home to less than a pound—though an American tourist had tossed in a couple of dollars.

The tramp's name was Herbert Gregory and he had been homeless for five years, living day to day off what he could scrounge, find, and occasionally steal. He was thirty-four years old, and had a bush of dark curly hair. His chin covered by a wild beard, which spread unusually far up his cheeks so to be within walking distance of his closely set blue eyes.

Though Herbert needed the money, he couldn't help but get the greatest joy when people would stop just to listen. Whether they offered money or not was not that important. Being able to play his music to an audience was.

As he continued to play, an elderly lady, with wicker bag over her arm, caught sight of him, and then started a detour around the bench so not to get too close. Herbert watched her pass, sad that people would make such an effort to avoid him. Noticing his eyes upon her, she visibly grimaced, turning her head and quickly walking away.

For many tramps, the company of a dog made life bearable. Herbert had no dog. He had an abundance of life living in his hair, but not the sort of pet that endeared people to him.

Two teenage boys stopped to listen to the flute. Herbert played with a little more enthusiasm, only for the boys then to start whispering to one another. One then stepped over, emptied his pocket of chocolate wrappers into the shoebox, and held his nose.

"He stinks like hell!" the boy said.

"Smells like a blocked toilet!" said the other. Herbert feigned getting to his feet, and the boys' smiles disappeared as they ran, shouting abuse as they did.

With nobody in sight, Herbert did now get to his feet, packed his flute away, and collected his belongings. A trolley with a blanket and various bits of junk he had found. A little food: half-eaten hamburgers and a couple of beers. He also had his instruments, which he had kept with him all this time despite the pressure to sell for food money. They were only a mouth organ and a violin, as well as the flute, and wouldn't fetch much. And, anyway, they were his love, the one thing that kept him sane. Selling his instruments would be the final acceptance of defeat.

He walked along the pavement, pushing his trolley, all the time aware of the people avoiding him. As he approached, the shopping precinct crowds parted to allow him to pass. People pretended not to see him, whispering behind their hands, some sniggered, some who got too close held their noses.

Then Herbert heard the sounds from the London Palladium. He was suddenly refreshed, the air he breathed full of hope. He smiled and continued towards the sound of music. As he reached the entrance, he stopped and listened.

The guards on the door—expecting his daily visits, but having been giving fresh orders about dealing with him due to the amount of complaints—alerted each other to his unwanted presence.

Herbert would just stand and listen to the beautiful orchestral tunes that escaped the building, absorbing and imagining the band playing. He remembered his own youth, when his one and only dream had been to play on that stage at the London Palladium. The British School of Musical Excellence accepted him at age twelve and he had attended the school briefly. He shared a room with four other boys that immediately took a disliking to him. He always thought it was because he was the most naturally gifted musician of them; capable not just of playing wonderful music on a single instrument, but on just about any instrument he should lay his hands on—a God-given talent with which he had been born.

Competition for places at the school, and then in the concerts, was fierce and jealously was unavoidable. But he had never imagined how far the boys would go. Danny Nile, Stuart Gilender, Peter Foot and Mark Forster were his roommates and they set out to jeopardize his chances. He had gotten the blame for flooding the toilet block, for which they had been responsible. They had planted *Playboy* magazines in his drawer just before room inspection. Then Stuart Gilender had claimed Herbert had beaten him up. He lay in bed for days pretending to be too badly hurt to move.

Herbert of course had denied the allegations but with the others as witnesses, he never had a chance. That had been his final warning, and then when someone vandalised the principal's car and twenty-five boys claimed to have seen him do it, he knew his days at the school of excellence were over.

As he listened now to the palladium music, twenty-two years later, he still thought *that* was the turning point in his life. If it were not for those spiteful boys, it could be him in there now, playing to an audience of thousands, accepting the applause, experiencing the thrill.

"Go and find somewhere else to stand!" the doorman demanded.

Herbert looked to him; he felt a lump in his throat. "But why?"

The shaven headed burly doorman stared hard at Herbert. "You're making people feel uneasy," he said. "Go on now...off you go!"

"I'm not doing anything wrong," he protested.

"Go on, piss off!"

Herbert turned slowly and pushed his trolley towards the alleyway. As he walked, he felt the anger raging inside. *It should be me*, he thought, *it should bloody well be me playing in there tonight.* And with that, he disappeared into the shadows.

The boys from The British School of Musical Excellence had finished their concert at the St John's school and now they, and the audience, began to disperse. One boy, Colin Gilender, walked alone. He was holding his flute in one hand and he waved both hands as if he were a conductor, dreaming, pretending, and hoping one day that he would be. He whistled some of the tunes they had played that afternoon as he entered the park. He cut across the grass as a light breeze disturbed the trees. As he continued to walk, smiling, he heard the music. He paused and turned on the spot. He couldn't see anyone. The park was empty. Where was it coming from? It sounded like a flute. His eyes drawn to the large bush in the centre of the park. He could again hear the flute's faint tune over the sound of the wind.

He slowly approached the bush, a little wary, taking a step at a time. The fear was starting to evaporate as he listened to the tune—a tune he didn't recognize but thought was incredibly beautiful. He had to see who played. He had to know. He reached the bush, parted the leaves and then stared in. There was a bearded man sitting on a branch, eyes closed, playing the flute. Colin watched for a while, mesmerized by the man. He marvelled at the apparent ease that the man could produce such heavenly sounds. He took his own flute out and started to play. The man opened his eyes and smiled. They played together, Colin approaching, getting closer, meeting eyes with the bearded man. Then the music stopped abruptly. If there had have been anyone passing, they might have heard the boy's muffled sobs.

Penny Nile, aged fourteen, was walking with a group of friends. They had just had a rehearsal for the upcoming school concert.

"I thought you did so well," one of her friends said to her. "That's the best you've played."

"Thanks," Penny said. She thought so too, but didn't want to sound arrogant. They walked through the town centre and then along the path the other side. They were walking together at their parents' request since the disappearance of local boy, Colin Gilender. Earlier that day the police had visited the school, to reiterate the importance of staying in groups and not wandering off alone.

The group of girls reached the junction.

"I'm going to go and see my dad," Penny said to the others. They looked around to each other. "It's okay…it's just over there—you can see the house, the one with the flowers on the windowsill," she said. "You can go—I'll be fine."

"Maybe we should come with you?" the red-haired girl said.

"Don't be silly," Penny said, waved and started towards the house. After walking a few yards she turned, insisted she was fine and they should continue without her. Reluctantly they did.

Penny skipped down the road, humming, looking forward to seeing Dad. Her parents were divorced and her mum didn't like her seeing him, but she would sneak around there and pretend she was having dinner around the house of a friend.

As she approached, she became aware of the music. She stopped, surprised. There was a woman carrying shopping bags on the far side of the road but she seemed not to notice. Penny thought it was coming from below her.

Then she saw the drain. But it didn't make sense. She slowly stepped over to the drain cover and listened. It sounded like a mouth organ, she thought.

"Hello," she called down to the drain, and then felt stupid.

"Hello," the voice from the drain said.

Penny waited, heart thudding.

"Can you help me?" the voice said. "I've got trapped down here…I can't open it from the inside. I've been trying to attract attention with my mouth organ."

"Why didn't you shout?"

"People get frightened if you shout…"

Penny got onto her knees and pulled at the drain cover. It came away with a clang of metal and with it a spray of dust. She blinked and then stared into the darkness below. Then the long hairy arm shot out, grabbed her around the throat and before she could release her intended scream, she had disappeared into the hole. Then the arm came out again, only this time to replace the drain cover.

The newspapers were crammed with stories of the missing children. The fact that no one seemed to have any helpful information only increased the spread of fear. The streets of the area were much quieter than usual; groups of schoolchildren no longer sat on the precinct benches and the arcade was virtually empty. Concerned parents collected their children from school and took them home by car, even if it were only a short walk for their children.

Weeks went by and more children disappeared. The police stepped up their efforts but to no avail. The only clue they had was one lady had seen a boy fitting the description of one of the boys who had gone missing. She had seen him walking alone down an alleyway. However, the strange thing was she could have sworn she heard violin music.

To lift spirits at The British School of Musical Excellence, and of those hit so hard by the tragedy of the missing children, the world famous Sergoni Orchestra was booked to perform. All proceeds would go to the prevention of child abduction. Seven children in all had gone missing. The link between them being their musical interest. It only seemed right that the tribute concert, the memorial, should take place at the London Palladium.

The seats packed, the rumble of conversation echoed around the hall. Stuart Gilender was present. His son Colin was one of those believed to have been abducted, and though it was ever so painful, he had to lend his support.

In the same row sat Peter Foot and in the row behind Mark Forster; the three of them at aged twelve having shared a room at The British School of Musical Excellence. They had remained friends ever since and even played together in several concerts. Danny Nile, the other dorm member, had not turned up—too devastated by his daughter Penny's disappearance.

The crowd waited expectantly for the show to start. In studying the schedule, Stuart noticed that there would first be a performance by the strangely named, Tramp's Orchestra. The name failed to fill him with much confidence.

Then a man walked to the centre of the stage, with the heavy crimson curtain behind. Whispers broke out amongst the crowd on the sight of the man. He was wearing an old tatty tuxedo and his hair slicked back with gel, his jaw clean-shaven. However, nothing could hide how scruffy he looked. He had a wide smile on his face.

One or two people thought he looked familiar, something about the eyes, but they could not place him.

Herbert stood on the stage, observing the crowd. Despite the whispers, he heard only applause, excitement about the show he would put on. He breathed deep breaths, enjoying the smell of the rich folk. He lifted his hands theatrically, and then brought his hands down to announce the commencement. The curtain began to rise and even before it had risen far, the crowd broke out in horrified gasps.

Herbert gazed upon his orchestra. It was set up like a drummer's kit and by sitting in the chair; he was able to blow in his flute, carved from a femur bone. He could bang his hands on the human drum skins that had been stretched tight so to make a hollow thud on impact. He could strum the bleeding tendrils that stretched taut between the bones of the rib cage, and he could tap his foot and the vein leading to the skulls would flex and cause them to knock together.

Doused in yells and screams, he started by playing an old composition that he had written and performed whilst living within the walls of The British School of Musical Excellence.

The crowd were now standing, shouting in protest, shock, not sure whether it was just a sick gimmick or…*real. Actual human body parts.*

It was now that Stuart recognized the tunes the man played. *It was him.* It was Herbert Gregory—the kid they had so spitefully seen kicked out of the school.

Then a woman called out: *"It's them! The children! It's the children!"*

Stuart gazed over to the hysterical woman. What did she mean?

Then he knew. He stared at the harp rib cage…and he could suddenly see his son materializing around the ribs—the ghostly form of his own flesh and blood. The sick truth begun to sink in…it was the missing children. He, the tramp, Herbert Gregory, had killed them and turned their body parts into his instruments.

Herbert continued to hear cheers as he began to pound on the drums—the children's skins stretched over the arrangement of bones. Even as the police were flocking towards him, he played, making the most of this, his dream—the opportunity to play before a live crowd at the London Palladium. And it was better than he ever imagined it could be.

They handcuffed and dragged him away…but still he played his flute until it was snatched from his mouth. As the curtain lowered on his performance, he smiled broadly and blew kisses to his adoring audience.

~Should Be Dead~

I had spent the previous three weeks backpacking around Britain and I was ready to return to my job as a director at Shopping.tv. The days leading up to my vacation had been a nightmare, with viewing figures dropping, backstabbing and bitching amongst the ranks, as well as talk of multiple redundancies. Maybe it should have been a time that I stood my ground and showed my commitment to the job, fought it out in the trenches to guarantee the future of the station and to save my own dwindling career.

But I just had to get away.

Thoughts of returning to work were buzzing around my mind as I had been following the grass verge down the mountain road, the sun burning bright in a blue sky and a light breeze refreshing my tired limbs.

As I stopped to take a sip of water, I could see the distant buildings of the TV studio and the town beyond. I relished the prospect of returning to civilization after three weeks in the wilderness; but having not been in contact with work, I had no idea what the position of the studio was, and of course, I had no clue to my own position of employment. Come Monday morning I might be skimming the Classifieds for a new job.

I should have been alert to the danger but my mind was drifting, pondering on my career options. When I saw the coach approaching much too fast, out of control, I hadn't any time to react—its huge mass swinging round the corner. I remember looking to the driver, who was desperately fighting the wheel; I recall the flat-nosed front of the coach, shiny bumper and circular glass lights expanding in my vision like huge terrified eyes; then I remember gazing over the cliff edge to see what fate awaited me if I jumped. All this in a split second and I hadn't actually the time to react as the coach skidded, the screech of tyres seeming to reach my ears even before the coach began its sideways slide towards where I stood paralyzed by fear.

The huge blue Euro Treks lettering on the side of the coach expanding in my vision as the massive metallic body swung towards me like a mechanical whip. Then it hit me with the force of an avalanche and all went black. It was as if the coach's hammer of a blow had knocked out, or paralyzed at least, all senses except for my hearing. I heard more screams, a screech of defiance as the fence tried to hold the coach's weight, and then the shattering of glass.

Then the falling—the wind sweeping around me.

Then everything stopped.

I was in darkness, trying to decide whether I had a chance of surviving the collision. The coach had been going so damn fast and though inevitably it would slow in its slide, the force of tons of weight would no doubt smash me to oblivion. I figured there was no way I would survive—the fall would kill me.

I opened my eyes and blinked in the bright light. I stared at the glowing sun, watched as a plane cut across the blue sky. It was then that I saw a dark shape high above, descending to where I lay. At first just a black spot, a spot that formed as it approached. For some reason I had no doubt it was coming for me.

The shape neared in a zigzag motion—a dark figure, I thought, riding a black horse. As it got closer, I could make out the thing's arms and legs, and the circle of darkness that was its head. At the time, I didn't think this was at all strange. It seemed the most natural thing in the world.

Then a face shot in front of mine; big blue concerned eyes and a fidgeting mouth blocked my view of the dark stranger and the sky.

'Jesus Christ, you're alive! I was sure you were a goner! You must be made out of steel!' the man said, and then leaning back, shouted: '*He's alive!*' using cupped hands to project his voice.

As his sweaty head slipped to one side and allowed the bright sun to sting my eyes, I saw the black figure on the horse, galloping—sky galloping—back up towards the sun.

I awoke in a hospital bed and it was whilst there that the doctor told me that the coach driver had suffered a heart attack. They don't know if the attack started before or after he lost control of the coach. He can't remember. He took a nasty bang to the head.

'It's a miracle you're alive. You should be dead,' the doctor said. But all I had were a few bumps and bruises. I thought I must have jumped before the coach crushed me. It might explain why I had managed to avoid serious injury. I would have fallen forty feet in freefall then slid and rolled down another fifty-foot or so.

But some of the passengers on the coach claimed I hadn't the time to jump—one passenger claims to have seen me getting crushed against the fence, then as the iron tore free of the concrete, the passenger says I was catapulted with the fence into the sky.

Obviously if this was true, I surely *would be dead*. Wouldn't I?

Luckily, the majority of the safety fence held strong—only the point that felt the brunt of the impact was blasted from the ground. Though the structure of the fence creaked under the bus's weight, it held. With the exception of the driver's heart attack, which might not have been as any direct result of the accident, and minor injuries, everyone had been incredibly fortunate.

I was allowed to leave the hospital after only a couple days of tests. I went home, where I had another couple of days to myself before returning to work. To my surprise, the shopping channel had started to make a profit again whilst I'd been away. I thought this might be enough to see me lose my job—I mean, I go away and profits rise. Maybe if I went away on a more permanent basis the profits would rise tenfold. To my delight, my job was not under threat.

The first day back was a good one. A lot of the tension had lifted and the production staff seemed to be working in near perfect harmony. It was the third day that things started to go wrong.

Jim from the sound department was by the coffee machine, trying to find the correct change.

'How's the world of sound, Jim?'

'Same old,' he said, lifting his head. He paused and gave a little sniff, his eyes then began to water.

'Are you okay?'

'Yeah fine,' he said. 'I'm due back…I'll have to rush.' He walked by me with his head slightly turned and entered the sound gallery.

I held my hand in front of my face and breathed, trying to block the escaping air so I could smell it. It smelled like rotten eggs.

I went to the bathroom and rinsed my mouth with water, swishing it then spitting. The egg smell remained. My face was pale; a slight bluish tint to my skin, almost translucent and the veins beneath seemed to push forward so to be seen. I wondered if I was having a reaction to the pain killing drugs given to me whilst at the hospital.

I didn't feel ill…I just looked it.

Nobody else mentioned my appearance for the remainder of the day, but the looks some were giving me spoke volumes.

At home that evening I studied my appearance in the mirror. My cheeks seemed somehow hollow, bones protruding. I thought I had the appearance of a man with a terminal illness. Then the doctor's words entered my mind.

It's a miracle you're alive. You should be dead.

By bedtime, my skin had further changed in colour. A green-blue shade. My lips were grey, my tongue felt too large for my mouth.

As I stuck my tongue out, clear fluid seeped from beneath and spilled into the sink—simultaneously more of the same clear fluid ran from my nostrils. I leaned over the sink, mouth open, allowing the liquid just to run its course. After a few seconds it stopped. I coughed; spitting what remained of the fluid in my mouth and wiped my face with a towel.

'Jesus Christ!'

The following morning I awoke in the rays of the sun. I could hear the birds singing, I could smell flowers in the yard and I could hear the children on the road waiting for the school bus. I rolled over and scratched at my stomach. It felt strange, as if I were scratching a beach ball. I gazed down to my inflated belly. It looked as if someone had pumped me full of air whilst I slept. I burped and as the air left my mouth, I again smelled the rotten eggs.

I leaped from bed, stunned by my overblown belly, appalled by the smell; I held my nose and ran to the bathroom where I vomited into the sink. More of the clear liquid squirted from my nostrils and I vomited again—this time upchucking last night's supper.

I rinsed the sink, leaving the taps on full to drink from. I put my dressing gown on—anything to cover the sight of my bulbous pregnant abdomen—then sat down and picked up the phone. I hoped Doctor Cowell would be able to come and see me.

An hour later Doctor Cowell arrived at my house. 'He doesn't do house calls,' the secretary at the surgery had said. After some gentle persuasion, the doctor took the line and I had very little difficulty in convincing him to come and see me.

The doctor sat in the recliner, rocking back and forth. I lay on the couch gazing upon the white ceiling of my lounge. I had never noticed the pattern before. It was white ceiling paper, in which were carved pictures of entwined flowers and vines.

'I think we will need to take you to a...a *specialist*,' Doctor Cowell said as he ran his index finger up and down his chin's groove. He glanced away from me, his head furrowed.

'What is it?' I asked. I had been expecting him to make further conjecture on my condition.

'What's that noise?' he asked. 'Have you a fan on somewhere in the house?'

Now my forehead was also home to grooves. 'A fan? No.' I sat up and listened. I heard the faint buzzing immediately and was surprised that my mind must have been so preoccupied with the patterns on the ceiling that I hadn't noticed it before. I stood, taking a few steps forward, listened, then walked on again, allowing my ears to guide me.

Doctor Cowell had stood also; his eyes were upon my inflated stomach, my gaunt frame, my blue-green skin and my gaping jaw, which remained open so I could breathe around my swollen tongue. The egg smell released into the room as my stomach rumbled.

Doctor Cowell used a hanky to cover his nose and mouth and followed my slow steps. I reached the living room window's blind; the buzzing was loudest there. I pulled the cord and the sight made me take a step back. Scattered over the window were dozens of flies dive-bombing into the glass, hovering and waiting as if to be permitted to enter.

An image came into my head at this point. It was of me lying in the desert, gasping for breath, fumbling around in the sand looking for water. Above in the sky, circled two vultures, just waiting…just waiting for me to die.

Doctor Cowell gave me something so I could sleep and then made some phone calls. A car came to collect us and I remember dozing off as the drugs kicked in. When I awoke, we were in the countryside, driving up a bumpy road towards a huge white building surrounded by electric fences. There were no signs, and no clues to where exactly this place was.

We pulled up outside and I was escorted down a long brightly lit corridor and into a waiting room. I sat watching the TV and waited in the room for the doctor to return with news. Apparently, they were in 'conference' about my condition. What seemed like hours came and went as I flicked through magazines, switched through the mass of TV stations. Then the door opened; the sight that confronted me sent my body into shock. I felt as if I were part of a 1950s Sci-Fi movie. Several people entered dressed in white uniforms that were reminiscent of those early cinematic spacesuits. The men's heads covered by masks, transparent plastic sheeting encasing their faces—their distorted eyes beyond.

I stood instinctively, obviously stunned, and I guess ready to fight off these alien beings if in fact they were not there to help me.

'I'm Doctor Kleinen,' the suited man nearest said, smiling through the plastic and holding out his hand. I leaned forward and shook.

'I'm sorry to alarm you this way, but until we know what's happening…what your problem is, it's better to be safe than sorry,' he said. 'But the suits are merely a precaution so please try not to be too alarmed. We need to take you for tests so we can establish your condition,' he said. Though he was dressed like a space invader, his words gave me some hope.

I went to what Doctor Kleinen described as a laboratory that specializes in skin conditions. They then escorted me into a room and offered me a cup of coffee, which I accepted. Then they left me in the bright room, sitting in a reclining chair. As I sipped my coffee, waiting for the doctor to return, my vision wandered. The first ominous sign was the bed. That suggested I would be staying in the room for quite a while. The size of the mirror struck me also. I had seen enough movies to guess that it was one-way glass and probably right now, as I began to come to terms with my situation and my probable quarantine whilst they ran tests, they were watching me.

But what could I do?

I sipped at my drink and walked around the room, dressed in white robes—my bare feet feeling the cold tiled floor. I tried my best not to look at the mirror. I don't know why, I just felt it was better they thought I didn't know they watched my every move.

The light in the room was so bright that in facing certain directions I had to squint. I held an arm out and gazed at my green-blue skin; the hairs of my arm all having died and dropped off—it seemed strange staring at an arm that was hairless...Just little holes where hairs had grown until a day or so earlier.

As I walked towards the door, I heard the bolt snap shut; I instinctively glanced to the mirror, then a crackle of static as the speaker system switched on.

'I'm sorry we've had to lock your door, but until we have established your condition, we cannot allow you to wander freely in the complex. Please be patient with us and hopefully we'll find a speedy solution.'

I didn't like the idea of being a guinea pig to their experiments, but as I've said, I had no choice. That is, if I wanted to be cured.

The hours of waiting turned into days. Occasionally someone would enter to run tests. Injections mainly, occasionally they wired me up like Frankenstein's monster and I felt sensations—such as pinpricks, electric currents and cramps, passing through my body. There were no explanations offered by anyone for their procedures. Just that they were doing all they could for me.

Disconcertingly, my daily visitors began to come armed with guns. I asked about their weapons and the response was they were just 'stunners' in case I had any adverse reaction to testing. They would smile and say things were moving along but I thought guns, 'stunners' or not, suggested bad times ahead.

Then I really did understand why they carried guns. The tests became more intense and I started experiencing side effects. The first was a fever that left me a shivering wreck for forty-eight hours, all the time feeling as if I would vomit—Followed by a period of paralysis down the left side of my body. The next effects were the hallucinations. I would see giant beetles crawling along the white-tiled floor, huge pincers that would tear at my skin. I would witness killer ants scurrying into my mouth and flies that flew about my head then tried to burrow into my eyes—I rolled on the floor wailing, screaming to be saved.

The following mornings I would feel normal. As if someone had rewired the loose circuits in my sanity. It was apparent that I felt okay when they were not doing tests on me—it was whenever the suited men came in with needles and cables, pushing trolleys with computer systems and other monitoring machines and equipment, I knew the suffering would once again begin.

The tests intensified further and I think they pushed me to the brink of insanity. It became like a continuous air strike in times of war, every time I seemed to escape with my life, another bombardment followed.

Time became relative and weeks might have passed whilst I was in a state of constant pain, disorientation and most of all misery. My mind wasn't even functioning enough to count to twenty. I was living in a limbo world.

Then I think the tests must have stopped as I regained hold on reality…of my senses. The fevers passed and though weak, I felt I was myself. I lay testing my memory, remembering as much about myself as I could

After a period without any contact with them, I thought maybe they had just given up trying to find a cure. Maybe I was the only person in the building still alive. Maybe what I had was contagious and the rest of them had dropped dead.

Then the light above my cell door flashed, and the door clicked to unlock and opened. One of the suited men entered and sat on the end of the bed I had slept in for days upon days. It was Doctor Kleinen.

'How are you feeling today?' he asked.

'Okay. A little disorientated. How long have I been here?'

'Two months,' he said. His face was unmoving behind the plastic face mask, his eyes dull. I sensed defeat in that face.

'Your condition does seem to be stabilizing a little. The decomposition has slowed greatly and I hope we can reduce it further.'

Decomposition. There…he had said it himself. The first time he had given my infliction a name. Reduce it further? Slow it down? No mention of making me better, just slowing down the disease as if it were a cancer.

'Out of ideas, huh?'

'Oh no, of course not,' the doctor said. His voice lacked any conviction.

'We've got more tests, more treatments to try,' he said. 'We just wanted to give your body a few days to…to recover.'

'I'm going to die, aren't I?'

The doctor paused. The hesitation was the confirmation.

'We start the tests again tomorrow,' he said, smiling and walked to the door. 'We'll step up our attempts.' With that, the door opened and shut, then locked.

I lay my head on the pillow and replayed the weeks of pain I had experienced because of their experiments. I felt my bones shaking, grinding, my flesh tingling with electric volts, I remembered the fever and hallucinations. I wondered if Hell itself could have filled me with more fear. And now they were to step up their efforts. They were going to crank the torture lever to full power. Really give it to me.

I was certain now, after this brief conversation with Doctor Kleinen, they had given up. I was literally a guinea pig they would do as many tests on as possible before I died, or cracked under the strain. I suspected the tests would no longer be designed to find a cure, but more in line with the discovery of the world's first man, first acknowledged man to decompose first, die second. This was big news worldwide. It had to be. They couldn't allow the opportunity to pass without experimenting with my body. The rest of my life, whatever remained, would be a continuous hell.

That is, if I were to stay.

That night, when I thought the fewest people would be in the building, the security at its most slack, I dropped on the floor and rolled about gibbering, wailing, screaming. I had a lot of experience of the pain so it wasn't hard. Two 'space suitors' ran in holding a straightjacket and tried to help me up. I snatched the gun from one, grabbed him round the neck and held the gun to his masked skull. I had gotten lucky. It was Doctor Kleinen. Surely they would not risk shooting me whilst their boss had a gun to his head. Maybe it was just a stun gun, but it might do some serious damage to a man's brain from close range.

I was able to walk free from the room, taking the straightjacket with me (It might prove useful, I thought). Those who were out in the observation room just watched wide-eyed, not wanting to risk their own safety.

I escorted the doctor along the corridor then out into the courtyard. We got in his car and I made him drive me back into town. Nobody followed us, I made sure of that when flicking the safety from the gun. I think they thought I must have gone crazy. Probably they had been expecting it anyway after all the tests they had run on me.

Doctor Kleinen stopped the car just outside the town centre. I put him in the straightjacket and left him.

'You can't leave me here!' he screamed. 'At least let me out of this damn thing!'

'I need all the time I can get,' I said, removing one of his socks and stuffing it as far down his throat as I could. It would not take long for him to spit it free, but it might give me some extra time.

After collecting my car and a few essentials, I drove night and day, only stopping for petrol, until I believed I was far enough away to live my final days or weeks in peace—without pain. That is all I wanted by then, no more suffering.

It has been two years now and I'm still alive! I set up home in a disused country barn and began trying all I could to improve my condition. It might seem a bit far-fetched but I sat myself down and thought logically about what supposedly slows decomposition. I now sleep in a wooden crate filled with soil! Sounds a bit vampire-like but there have been dramatic signs of a slowed decline. Month to month there are changes, further decomposition to my body, but no longer day to day. My body is frail, my skin blistered and blue. My stomach sometimes inflates, sometimes does not. When it is bulbous, I secrete that stench of rotten eggs.

My body is totally hair free, and my nails have long since broken away.

Actually, my final nail came off this morning, leading to me writing this account of the last two years of my life. But I'm happy. I haven't been in actual contact with a living soul for all this time. I've seen only one person, which was a hiker on the ridge of the hill that overlooks the barn. He had seen my home and started to come down—probably looking for shelter for the night. I gazed up towards him with the gun from the lab in my hands. He turned and ran and I haven't seen him since.

So far, in fact, my main concern has been the flies and bugs that seem attracted to me each time my stomach inflates and I start releasing that toxic smelling gas into the air. They come in their droves and I have to keep on the move so they aren't able to pin me down. God only knows what they would make of me if I just lay back and let them get on with it.

It is only three days since I last wrote, but now I'm sure this will be my last entry. I was walking down towards the river for a night swim. I swim every night, once the sun has gone down—the water I think, helps to preserve my body. But on this occasion as I walked through the long grass, a sudden bolt of pain fired through my body, I collapsed and suffered wave after wave of agony, as if fire were passing through my veins, swamping me—as if the coach smashing me through the railing and down the cliff had finally caught up with me. It had been following me like an invisible fist for two years and had finally found me. WHAM!

As I lay in the grass, I could see the coach sliding towards me; I could hear the screams and smell the burned rubber. Then the sensation of falling and as I landed more pain fired around me. Then my bones began to snap and crack one by one. Then the pain went and I was alone in the long grass. It was as I tried to stand that I realized my body really was now a mass of shattered bones. My neck broken and unable to hold the weight of my head. I've crawled to the barn and pulled down this paper to the floor and I write now, my fingers breaking like pencil led. As I gaze down to my leg, I see it crumbling as the bone goes brittle…now I again see that black figure in the sky, illuminated by moonlight, riding the dark horse, galloping on air as he spirals down towards me. Only this time, I have no doubts, he won't be returning to the stars alone.

~*Six Separate Pieces*~

Every seat of the dome-shaped auditorium is full. The crowd waits eagerly for the entertainment to commence. The air is barely breathable; teeming with body odor, beer breath and cigarette smoke.

Just in front of those rowdy spectators is the commentary team for the evening. There is only radio commentary because the major TV networks have boycotted the event, deeming it sick and an utter disgrace.

"Hello, this is Jim Boyd here at the auditorium, and with me tonight my co-commentator Art Mayweather. Thanks for coming, Art."

"My pleasure, Jim. Wouldn't have missed it for the world!"

"Well, folks, you can probably hear the atmosphere—no exaggeration to say it's deafening! Absolutely incredible! I can barely hear myself speak."

"It's amazing," Art adds. "I think—"

"For those folks just tuning in, unaware of tonight's historic occasion," Jim interrupts. "I'll quickly fill you in before we get underway. We're hoping to witness a world record here tonight! That record is for the amount of human bodies that can be 'de-limbed' in the space of sixty seconds—that's *one minute*. To be categorized de-limbed, the body must be chopped into six separate pieces. That is the head must be amputated, as must both arms and legs. That's five pieces and then the torso makes the sixth! Jake Cummins, our competitor tonight, will need to de-limb eleven people to break that long-standing world record!"

"It will be interesting to see how he fares," Art says.

"Yes it certainly will! The bodies are in clear view just a few yards ahead of us, really great seats we have! Eleven naked individuals flat out on their stomachs, lined up on the tables. Arms and legs stretched out. It's also important to mention that these people are not actually dead. They are though of course sedated. But don't you folks listening at home worry yourselves; only people on death row have been selected, so there's no need to feel bad for them…they are *all* destined to be killed regardless of the success of Jake Cummins' record attempt tonight!"

"And those buckets beneath the tables…" Art says, taking advantage of Jim's pause to sip water, finally getting a chance to speak uninterrupted. "They've been positioned to catch the amputated heads. This safety procedure introduced because a Frenchman trying for the record managed to trip on a head as it rolled under his feet, wrecking all hopes he had of breaking this long-standing record. It will—"

"Got to interrupt you, Art, as Jake Cummins has just come through the curtain. The atmosphere absolutely incredible as I'm sure you can hear! And you folks listening at home, probably sitting with your families around the radio, perhaps just having finished your supper, you can enjoy all the action here with us! It promises to be quite a show!"

"Jake Cummins is wearing a white vest," Art points out.

"I think we could call it a Bruce Willis style vest, don't you, Art?"

"I think that's a fair description, Jim."

"He's holding the short-handled axe," Jim comments. "The countdown clock will start as soon as Jake takes the first swing. *Wow!*…the hair on my neck is standing on end. It really is *that* exciting! You could cut the tension with a knife! Or maybe I should say with an axe!"

"*And we're off folks!* Jake with a powerful swing—the first head pops off and cleanly lands with a rattle in the bucket! Fantastic stuff! He's around to the legs and takes one and two off, then onto the arms—incredible, so fast, *so precise! So messy!*

"Onto the second body—he's already taken the head and one, and now a second arm!"

"He's really going for it, and look at the concentration on his face, Jim."

"Incredible! What a competitor and he's already on to the fourth body, though it takes him two strikes to remove the right leg! And listen to the crowd now, chanting Jake's name, absolutely deafening sound! They're right behind him folks! And why not—they want to see the world record smashed!

"At the halfway point he's already de-limbed six people. *Incredible! Wow!* The head on the seventh body drops then hits the rim of the bucket and fortunately rolls under the table and away from Jake's feet! The floor is wet and slippery with blood. He's on to person number eight as the clock ticks down, twenty-one—twenty—nineteen."

"Number eleven is stirring, Jim."

"*What? Jesus Christ!* Excuse my language, folks, but my co-commentator is absolutely right! The proposed eleventh and would be record-breaking body is as I speak crawling to the edge of the table! He slumps onto the floor and now staggers towards the exit! *This is awful! Terrible!* But don't panic, folks; he'll be shot as he tries to leave the building!

"But Jake continues, unfazed, but seems now destined to fail! On to number ten—*head off! Legs off!* And arms…Arms are off with a spray of blood! But now what? It's hopeless—with nine seconds remaining, he has only equalled the record! Looking bemused as he stares at me…he's coming over to the commentary box, Art—*wait! He's got me, dragging me!*—"

"*He's got Jim!*" Art cries, taking over. "Thrown him on the table—the axe comes down!—*Jesus!* Your commentator's head has just been sliced off—his blood splashing my face! And his arms are off with three seconds to go, and on to the final leg…two—one…*he's done it! Jake has done it with only a second remaining!* Eleven de-limbed in a single minute! The eleventh, amazingly, your commentator for the night, Jim Boyd—still fully clothed!

"The crowd goes wild, screaming—so very excited they've witnessed a world record here tonight! Oh but the referee is waving his arms for the crowd to quiet down. He's checking whether your commentator for the evening, Jim Boyd, was correctly dissected. One of his legs remains on the table and inside the trousers. The referee pulls at Jim's leg and it resists. Oh dear, it's not looking good. The ref is rolling up the trouser leg to examine the cleanness of the cut. Is it a proper amputation? The auditorium is silent—you could hear a pin drop. Is it good? *IT IS!!* Jake

Cummins has done it! Oh and does he look pleased with himself, drenched in blood, grinning, and so he should be—he's just written himself into the record books!

"What a night, folks—and thanks for joining us on this historic occasion! Until the next time, good night! And please, don't have nightmares."

~Rotten Core~

As I waited for the train, a gust of wind shot through the station and cut across my throat. I dipped my chin into my coat and rubbed my hands together—noticing the snake sliver from a box into the long grass behind the stationmaster's hut.

"When does the train arrive?" I asked the stationmaster as he swept the floor.

"Anytime now, sir."

The stationmaster looked up, leaned on his broom and pointed. The train approached, it braked and slowed...slowed...then stopped next to the platform with a thin layer of snow on the roof.

I walked over to the door, opened and entered. The door clanked shut behind me and I found a seat, rubbed my hands together and blew on them to generate heat.

Outside, the snow began to fall, floating down and landing on the tracks.

The train jerked and started. It increased in speed, passing snow-covered fields as the late afternoon sun began to edge down for the night. The chugging train's rhythm began to relax me and I closed my eyes to rest. Feeling warm and comfortable, I unzipped my coat a little and leaned my head back against the soft blue cushion. The train shuddered over a bump and I opened my eyes. The head cushion on the seat opposite was torn, yellow sponge exposed. Two balls of chewed, chewing gum sat on the seat.

I turned my head to the only other passenger in the carriage. She was an elderly woman of over seventy. Her hair sprouted uncomfortably in white, wispy spirals; the hair so thin, the carriage lights glistened off her pink scalp. Her face sagged under the weight of her wrinkles and a smile stretched across her cheeks.

She was staring hard, focused, upon her knitting. The black wool she used was beginning to take the shape of a glove.

She looked up to me. I smiled and she smiled back revealing a toothless all-gum grin. Her eyes then left mine and returned to her knitting. She was now knitting even more intensely.

I turned back to the window and watched as the snow continued to fall. In the distance, the tops of the trees wore white wigs and lights began to blink on in the passing farmhouses. The wind whipped against the window—it was not closed properly and made a high-pitched whistle. I got to my feet and tried to shut out the wind. The window was broken and resisted my attempts. The wind continued to whistle as a kettle does en route to boiling.

Then the carriage door opened and the ticket inspector stepped in wearing a navy, flat hat and a bulky ticket machine, which was supported over his shoulder by a strap. As he turned, I gasped at the sight of the eyeball-less black void that sat next to his pointed nose.

"Tickets please," he said.

I sunk my fingers into my pocket for my ticket, whilst I tried to stunt my shock. I handed the ticket over and stared as he checked. He punched holes in the ticket then handed it back.

"Thank you," he said.

My eyes darted from the ticket inspector to the floor and back again, unsure where to look. He turned towards the elderly lady.

"Ticket please."

I felt bad. It must have been obvious that I was uncomfortable with the sight of his...eyeless hole. But I wondered what was in there? It looked deep...black...bottomless. If I had shone a torch into the hole, would I have seen his brain? I shook my head to clear my thoughts. The poor guy must get the same reaction every time he asked to see tickets.

The elderly lady placed her knitting down on the seat and plunged her hand deep into her handbag. She fumbled about, and then her fleshy, veined fingers reappeared holding the ticket. She handed it over, grinning her gums.

"Thank you," said the one-eyed ticket inspector then handed her ticket back. She tucked it into her purse then continued to knit. The black glove was taking shape.

The ticket inspector walked over to the door, dragging his leg in a limp I hadn't noticed before. He opened the door, and then glanced at me for a second before leaving—glancing at me through that black void! He smiled then departed. A shiver ran up and down my spine. He had smiled as if he had seen me, but from the angle he had looked at me from, he wouldn't have been able to see me from his good eye. Only from the…the empty socket. The icy shudder returned.

I shifted on my seat, looked up and met eyes with the toothless elderly lady. She grinned, and then allowed her eyes to concentrate on the woollen glove she knitted.

"Cold night, isn't it?" I said, smiling.

She took her eyes from her knitting and met mine. She didn't respond.

I shifted further and gazed out the window as the train began to slow, approaching a station. The train stopped. There was only a single person on the platform. He stood wrapped in a dark scarf and wearing a bobble hat. His silver, puffy jacket pulled right up and only his nose and eyes were visible. He picked up his backpack and stepped over to the train, opened the door and came into the carriage. He smiled at the elderly lady, who looked up from beneath her eyelashes. He tilted his head around to survey the carriage and then walked over and sat down in the seat opposite. His head back against the yellow sponge that spilled from the head cushion. Remembering the chewing gum, I looked down to the seat.

He had sat on the chewing gum.

He stared at me through the slit left between his hat and the scarf, and then closed his eyes.

"Sorry to bother you, but I think you've just sat on some chewing gum," I said.

He looked at me through his dark, dull eyes—then closed them. I assumed he must have been foreign and not understood me…I was about to try again when he began to snore. I was surprised anyone could fall asleep in such a short space of time.

I gazed out at the falling snow as the train pulled away from the station.

The train was soon cutting through the countryside again, the sun having dropped below the horizon for the night; darkness blanketing the sky.

I yawned and then looked to the man who sat wrapped up opposite me. His nose was bleeding. A thin, wet trail ran down from either nostril. I again considered waking him when he, sleeping, lifted his hand and wiped at the blood with his fingers. The blood smeared across his fingers and then as he scratched at his cheek, he left a crimson smudge.

The man with the nosebleed was still snoring.

The elderly lady was still knitting.

I got to my feet and went in search of a toilet. The light in the corridor flickered and sparked out as I walked. Shadows spread over as I passed the first class seats. I saw the toilet at the end of the carriage, and then froze as I heard banging. I listened. The bang, then again...again...bang...

I carried on, stopped, shocked at the sight of the teenage boy sitting in an electric wheelchair, driving directly into the door. His legs banged into the wood. Then he reversed and the back of his head smashed into the far door. Then he sped forward again, crashing into the door behind which I stood. He paused, took his chubby fingers from the control stick and looked up to me with angry eyes and a forehead of creases. His face was fat and his chin sat in folds above a polo neck sweater.

"*Go away!*" he screamed. "*Get lost!*"

The light flashed back on and I made my way to the toilet. I pissed in the bowl, wobbling as the train jerked. Off balance, I squirted urine on the floor. I shook off then allowed the cold tap water to clean my hands. I flushed, and then walked back along the corridor. The lights flickered off...I waited and they flickered on again. As I passed the wheel-chaired boy, he reversed into the wall with a thud, then forward again smacking his legs into the door with a crack.

"*Go away!*" he shrieked, his flabby cheeks red and trembling.

I quickly passed and continued back to the carriage—baffled by what the boy in the wheelchair hoped to achieve. He was like a trapped animal, desperately trying to ram his way to freedom.

I sat down in my seat. There was an icy puddle of water around the man's feet where the snow had melted from his shoes. His nose was still bleeding, drips continued to flow and he continued to wipe at the nose, each time spreading more blood over his face. He was beginning to resemble a clown with a red painted face.

He still slept, snoring.

The old lady stopped knitting for a moment and rummaged around her handbag. She pulled out a red apple and began vigorously rubbing it on her cardigan. A single bead of sweat on her forehead dripped down and her deep facial wrinkles ambushed it.

She eyed the apple carefully and then pulled a set of teeth from her bag. She forced the teeth into her mouth, stretched her jaw, and then grinned at me. I smiled back.

She bit into the apple and a chunk came off in her mouth. She chewed.

The train jerked and the apple wriggled free of her vein-ridden hand and fell to the ground. It rolled steadily toward my foot, then stopped. The missing chunk faced me. I glanced to the lady. She was again knitting, her teeth still chomping the single mouthful she had taken.

"It has rolled into some dirt," I said.

She did not respond.

I took a final look at the red apple, then realising she'd given up on it, I rested my head against the head cushion. My eyes were heavy, tired.

The man's nosebleed had stopped, and the blood was drying.

The apple remained covered in dirt in the centre of the aisle. A bruise had begun to form.

As I drifted towards sleep, I noticed a snowman in one of the white fields. The snowman wore a black hat and had a carrot for a nose. As the rhythm of the train began to lead me towards sleep, I thought I saw the same snowman, only I couldn't have, as the field was long gone...I slept...dreamt....

...I was on a cloud floating through the red sky. On the cloud opposite, I saw the elderly, wrinkled lady. She was eating the apple, chewing—but her teeth were resting on her knee...her gums began to bleed and the blood trickled steadily down her deeply grooved chin...then the man with the nosebleed appeared...only then his head was just one giant bleeding nose...bleeding...and the wheel-chaired boy laughed, croaked: "Leave me alone! Go away!"...Then ahead, the ticket inspector's eyeball-less socket got ever closer—like a black hole in the red sky…the cloud drifted towards…nearer…inside….

…I awoke and steadied my breaths. Relaxed…ran my hand back through my moist head of hair.

"Just a dream."

The train was stationary. I yawned, rubbed my eyes and blinked. The man with the nosebleed, scarf, and silver coat had vanished. The puddle where his feet had been, remained. I stretched, then turned my head towards the old lady. She had gone too. I pressed my face against the window and tried to make out which station the train had reached. I couldn't see any signs. It was so dark I couldn't see at all.

I got to my feet and walked along the aisle to the carriage door. I opened.

Ahead I could see only a thick, white fog—so thick that my eyes were not able to penetrate. Below, I could see the edge of the platform and the yellow safety line. I stepped down, hands out in front of me as I passed through the fog.

Beyond the fog was a graveyard. A single tree hung over one of the gravestones. On a branch, a red apple swayed in the light breeze. As I took another step forwards, I noticed the missing chunk from the apple. The apple dropped, split as it hit the headstone and plummeted into a freshly dug grave. I leaned over and looked down to where the two halves of apple had landed. Maggots had spilled from the rotten core and begun to burrow, dig, down into the soil.

The train screeched, then began to leave.

"*Don't go without me! I'm not ready!*"

The train pulled away and then vanished into the fog.

~*Bellybutton*~

A blanket of mist entombed the grassy Derwent Valley and the sun was gradually climbing to its seat in the sky, as Pam noticed the light beaming from her husband's stomach.

She blinked hard, using her balled fists to remove tiredness from her eyes. The vision that she had questioned, remained. Light shone faintly from her husband's bellybutton.

She looked from his bare stomach, up over his hairless chest, and to his peaceful face. His closed eyelids flickered ever so gently, breaths exhaled, air inhaled in unison with the rise and fall of his chest.

She glanced again to the bellybutton—squinting to penetrate the beam of light. Not a bright light, not a blinding light, but a glow, like that from the bulb of a dying torch.

She leant forward, lowering herself, her face closer to the light source, her eyes darting back and forth between the hole and her husband's face.

As the light hit her eyes, she could see dust particles within, floating aimlessly, illuminated and spotlighted.

Twelve inches from the bellybutton, she continued to lower her face, hands either side of her husband's waist, her hair hanging and almost touching his stomach.

Ten inches, her hair touched down.

Six inches, the beam of light shining in her face, still not bright; there wasn't the need to blink, to turn away, or to cover her eyes.

She pressed her eye against the hole and gazed in. It was dark but she could see bright dots of light amongst the blackness. Like stars—was she looking into space?

Heart thumping in her chest, she swallowed. In the distance something was forming. White mists materializing from deep within the vision, sucked to the forefront, forming and creating. The mists condensed, the stars brightening in the blackness. Then she saw it; the illuminated mists created a face that brought only one name to her mind.

'What are you doing?'

She sprang away, gazing at the light projecting bellybutton.

The voice again. 'Honey, are you okay?'

She looked up and for a moment met eyes with her husband.

'What's that light?' he said, yawning.

She held her husband's hand and squeezed. 'Jesus Christ,' she muttered.

'You're sweating,' he said, sitting up and gazing down to where the light shone. He glanced around the room for the source. His forehead creased in puzzlement. *He* was the source.

Jack and Pam Stoud held each other. Jack ran his hand over his wife's woollen sweater. She had her face pressed against his chest, feeling his heart's drummed beat. She had told her husband what she had seen. He had tried to see also, but he had not the agility to get into position to see down his bellybutton. He had to trust his wife, and he did, unequivocally.

The initial fright had passed for both of them; they were in a warm embrace, silent. Physically inactive, motionless, but mentally thoughts darted, tangled and ricocheted in every direction.

'What shall we do?' Pam asked. She felt her husband's chest depress as he released a long sigh.

'I don't know,' he muttered. 'I really don't.'

Pam took her hand away from his chest and ran her fingers softly over his face.

'Do you think it's a sign?'

'Maybe,' he said. 'But why now? Why today? If it is a sign from...' He could not bring himself to say the name. '*Him*...are we supposed to tell people? And what would we...*could* we say?'

'But it's his face, isn't it?'

'I guess so.'

Pam gently lifted her husband's sweater—the faint light released, hovering in a tube-like beam from the exposed bellybutton.

Heart pounding, head heating, she lowered her eye to the hole once again. The feeling of trepidation, she thought, a thousand times worse than in a job interview; this was a…an audience with Jesus Christ. At least it seemed that way. She pulled away, taken over by fear.

She need not look again; she knew what was there.

Though it may have only been a picture, she could not dissuade herself from believing the misty face was home to thoughts, to sight—to his, *Jesus Christ's mind*. The thought terrified Pam. Were they to be judged?

The Stouds kept the information a secret for six weeks. However, their lives had become unbearable with the secret hanging heavy around their necks.

They had to talk to someone, somebody that had some answers.

In those weeks, they had both avidly read the Bible in search of an answer; Jack had regularly confessed his sins at the local church, paranoid, convinced it was some kind of punishment for something. He had no appetite, grown thin, pale, and weak—he had been off sick from the bank. He had claimed that personal problems had arisen and the bank's management had given him time off. He had been at the Simpson's Bank ten years with barely a sick day to his name, so they knew it must be something serious.

Over the weeks, he spent his days in bed, wrapped in blankets, bandage around his stomach covering the hole, the face of Jesus. He was breaking down—in the middle of some kind of nervous breakdown. It was a curse—a punishment for sleeping with so many women behind his wife's back. He should have known that those infidelities would come back to haunt him. He felt numb, hopeless.

Pam had decided that it was a good sign, a positive phenomena; a miracle that proved that Jesus had once lived and that they must change their lifestyles to accommodate Christianity. Pam prayed several times a day, asking for an explanation, begging for God to speak to her and tell her what was happening, asking what they were supposed to do about the phenomena. They had not been able to have children of their own, her fault not his, and it played on her mind. Her thought was that this might be the rebirth of Jesus Christ, born from her husband's stomach.

Unlikely. Perhaps that was just the sign to warn her of an imminent pregnancy.

She had taken a pregnancy test herself once a week—just in case it was a vision of *her* future—fingers crossed, not knowing whether she wanted the test to be positive or negative. It was negative each week. She chose not to tell her husband about the tests. The idea that they might be about to give birth to the Son of God, probably would have given her husband a heart attack.

She was worried about her husband. She had begged him to see a doctor, but he refused. After six weeks of life with the phenomena, with her husband's condition worsening, she had decided it was time to seek advice. But who do you seek advice from about something like this? There was only one option and that, she knew, was the Church.

Sunday morning. Pam had convinced Jack to come with her to the church and speak to Father McFadden. Jack was a shell of himself, bags under his eyes, his hair dishevelled and his chin unshaven for two weeks. He held a handkerchief by his mouth to catch each of the spluttered coughs that escaped. He felt like absolute shit. He had not really wanted to come to the church with his wife, but if he was to die, he had at least to show he was going to fight death off as long as he possibly could. He had come into this god-forsaken world kicking and screaming, and he intended to go out the same goddam way—Even if he had to stand toe-to-toe with the Grim Reaper. The vision in his mind's eye of getting involved in a scythe contest with Death brought the first smile to his face for many days.

'I love you,' he said as Pam helped him into the car.

'I love you,' Pam responded. 'You know this will all be okay, right? I mean, someone connected to the church will know about this. It just has to be a good sign—I'm a hundred percent sure of that. You have nothing to worry about,' she said.

'I hope you're right,' he said, smiling and squeezing her hand. His grip was weak; his strength diminished by six weeks of worry—worry that had eaten him away, devouring his heart and more significantly his hope.

Jack had already accepted his fate, but he would try to stay strong for his wife. The poor bitch was still under the delusion this phenomenon was for the good of the world. The reality, he *was* dying. Surely, God would not send a sign that would cause him to suffer, slowly tearing him apart until the day his family, the ones he very rarely saw, might even enjoy shovelling soil onto him. Good riddance to the worthless shit, they would probably be thinking. That is, except for his wife. She loved him with all her heart. Despite his misdemeanors, he loved her.

By the time they arrived at the church, the service was well underway, but Pam refused to wait in the car—she thought they could slip in at the back. She pushed open the church doors, walking in quickly with her husband. She wrapped the scarf that had come loose, tightly around her husband's neck, and kissed his cheek. His face was cold.

'Come on, darling.'

They quietly sat at the back of the church as Father McFadden continued the service. Until six weeks earlier, she had never believed in God. Now she had no doubts about his existence. She had attended as many church services as she could, and she had gotten to know Father McFadden. She had to speak to him about Jack.

The Bible reading was from Corinthians 14.

'Follow the way of love and eagerly desire spiritual gifts, especially the gift of prophecy.'

Jack had difficulty keeping his eyes open—he had lost so much sleep. She gently ran her fingers through his hair, closed her eyes and prayed.

'Amen,' Father McFadden said. The church of people began to collect their coats and slowly walked from the church in quiet, polite conversation.

Pam helped Jack to his feet and walked him towards where Father McFadden was collecting his reading materials.

'Hello, Father McFadden.'

He turned with a smile that dropped from his face as he saw Jack Stoud.

'My heavens, you do look poorly,' he said.

'Please, Father, you have to help him, *help us.*'

Father McFadden brought his hands together, as if in prayer, and then raised them to his mouth, his head furrowed in thought.

'How can I help?'

'My husband's very unwell, as you can see. Please do not suggest a doctor because he will not go. We think that you may be able to help though, Father.'

'Please, come into my office and we can speak in private.'

Pam told the Father every last detail of the phenomena. Jack had nodded weakly throughout, confirming to the Father all his wife said, just in case he thought her crazy.

'Will you take a look for us, Father?'

Father McFadden sighed. He rubbed his face.

'It's an incredible claim…but the Lord does move in mysterious ways,' he said, smiling. Never had the words seemed more appropriate.

He agreed to look. Jack lay on his back on the sofa; Father McFadden bent over him, cautiously moving his head into the light beam, doubts firing around his mind. Pam Stoud's fidgety eyes and worried gulps urged him forward. He pressed his eye against the bellybutton and watched.

His head shot up. He panted. He reached for a glass of water and sipped.

'I don't believe it. *It's true.*'

Johnny Eastman had just come out of the church toilet when he had seen Father McFadden talking to a couple. The husband had looked half-dead.

Johnny was a journalist for a local paper. He had graduated from university with ambitions of becoming an Investigative Journalist. Five years in journalism later, he seemed to have hit a brick wall—stuck in the local press.

The newspaper asked him to do a story about the Sunday service at the church. Father McFadden had contacted the newspaper about getting some much-needed publicity. Johnny was not sure whether money had been exchanged, but here he was, bored shitless, listening to Father McFadden prattle on about love. He had been relieved to slip away to the toilet to pour cold water over his face.

Nevertheless, this was interesting; the wife had seemed desperate for help. *So,* Johnny had followed them to the Father's office, and watched through the window as the incredible events unfolded, tape recorder in hand, camera at the ready. This was a story with *real bollocks*. An apparent insane couple convinced Jesus Christ of all people was hibernating inside the husband's stomach or something along those lines.

Then the Father had staggered away, shocked. Johnny's eyes sprang open, ears pricked up.

'It's true!' he had said.

Jesus Christ, he thought. Johnny 'Sniffer Dog' Eastman, as his friends had dubbed him at college, had a goddam hot story. As hot as fresh shit! Big. Real big.

As he took the digital photos, Jack noticed him, camera in hand. Jack pointed an unsteady arm. Father McFadden turned to look. Johnny though had what he wanted—he ducked and ran along the church aisle and out into the warm summer air.

'*Yes! Yes!*' he screamed as he dashed across the road, trying to decide how much he would demand for the story.

'*I'll be rich!*'

The following morning, Jack and Pam Stoud woke to the sound of voices. The Press lined the fences of both front and back gardens—local, national and even some international. On seeing Pam peering out from the curtain, the click-clicking of cameras fired.

'*Mrs. Stoud, is it true?*'

'*Can Jesus Christ be seen?*'

'*Does this sign relate to your husband being unwell?*'

'*Have you been visited?*'

'*Mrs. Stoud, is this a publicity seeking hoax?*'

'*Mrs. Stoud?*'

'*How is your husband?*'

Pam shut the curtain and sat on the end of the bed. Jack lay on his back, eyes upon her.

'You'd better call the police,' he said. He had declined further during the night. His eyes blood-shot; his hairline had begun to drift away from his forehead, the evidence of hair loss sprinkled across the pillow. His face grooved with dark lines. He literally looked like he was decomposing in life—a gaunt and ill man, something that had escaped its coffin, taken a wrong turn, and walked into the world of the living.

Pam Stoud picked up the phone, trying to compose herself, trying to fight away the tears. The line was dead. She pressed the button repeatedly—she had seen that in movies. Like in the movies, it was of no use.

Pacing the room, biting her nails, she tried to select their best option. The press had found out about the phenomena—no doubt from that intruder in the church. Father McFadden had feared this would happen. The Press knew—how could they possibly conceal the truth? The Press are bastards, they would wait and wait, ignoring the need for food and drink—resorting to cannibalism rather than losing prime photograph positions.

She would have to face them. They might then leave them alone. Or at least give them a little time to escape.

'*Mrs. Stoud, it is Father Hanley from the church.*'

Pam got to her feet and poked a finger between the curtains to open them enough to see through. Pushing through the crowds, Father Hanley forced his was into the garden and up the path. Pam dashed around to the door and allowed him in, deafened by the roar of requests from the lurking vultures.

'Mrs. Stoud, I'm Father Hanley—a colleague of Father McFadden...he sent me to collect you after seeing the revelations in the morning papers. Are you ready, how's your husband?'

'Not too good,' she said, leading Father Hanley into the bungalow's bedroom. Jack had already gotten out of bed and was dressing.

Jack stepped weakly over to Father Hanley and shook his hand. 'Thank you for coming,' he croak-whispered into Father Hanley's ear.

The three of them ventured out into the garden, photographed by a hundred cameras. Father Hanley led the way, doing his best to shield them. A black Ford awaited them.

Inside were two other members of the church. One in the driver's seat; he was a chubby man with dark hair and beard. The one in the passenger seat was red haired, his cheeks flushed with colour. All three dressed in black, wearing the white collar of the church.

Pam and her husband sat next to Father Hanley on the back seat. He smiled kindly.

'Better put your seatbelts on,' he said.

The Press shouted outside, cameras thrust in front of the car, pictures taken. The car revved into life and accelerated away from the scene, leaving the smell of singed rubber in the air. Soon the crowds were out of sight—the driver however did not let up on the pace he was setting, taking lefts and rights, trying to lose any pursuing vehicles. The car sped along the country roads; the wind rattled the back shelf of the Ford as it navigated the bends.

'We are to meet Father McFadden at his home—the church will be swarming with the media. They were waiting outside this morning, snapping shots, piecing together stories from what evidence they have. The news of your husband's gift has spread like wildfire. Now we must contain it,' he said as he closed his eyes and put his hands together. Pam realized he was praying and stopped herself from asking if he was okay. Instead, she gazed at her husband. He smiled, and then rested his head against her shoulder. She could not believe any of this was happening, and why to them?

A line of drool was hanging from his gaping mouth. She noticed for the first time how his jaw-line now jutted out, the veins in his neck protruding as if they were stretching the skin, trying to break free from his dying body. She swallowed hard, trying to hold off the tears. They were in safe hands now; they *would* be protected. That was their hope. *God.* He would help them, she was certain of that.

After twenty minutes, the car slowed and they drove up a gravel drive. Pam looked out the window; a little surprised they had taken the turning. She could not see a house, just a large farm barn. Hairs began to spring up over the back of her neck. She glanced to Father Hanley. He had a gun in his hand—he pointed it at her heart. She froze. Swallowed hard. Released air. She was glad to see her husband had fallen asleep.

'What's…what's happening?' she asked.

The redhead in the passenger seat leant back holding a gun of his own.

'Business,' the man said, grinning.

They drove along the gravel drive. In one of the surrounding fields, a single goat munched on the long grass. It lifted its head and gazed over to them as they passed. It finished chewing, swallowed, and then dipped its head into the grass for another mouthful.

Their captors escorted them through the empty, high-ceilinged farm barn and to a small door that a stack of hay partially concealed. Behind the door, stairs spiralled downward to a white door. Father Hanley knocked on the door. Silence for a minute then the door swung open, inwards, and a bespectacled man with a flock of static grey hair blinked dumbly.

'Good! Come in, please, do come in!'

The 'priests' pushed Pam and Jack forward, waving their guns in the direction of the grey-haired man. He wore a tweed suit and purple tie. His glasses were silver rimmed, the lenses small and circular.

The room was small; there were bookshelves on the wall, a desk of papers and a bed in the corner.

'Is that where you *fuck* Father Hanley?' Pam asked.

'No,' he said. 'I'm sorry about the rough stuff,' he continued. 'I tell the boys to take it easy, but they are bullies by nature, all in the diet I say. Not enough wheat.'

'Why have you brought us here?'

'Research,' the man said. 'My name's Franklin, Bruno Franklin.'

'Are you a mad scientist?' Jack croaked; he wished he had the strength to beat the shit out of these arseholes.

'No…I'm a religious education teacher by profession, but I spend long periods travelling—looking for religious artefacts, searching for miracles. My travels have uncovered many things that certain religious sects would not wish for me to unveil. Meddling in religion is one easy way to make enemies. For example, what sort of affect would it have on mankind if I were to disclose the contents of missing pages from the Bible?'

'You have missing pages from the Bible?' Pam asked.

Bruno smiled. 'Let's just say I have made many discoveries in my time and have a lot of people who would like to see me dead. Hence the muscle,' he said, glancing to his bodyguards.

'Do you know what's happening to my husband?'

'No…*not yet*. But I will,' he said. 'But you must believe me when I say I wish neither of you any harm. If you cooperate—'

'Cooperate? You mean if we do as we're told you will set us free?' she asked.

Bruno sighed. 'You must understand…I am the least of your worries. I just wish to discover the *truth* and if I am able to, I will tell the world!' he announced, smiling, looking beyond the walls to a billion people cheering his name. He blinked and looked to Pam. 'I wish you no harm. However, there will be countless people hoping to…*eliminate* your husband.'

'But why would anyone want to hurt my husband…destroy this thing? Surely it could be seen as proof of Jesus Christ's existence?'

'If only it were that simple, my dear woman. Remember, not everyone will be pleased if Jesus really had once existed. For everything this miracle may prove, it therefore has to disprove also.'

Bruno's eyes now fixed on Jack's stomach. He had talked himself into a feverish need to witness the miracle for himself.

Pam noticed the glazed, slightly insane glint to Bruno's stare, as she scanned the room. Bruno grinned. 'I shouldn't bother. There is no way you can escape. I also suggest you don't waste your time yelling for help, we are miles and miles away from civilization—all screaming will get you is physical abuse from them,' he said, gazing at the black-clothed guards. 'And, I should imagine, a sore throat.'

Pam nodded.

'Right. I think the time has arrived. You can go now,' he said to his guards. Father Hanley was the last out, shutting and bolting the door.

'I have had dreams—dreams my whole life about being the *One* to discover the greatest mysteries in religion. I knew I was different. *Special.* Now the opportunity has arisen. Again, I'm sorry for the rough treatment, but I knew you wouldn't allow me to study this phenomenon any other way.' He was staring blind again, lost to the world. '*My God*, this could change the way mankind views the world. This could have significance to the *Second Coming*. At this stage, who knows? Oh, but I will dedicate my life to this phenomena if need be, and maybe, just maybe, I will find answers that are so mind-blowing, we cannot even begin to imagine.'

Bruno took a handkerchief from his pocket and approached Pam. He brought it over her head, towards her throat.

'*No!*'

'I'm not going to hurt you or your husband. I'm just taking precautions,' he said as he gagged her. 'As I have said, nobody can hear your screams anyway, but I could do without the headache.'

Just then, the three of them paused as they heard the approaching vehicle. Bruno's face suddenly aged by twenty years, his eyes darting around.

Shouts penetrated the walls, followed by the screech of tyres and gunfire. Gunshots echoed around the barn, screams and then what sounded like a grenade exploding, followed by an agonized wail and more gunfire. Then there was silence. Bruno ran to his desk and withdrew the semi-automatic. Sweat had sprouted over his forehead; his gun wielding hand shook violently.

'What's going on?' Jack said. Bruno looked to him, biting at his lower lip. A trickle of blood ran down his chin as he sucked air and dabbed the blood with trembling fingers.

Jack had moved nearer to his wife. He wanted to be close to her. The door swung open and a tall, bald man entered, wearing a white suit and black tie; a scar ran from his right ear down to where his upper and lower lips met at the corner.

A piece of the brick exploded just above his head—he ducked, swivelled and fired towards Bruno, who stood wide-eyed, gun at the end of outstretched hands. The bullet erupted in his chest, covering his face and static grey hair in blood. He wheezed a groan as he collapsed and fell backwards onto his desk. He slid and slumped onto the ground, a gentle murmur left his lips as he twitched dead.

The new arrival covered both Jack and Pam Stoud with his gun. He looked around the room. He sighed as he collected Bruno Franklin's papers and stuffed them in his jacket.

'*Yes, yes. Good,*' he said. Then he scratched his facial scar and turned.

'Don't move,' he said, scratching his scar again. 'It tends to itch in the heat of battle,' he said, smiling. The light from the bulb above his head glistened off the top of his pink mottled scalp.

'Do you know what I see when I look at your husband?' he asked. He did not wait for a response. 'I see a dying man…a pitiful man who for some reason has this miracle growing within him. But beyond the broken shell that is your husband,' he said. 'I see riches. I see more money than you can dream up. Imagine the appeal to see a man who has a vision of

Our Saviour inside his stomach. I will take him the world over—to the Americas, Asia, and Australia…even to the fucking Antarctic! He will be like the circus freak that everyone just has to see. I would be a fool not to take this opportunity.'

He stepped over towards Jack. *'Get up!'*

Jack forced a smile. *'Fuck you!'*

The bald man's head fell back as he laughed. He shook his head. 'Now don't be an idiot,' he said, holding the gun aloft.

'Go ahead, shoot me—you would be doing me a favour!'

Pam looked to her husband, her eyes filled with tears. She began to sob. *'Please just leave us alone! For God's sake!'* She wanted to say more, the rage and hopelessness of the situation building up inside, ready to explode, but there was nothing more to say, the whole thing was just so ludicrous. She wept hard, holding her husband. One bastard dies and another is born.

'Jack, be a good boy and do as I say,' the man said. He was no longer laughing. He had the look of a man who was beginning to lose patience. 'I said, *get the fuck up!*' he shouted, as he stepped forward and grabbed hold of Pam and flung her across the room. Jack gasped, grabbed for the man's leg, but his hand kicked away.

He took hold of Jack by the collar and pulled him up, as he did so, with his back turned to Pam, she tried to lunge for him. In a seamless swift motion, the man heard the approach, dropped Jack back to the ground, span and fired. Pam plunged forward and smacked down against the floor.

Jack stared in disbelief. Heat fired around his body, his heart pounded as he tried to comprehend the sight of his wife laying face down, eyes wide-open but unseeing, handkerchief around her throat, the hole in her forehead.

As he regained his grasp on what had just happened, another gun fired. As Jack turned, he saw the shock spreading across the face of the tall scar-faced murderer of his wife. He staggered forward and fell. The blood from his back was spilling and staining his white jacket. His lips trembled; blood ran from his nose.

As the final breaths left his body, his head slumped. Behind him,

Bruno was lying on his chest, face down in the gap between his arms. His fingers loosened and the gun clanked as it hit the floor.

The room filled in the silence made by the dead.

Jack crawled over to his wife. He lay across her back as he cried, rocking her back and forth, praying, and begging for her to be given life.

He held her tight against himself. In his mind's eye, he saw many of the highlights of their marriage…of their love.

After what might have been hours lying with her, he climbed to his feet. He scanned the room. Three dead bodies: Bruno Franklin, the scar-faced man…his wife.

He could not just leave her there. He had to find some way of getting her out. However, he had not the strength left to carry her. As thoughts fired around his brain, he decided his only hope was to find a phone.

Remembering the earlier gunfire, he took the gun lying by Bruno's hand. It was the first gun he had ever held. He climbed the stairs and weakly stepped out into the barn. Scattered on the floor were the bodies of the other three black-clothed guards and four white-suited men. Blood flowed across the stone ground, trails merging to form streams that ran away into the farmyard. Black smoke spiralled from the Ford; the burnt out remains still illuminated by the dying flames. A jeep had crashed and the front bumper imbedded in the fence.

Jack walked over to the jeep and looked inside—in the hope of finding a phone. His search was in vain. He leaned against the fence that bordered the field of grass on which the lone goat still feasted.

For a moment, he would have done anything to be that goat. Just out in the sun, eating to his heart's content—not a worry in the universe.

The warm breeze brought with it the smell of death. He could not erase the vision of his wife lying lifeless with the circular hole in her forehead. Jack slumped against the fence, tore the bandage from his stomach and released the beam of light. He poked the gun barrel into his bellybutton; his finger trembled on the trigger. He closed his eyes ready to squeeze, then he realized he had already experienced enough suffering. He would not delay the end. With that thought, he lifted the gun to his skull and pulled the trigger.

~Strapper~

When I first arrived at the warehouse, I had only a vague idea to what I would be doing. I was to "Strap" the night manager had said. I nodded, trying to show interest.

"You ever strapped before?" he asked.

"Err...no."

"It's a piece of piss," he said, walking away from me. I followed as we negotiated the various noisy machines, from which newspapers and magazines shot out into piles. Most of the people present were standing around in conversation, smiling and only occasionally concentrating on their work.

The night manager said something else as we walked, tilting his head back.

"What?" I said, unable to hear due to the commotion; he then stopped and pointed to the strange looking contraption. Standing upright on a table was what looked like a metal picture frame or a window frame without any glass,

"This..." he said, "is the Strapper."

He grabbed a bundle of newspapers and placed them on the machine, pushed them halfway through the metal structure, and at that moment a whoosh of sound made my heart pound—something shot out of the machine like a whip. Within a second, I was aware of what had happened. Plastic strips that stretched around all four of the inner sides of the metallic frame, had shot out when the newspapers were placed on the table, and those plastic strips had wrapped around the newspapers like a lasso—all in a split second.

The night manager, with a grin on his face, held the bound pile of newspapers for me to examine. Bound tight; it would take a blade to slash the plastic strips.

"Now it needs another," he said. "Each bundle should have two strips of plastic; the other should go across the width so you form a cross with the plastic strips. That way the papers are bound good and tight. No fear of them coming loose during delivery."

He motioned for me to have a go; I hesitated, fearing I would get my hand sliced off, such was the incredible speed and apparent power that the plastic strips scythed through the air.

"It's perfectly safe," he said. "Nothing whatsoever to worry about." He took the bundle and placed it on the table, on top of a button I noticed. *Whoosh!*—and strips bound the newspapers.

"Easy, totally harmless," he said, but I couldn't help think the smirk on his face suggested otherwise.

To prove just how harmless it was, he grabbed my wrist and moved it towards the machine. I resisted, feeling my heart in my mouth, the sweat dripping down from my armpits.

"Don't be frightened," he said, smiling, almost laughing at what he obviously thought was my irrational fear.

Just as I was about to really use force to wrench my hand free, he let go and shrugged. "Okay, that's fine," he said and placed his own hand in the Strapper.

Whoosh!

He retracted his hand with a strip of the white plastic tightly wrapped around the skin. Like an extremely tight bracelet.

"See, it doesn't hurt," he laughed, then cut the strip with a penknife and tossed it into the bin. "You think you'll be okay?"

"Yeah, sure," I said.

"I'll leave you in the capable hands of Frank. Frank, this is Ray, he's going to working the night shift…you can show him the ins and outs, right?"

Frank was a grey-haired man with glasses. He was short, and winked as he met eyes with me.

"Leave it to me, boss," he said, giving the night manager a wink and a smile.

The night manager strolled away; Frank had leaned across the table to shake hands.

"Nice to meet you," he said. And that's how I met Frank, and he was always just Frank, as we never exchanged surnames.

During the following weeks, we worked together each night through until sunrise. He one side of the table forming the bundles of newspapers and magazines that the newsagents had requested, and then feeding them across to me, often with a wink, and then I'd put them in the dreaded Strapper that turned out to be not all that dreaded—in fact, harmless, like the night manager had promised.

With regular coffee breaks, the job was bearable, though the monotony was a problem at times. The pay was not great, but it covered the bills and left a little to save.

After returning from work one morning, I unlocked the apartment door, stepped in and yawned. The newspaper was on the mat.

"I'm home!"

Kim came rushing out into the hallway. We had been dating for two years, living together for one of those. "Have you seen my other shoe?" she asked.

"No."

"Damn it! I'm gonna be late!"

I checked my watch, pushing back another yawn. "You've got time…don't panic."

"*I am fucking well panicking*…I'm supposed to be meeting my boss before work!"

"What for?"

"He said he wanted to chat about my future."

"What does that mean?"

Kim ran her hand through her hair, and then stared at me, blowing out air. "*Look*, I have to find my shoe. Are you going to help me or just stand there?"

I kicked my shoes off and helped her look for hers. I found the missing shoe under the dirty laundry bag.

"Why's it under there?"

"I don't know."

She rammed the shoe on her foot and grabbed her bag, virtually knocking me flat as she ran out the door, not bothering to close it behind her. She came rushing back—I thought to give me a goodbye kiss, but instead she snatched an apple and left again.

"Oh fine," I called after her.

"Now what's wrong with you?" she asked, turning.

"Nothing."

"Well don't hold me up then…and it wouldn't hurt you to do the laundry once in a while." With that, she exited the building before I could think of a witty response. The apartment was silent and empty. I got changed and went to bed.

The problem with our relationship was that when one of us would be going to bed the other would be heading to work. This was an everyday occurrence with her working daytime hours at the TV studio, while I worked nights at the warehouse. We only ever seemed to meet in passing.

It was over coffee that Frank and I, three weeks into the job, first mentioned a topic that wasn't newspapers, wasn't strappers, wasn't warehouses, wasn't sport, wasn't the damn night shift and wasn't the porno magazines that were scattered around the building.

"So I don't know what to do," I said. "I love her still, you know? I just want to see her more often. She's always so busy." This was the end of a minute summary I had given Frank about me and Kim.

Frank nodded, smiling as if he had heard the story a thousand times before, and he probably had.

"Maybe I should quit this job and find something else, something that will enable us to spend more time together? You know, a regular nine to five job. At least then we'll have the evenings with one another."

Frank pondered for a while, sipping his coffee. "You know what you should do?"

"No. What?"

"I think you've just got it into your head that it won't work—that it can't work while you have these jobs. It is like a barrier between you that you have accepted, and have not really tried to break down. For a start, you say she only works seven days out of fourteen. That means seven days off for Christ's sake! It's just you don't manage your time well enough."

"How's that?"

"I'm saying, I'd bet if you worked out how many hours you spend together at your apartment, you would be bloody surprised. What happens with those seven days she gets off every fortnight? You *do* have the time; you just need to make the most of it. Plan ahead so days don't get wasted."

I thought about his advice and couldn't help but agree. I felt new hope.

"You should make a living out of giving relationship advice," I said, smiling. "One of those Agony Aunts."

Frank nodded and smiled. He gave me a wink, then leaned over the table and motioned for me to near him. He looked around to make sure nobody was watching, then licked a finger and flicked through the newspaper in one of his piles. He found the page and pointed, again gazing around. I stared at the page, puzzled. It *was* one of those Agony Aunt pages, and I thought for a horrific moment, he had written in about my problems. Mr. F was the expert giving the advice to readers' letters. It didn't take long for me to make the connection.

"You mean…" I said. Frank put a finger over his lips to hush me. He nodded then winked. "It's a secret, you mustn't tell anyone, okay?"

"Sure thing, Frank," I said. "But why?"

"Why don't I tell people?"

"Yeah."

"Reputation," he said and winked. "I can't let the guys know I'm sensitive at heart, they'll take away my membership at the working man's club," he said and winked.

"Does the newspaper pay you?"

"Only fifty pounds a week," he said with a shrug, and then brushed across his grey hair. "Beer money you might say. But I enjoy doing it."

What neither of us had noticed was the night manager sitting on a crate reading an edition of *Playboy*, and he had heard the bulk of the conversation. He had struggled to stifle his laughter, he had told me later.

Wait until I tell the guys about this! he had thought. *Frank, the so-called hardened ex-marine; the guy who can guzzle a dozen pints without getting pissed; the guy that got all his teeth knocked out in fights by the age of fifteen—that Frank is an Agony Aunt and is deeply in touch with his emotions and gives love advice! It's the most hilarious thing I've ever heard!*

Over the following days, we noticed the change as people came over and asked for hints and tips on relationships and other sensitive issues. Frank would accusingly look to me, thinking I had told of his secret—but I insisted I hadn't. Then one night as we clocked in, Frank found an inflatable doll on his worktable, and a note taped to it. It read: *Please Frank, you just got to help me. I can't take all the sex no more. I never get the chance to leave the bedroom. My owner's cock is always in me!*

Frank looked around and saw the entire warehouse staff watched, trying hard not to laugh.

"Screw you, shitheads!" he said, then picked the inflatable doll up and stood her by the table while he checked newspaper bundles.

I thought I should put into action the advice he had given me. I had to do something to save mine and Kim's relationship.

When I arrived home from work one morning, instead of going straight to bed I started preparing for Kim's arrival that afternoon. I dusted the flat, I polished, I vacuumed, I did the laundry and I even went shopping. All things that in the past I had tended to leave to her. I hoped it would put a smile on her face.

I also cooked dinner, carefully following the instructions from the recipe book. I lit the candles, sat back and waited. When she didn't arrive, I began to worry. I turned the temperature down on the oven. When she still hadn't returned after an hour, I called her at work.

"Hi, Kim, it's me. I was just wondering what time you would be home?"

"Oh, not until late," she said. "I agreed to stay on and help out with the lighting…we've got this—"

"So when will you be home?"

"Probably not until after you've gone to work. What do you want?"

"I didn't *want* anything…well, except for my girlfriend to come home when she said she would."

I heard heavy breaths down the phone. "What's the big deal? I am old enough to choose when to do overtime…*this is my fucking career!*"

"Okay."

She slammed the phone down without a reply. I stared at the phone I held and was tempted to smash it on the floor. I resisted, and then tipped the dinner I had prepared into the bin.

I did have to go to work before she returned home, so it wasn't until the next morning that I saw her…just as she was leaving the door. I said: "How did that meeting go with your boss?"

"Fine, I haven't got time to talk about it now."

"Can I make an appointment then?"

She glared at me as she put her earrings on. "Is that supposed to be funny?"

"Yes," I said. "I just want us to arrange to spend some time together."

"Okay, I'll talk to you tonight."

She collected her bag then span on the spot, scanning the flat for anything she may have left behind.

"Oh, I should probably tell you…I've been offered a job in Peterborough," she said, her eyes suggested she had already decided to take it, and that she would do so no matter what my feelings were. There certainly wasn't any hint of tears despite the fact that it would mean moving two hundred miles away.

"Peterborough. Well…how's that going to work?" I asked. "I mean, I have only just started this new job."

"I know. We can still see each other on weekends or something."

I stood, gazing at her as she swallowed the remainder of a glass of water.

"That's it then? You're going to accept the job without even consulting me?"

She shrugged, sighed. "I really need to take this job. It's what I've been waiting for."

"You once said that about me," I said, the words sounded hollow to me now.

"I'll speak to you later," she said and dashed past me, her excessive perfume irritating my nose. I couldn't believe we had drifted so far apart.

I took Frank aside that night at work with our coffees. I remember the bright full moon, and a breeze that disturbed the fern trees. Frank's face partially covered by shadow.

"Frank," I said, unable to hide my frustration. I had suffered severe headaches for days—due to the worry I suppose. I'm sure Frank guessed there was something wrong.

"Kim's got a job in Peterborough."

He put a hand on my shoulder. "Ray, you really are up shit-creek without a paddle, aren't you? You need a lucky break and it just isn't coming. See how it goes, is what I suggest, and then, if it isn't working, then maybe you have to decide just how much you love her and how much you want to be with her. Moving up to Peterborough might be the only way to save your relationship. I don't want to put down this job we've got, but it isn't exactly the best, is it? She sounds like she's doing pretty well: new job, good pay and so on."

He needn't say anything more. But I could tell he was worried for me. We were definitely now friends, I thought, not just work mates but true friends.

"What about you, Frank, what's your story? We only ever seem to discuss my problems."

"Not much to tell really. I live alone. Was married once—she left me for another woman. Yep, that's right, turned out she was a lesbian."

My jaw dropped.

"That was when I started getting into the Agony Aunt routine—a desperate attempt to figure out what had gone wrong with my life I suppose. And I used to be a Strapper just like your good self, until I got promoted to my current position as a stock checker and sorter," he said, trying to sound posh. "I did your job for five years after leaving the armed forces due to my back problems. I actually preferred the strapping job to this current one, but the pay was shit, as you know only too well. In fact, I know all there is to know about strappers: the different models, the mechanics of how they work," he said, smiling, winking.

Even after he had explained the strapping machines to me, I wasn't sure I understood. And when he spoke of them, he almost went into a trance. He spoke about them as if they were extraordinary artifacts. Maybe the intensity to the way he spoke should have given me fair warning of future events.

I decided I *did* still love Kim, madly in fact, and couldn't imagine life without her. I knew what I had to do: I would go with her to Peterborough.

"I think you should take the job, Kim," I said. "I really do…and I think I should quit my job and come with you. I'll find work in Peterborough, it shouldn't be that hard."

She grimaced, and then took a deep breath. "Ray, I don't think you should quit your job."

I was perplexed. Why shouldn't I? How was it going to work otherwise? I stood and waited for her to elaborate.

"Ray, I think I've known this for a while, but…I've found it difficult to say."

I swallowed hard, I could feel the temperature rising in my head, I could hear my heart's beat.

"I don't love you anymore. I'm sorry…I…I don't know what to say." She looked down to her toes and waited for me to respond.

I couldn't find anything to say. Her words had sliced into my heart as effectively as a machete would have. She went to work and then phoned saying she was going straight up to Peterborough and would send her dad around to collect her stuff. Just before she ended the call, I heard her snigger, and then her boss's voice. I don't know if anything was going on between them, but I imagined him kissing her neck. Nightmares tormented me that night and for many after—of them rolling about naked in bed, laughing at me.

I told Frank the news, and he shook his head. I could see the tenseness to his jaw as he digested the information. He had a rage in his eyes that frightened me.

As we worked that night in silence, I found my mind full of thoughts about Kim. I did love her so much and each memory of her brought butterflies to my stomach. A kind of nausea, knowing I would never again kiss her and would never again make love to her. I was still in shock of course, almost unable to eat. This seemed to make Frank angrier still, and when we spoke about her, he did so through gritted teeth; he hated her, which was plainly evident. But I loved her still. I had no doubt about that, and I was considering the crazy idea of quitting the job and going to Peterborough in a last ditch attempt to sort things out. Then Frank led me out into the parking lot. We stood in silence for a while, but I knew he had something on his mind.

"Ray, I've got an idea…and I think it's the only thing to help you right now. I've witnessed these past weeks…how you've been. You look like death warmed up for Christ's sake! I want you to come over my place this weekend and we'll talk things through."

As he touched my shoulder, I shuddered.

"What do you say?" Frank asked. "We'll have a few beers and talk it over some more. I have a way of making you forget Kim, erasing her from your life once and for all," he said and winked.

So that weekend I drove out to Frank's place. It was a lonely property in a poorly lit avenue. His house was small and gothic in appearance— light came from the crack beneath the garden gate. I took a few deep breaths and then knocked on the door. I still felt uneasy. Frank was a good man, and my friend; he would only have everyone's best interests at heart. And I still believe he did, even now, retelling the story.

"You made it!" he said and winked. He dragged me in, took me into the living room and passed me a cold beer.

His spirits had change dramatically; he was excited, eager, in contrast to how tense he had been at work all week.

We drank beer and watched the football before he turned to me, locking eyes.

"Now down to business," he said. I swallowed hard. "You know you're my friend, Ray—a damn fine friend and I want to help you deal with the problem. And you are in luck, I happen to be a pretty fucking special Agony Aunt…just read some of my fan mail if you need proof," he said, suddenly tender and caring. The sudden change made the hair on my neck stand on end. I wanted out of his home. The burning logs in the fireplace and the shadowed corners of the room didn't help the eerie atmosphere.

"Come with me," he said, and led the way up the stairs. We came to a white door. He smiled and then opened…

And the sight behind the door shocked me. Illuminated by moonlight in the centre of the room, was a Strapper. It was a much older model than the ones used at work, but it was clearly a Strapper. The metallic window frame appearance and the coil of white strip-plastic beside it. My heart pounded hard. I knew now—I was certain he intended for me to lure Kim to his home so we could bind her, maybe then drop her helpless body into the ocean. Or was it her boss he wanted us to murder? I had to tell him immediately that I could never commit such an act.

"I…"

"It's a Strapper, you see?" Frank said, wide smile on his face. He led me over and showed me it in action. *Whish!*

He turned to me, hands on each of my shoulders, eye to eye. He looked so concerned that moment—as if he would do anything for me. Then he opened the cupboard door…

My jaw dropped, my body began to shiver then shudder then shake—so much that it felt as if the house was trembling. I found my breaths quickening, my heart jolting behind my rib cage. There were jars of clear liquid on the shelves in the cupboard; each was home to a human heart. Each heart strapped in the telltale white plastic strips—lengthways and widthways.

"There's no need to be afraid," Frank said softly, so softly that gooseflesh sprouted over my skin. "Kim's done a terrible thing to you, Ray, and you know as well as I, she's broken your heart. She's torn it to pieces and it needs fixing," he said. I couldn't meet eyes with him, but he lifted my chin so I had to. "Really, Ray, it's the only way for you now…we must fix your heart."

I wanted to run but I couldn't. It felt as if my feet were stuck in cement. Frank saw my concern. "These hearts," he said. "These are the hearts of those that needed my help the most…there's only so much I can say on the printed page of a newspaper. And each of these hearts has been mended, and they, the owners, can move on with their lives."

He paused for a while, just staring at the jars of human hearts, not blinking, and just staring as if remembering each of the people that had once possessed those hearts.

"We'll take yours, Ray…and fix it," he said, pointing to the Strapper. "Then you too…can move on."

This is when I found my strength, when God returned control of my body. I shoved Frank away and ran to the door, and as I slammed it behind me, I could hear his calls: *"Ray! Come back, Ray, I want to help you!"*

I ran in a haze, unsure of where I was going—everything was blurred and surreal; I couldn't stop thinking about what I had seen, had discovered, and even that left me unprepared for when I forced open another door. There were bodies in various stages of decomposition spread evenly across the basement floor. The oldest of which were no more than skeletons. Each had a hole smashed through the ribs where the heart had once been.

In the time I stood in the doorway, I think my whole knowing of Frank flashed before my eyes. I searched for clues that might have warned me of the monstrosity I now faced. And I couldn't help notice the little engraved plaque standing by each.

Mary Robinson: 1973–1999. Ben broke her heart. It was fixed on April 7.

Jack Cotton: 1982–2002. Amy shattered his heart. It was mended on November 14.

I could take no more and ran from the house and far away, leaving my car behind in noticing Frank standing beside it. As I ran into the dark, I heard his call: *"I just want what's best for you!"*

I have never believed anything other than that.

The police took Frank away. He hadn't even tried to escape or hide. They found him crying, sitting by the Strapper.

I often wonder how someone's sense of duty can be so badly twisted and distorted. It is hard to comprehend the lengths Frank had gone to make people happy. To help people he barely knew.

And I live on, thinking about him often, wondering how I could have done things differently. They locked Frank away at a mental institution. He was devastated he could no longer help people. So I've heard, he sobbed day and night until one day the sobs just suddenly ceased. The staff assumed he just had tired of sobbing but went to check just the same. Frank was dead, the cause: heart failure. Apparently, he felt no pain—his heart had just stopped. And it is not easy to live with myself knowing that I was the cause, I effectively killed Frank, for I destroyed what kept him alive. I broke his heart.

~*The Beating Heart*~

You might think Gerald Littlehampton would be panicking, having killed his landlord by way of a blow to the head with a sledgehammer. You would be wrong. Gerald is extremely calm. He is quite content. Relaxed...despite the two police officers currently searching his home.

"Would you like a drink, Officers?" he asks, casually. "Coffee perhaps or orange juice?"

The taller of the officers, who has a baldhead and goatee beard, looks to his colleague—an altogether more compact man, with less height and more stomach.

"No thank you," the taller cop says.

Gerald smiles inwardly; even he hadn't realized he would be *this* relaxed. He had spent hours in front of the mirror practicing being normal. He knew at some point the police would visit and he had to be ready for that visit...and he is.

He had done the wicked deed a week ago. He crept up behind his landlord just as he was approaching the top of the stairs. The landlord had been calling for him—asking where the hell his morning cup of tea and newspaper were. Gerald had tiptoed closer, closer, closer and then WHACK!!

His landlord toppled down the stairs, somersaulting; his skull cracking on every fifth step. However, he surely would not have felt a thing, for the first blow of the sledgehammer shattered his skull. *Oh, how easy it had been!*

"Mind if we take a look around?" the fat, short cop asks.

"Be my guest," Gerald says, smiling. "I have nothing to hide," he adds, raising his hands to highlight the point. Of course, he has; he has his landlord's body to hide and he just happens to be buried under the floorboards right beneath where the taller police officer now stands. But Gerald is secure in the fact that he is well hidden. And he doesn't believe in life after death, so he has nothing at all to fear from the police searching the house.

The taller cop gazes over to where the fire burns; the logs sizzle and pop. The cop sees the stuffed raven sitting on the windowsill.

He looks to it and then to Gerald. "Into taxidermy, are you?"

Gerald shrugs. "Not really…the raven is all I have. But I find him quite striking."

The tall and bald cop nods. He stares upon the raven, scratching at his goatee beard. He then allows his eyes to drift over the rest of the sitting room. He stands in the doorway; shadows cover the near side of his face. He appears to be considering whether to enter the dimly lit room—lighted by only two candles that stand on the mantelpiece. Then he does enter and the small, fat cop follows, as does Gerald.

Gerald rubs his foot against the area of floor where he has buried the body, just to reiterate his confidence in escaping undetected. *Oh, what a delightful criminal I make!*

The fat police officer is examining the bookshelf: he pulls out *Tales of Mystery and Imagination.*

"Edgar Allan Poe," he reads then glances up to Gerald. Gerald feels the first bead of sweat run down from his armpit. He is now aware of his own heart's beat. He has been waiting for this moment…he knew his heart would start to interfere, but he also knew it was nothing to fret about.

"He wrote a story about a raven, didn't he?" the cop asks.

"No…that is, he wrote a poem—'The Raven.'"

"That's right," the cop says, nodding. He places the book back and then half withdraws another Poe, and another, and another, and now Gerald does feel the strain a little—he notices his heart beating faster…there are now more drips of sweat running from under his arms.

Nevertheless, he is still in control…he is still calm. And he knows not to crack like the narrator in the Poe story who is driven to confession by the sound of his own beating heart when convinced it's the heart of his dead victim.

No way will he let his heart's attempts to expose his crime bother him.

No problem at all—he's very aware the beating heart he hears is his own and he is far too clever to let his guard slip. That isn't to say he's not crazy—he's very aware he's crazy. Why else would he smash his landlord's brains out with a sledgehammer? The bastard didn't even have a hideous glass-eye to provoke Gerald into killing him, for heaven's sake!

"Poe wrote the one about the guy who buried his landlord under the floorboards, didn't he?" the taller officer says as he turns from where he has been warming his hands beside the fire. His tall black shadow cast across the room, stretching over the floorboards and climbing the bookshelf. Gerald swallows.

"'The Tell-Tale Heart,'" Gerald says, but now he can hear his own breaths as they leave his nostrils. *Oh, God, how noisy they are!* He opens his mouth a little to make breathing easier—more ventilation. He crosses his arms in an attempt to cover the growing amounts of sweat.

"You haven't murdered and buried your landlord, I assume?" the smaller cop asks, his lips raising into smile as if it had been a throw away remark, a joke, but his eyes give him away... *the devious little bastard!* His eyes lock with Gerald's, searching for a flicker of weakness.

"Please..." Gerald says, raising a hand to cover his mouth. "You shouldn't be so insensitive...my landlord was a dear friend of mine."

The police officer nods and gazes to his feet. "I'm sorry...I shouldn't have said that."

Gerald can barely contain his laughter—he has really fooled the idiots! They really believe he cared for the stupid bastard who would demand breakfast in bed, demand he scrubbed the kitchen floor, demand he mowed the lawn!

The taller cop walks across the room and looks at a picture that hangs on the wall. It's of a desolate, dying land, which is home to a castle that is in vast disrepair...a huge fissure runs down one of the walls.

"*The House of Usher,*" he reads out, his eyes widening. "There sure is a lot of Poe around here," he says, smiling. "Maybe we should lift the floorboards after all?" he adds and stamps his foot. Then he listens. For a moment Gerald thinks they are on to him...but he knows not to panic, he knows *that* is the worst thing he could possibly do. He is crazy, admittedly, but not stupid.

"*Oh, but, Gerald, you won't get away with the horrible crime you've committed. Never in a million years. I think you are stupid!*" the voice says.

What has Gerald's pulse racing is that the voice has come from neither of the police officers, for he is watching them and neither mouth moved. The voice has come from much closer to where he stands.

Who the hell said that?

"*It was me, your heart,*" comes the reply. Gerald's skin is now alive with goose bumps—the hairs on his neck springing up. He lowers his head so to be looking at his chest elevating and depressing. His body begins to shudder; he is suddenly dry in the mouth, sweat gushing from his armpits.

"Are you okay, Mr. Littlehampton?" asks the tall cop, as he idly flicks through a collection of Poe stories. The way he asks implies he knows something is seriously wrong, that he knows what Gerald has done—but is playing games with him, messing with his mind. Like the cat that paws the mouse.

"I…I'm fine," Gerald says, and then rubs at his neck.

Oh, God, I'm drenched in sweat!

The taller officer walks over, placing the book back on the shelf and stands before Gerald. "Are you sure there's nothing you want to tell us, Mr. Littlehampton?" he asks.

Ha! What an idiot he must think me! I shall not be so foolish!

"*But you are foolish, Gerald, and they know you did it. They're just playing games with your mind…because they know you're nuts!*"

"*Shut up!*" Gerald hisses.

The tall cop leans away, surprised by the outburst. "I think we'll take a look around," he says.

"*They know he's under the floorboards, Gerald…they know!*" his heart spits.

Leave me alone—for the love of God, leave me alone!

"*You think you're clever, thought you would get away with it…oh but you won't.*"

"I…"

The two cops turn suddenly, silent—eyebrows raised, waiting for the confession. The smaller already has his hand near his gun.

"I need to go to the toilet," Gerald says.

The police officers exchange glances. "Okay," the taller says and follows Gerald to the bathroom and has a quick look inside.

"I'll be waiting just outside," he warns.

Gerald nods, enters and shuts the door, trying his best to stifle the huge sigh of relief. He looks at himself in the mirror: his eyes bulge in horror at the amount of sweat across his forehead. He wipes the sweat away then sits on the toilet, head between his legs.

"*You won't escape!*" his heart insists. "*It's obvious you're hiding something!*"

"I'm not," he mutters. "I mean…they don't suspect—stop saying they do!"

"*Don't you think they've noticed your profuse sweating? Your heavy breathing? And asking to go to the toilet for Christ's sake!*"

"Shut up shut up shut up!"

"You okay in there, Mr. Littlehampton?"

"Yes. Thank you."

He flushes the toilet then leaves the bathroom. His legs are weak and he feels sick…as if he may vomit any moment.

"Okay, we'll leave you in peace, Mr. Littlehampton," the taller cop says. Hope suddenly injects Gerald. He follows the officers to the door. As they walk out into the rain, the taller turns.

"If you remember anything you haven't yet told us," he says then hands the card to Gerald with his number on.

"I will, Officer," Gerald says. "I hope you find him…he really was a dear friend of mine."

"Was?" the small, fat cop asks. Gerald can feel the blood boiling in his brain but knows to fight it; he knows not to panic, not now—having come so far undetected.

"I just hope he's okay," Gerald says. "But I've never known him to go missing like this before."

The smaller cop smiles. "We'll do our best to find him."

Gerald raises a hand to wave and then shuts the door and slumps to the ground, weeping. *I've done it…I've survived!*

He walks into his dining room and over to his brandy. He pours himself a glass and swallows and then another, smiling. He returns to the area of floor his landlord's corpse is beneath. He stamps his foot.

"I told you! I told you I would stay calm, told you I wouldn't let a damn beating heart give me away!"

"*That you did,*" the voice says, but it isn't his own voice and it isn't his heart's either. Gerald freezes, gazing down at the floorboards.

"No...*this can't be happening!*" he yells.

"*But it is Gerald,*" whispers his heart. Gerald watches his own heart beating hard—so hard that it hurts his ribs. He pants, doubling over, fighting the pain and gazes down and now is horrified to see the floorboards contracting, rising and falling, as if being stretched by the beating heart of his dead landlord.

"*You thought you could kill me but you failed!*"

"*You fail!*" his own heart adds.

"*No!*" Gerald screams, running to the cupboard and collecting his sledgehammer. He swings at the floorboards, again and again, smashing through the wood, all the time listening to laughter, laughter all around, coming from his own heart—from his landlord's heart under the floorboards.

"*Stop it I tell you! Stop it!*" Gerald shouts. And then he hears the knock on the door and freezes.

"Mr. Littlehampton, open this door immediately!"

Gerald whimpers, shivering, he looks down to the broken floorboards and the bloody corpse that lies below, and still he can see the heart down there...and it beats, pulses with life. Taunting him, teasing him, after making him think he had succeeded!

Then his attention is on the door as he hears the police officers trying to ram it down. He runs for the kitchen and grabs his sharpest knife, then drops to his knees and stabs and stabs at his landlord's heart—blood spewing out over his hands and showering his face...but he must kill it—he must kill his landlord's heart otherwise the police will know...they will hear it—it will tell them of the hideous thing he has done!

"*It's too late, too late!*" mocks his own heart and he turns the knife on himself and thrusts it into his chest...even as he's taking his death bow he slices, attempting in his final moments of life to murder his own tormenting heart.

The police officers break the door down and dash through the house. They find Gerald's lifeless corpse lying sprawled across the hole in the floor. Directly below lays the decomposing landlord.

"Jesus Christ," the smaller cop mutters. He slowly, taking deep breaths, lifts his radio to call for assistance. But neither of them can bear to wait in that room, so they go and sit in the living room by the fire—unable to take their eyes from the stuffed raven.

The taller officer believes his own heart is beating unnaturally hard and fast. He puts a hand to it and tries to steady its beat. The smaller cop, his hands shaking, picks up *Tales of Mystery and Imagination* and begins reading by the light of the fire.

~*Whispering*~

My wife saying she wanted to learn French seemed reasonable enough. I had no reason to think otherwise. I was glad she had found a hobby— I worried she spent too much time watching soap operas. Even her request for me to "make myself scarce" was fine. I dabble with painting myself and I know how difficult it can be to concentrate when there's somebody scuttling around the house. Of course, those people usually don't mean to disturb…they just do.

"You could go to the pub," my wife suggested on that first occasion she had unveiled the "Learn French Fast" language book. She had a pad of A4 paper on the table next to her fluffy pink pencil case, a new packet of chewing gum and a glass of water. I quite admired her commitment— she was certainly prepared.

Therefore, I went out, but not to the pub. I went to relax in the park and to think about my latest project. The sun was out, the autumn leaves blew over the grass and the fountain's water sparkled in the late morning light. It was a very productive day for me and I returned home with a clear picture in my mind's eye of what I wanted to paint. To my delight, Lucy was in great spirits also; she gave me a big squeezing hug and a kiss on the cheek. She even had a banana and raspberry smoothie waiting for me in the fridge.

"What have I done to deserve this?" I asked.

"Oh nothing…just a thank you for, well you know, giving me some space."

"Well that's fine," I said. "I had a good day too."

And that was that—a nice roast beef dinner, followed by mint ice cream and coffee on the balcony, as we watched the stars. The perfect day.

When the following day arrived, it was terribly bleak out—the black clouds looming, the rumble of thunder. I had planned to go sit under the same oak tree in the same park as the previous day—to see if I could discover further inspiration. However, with the horrid weather I hastily dismissed the idea.

"Will you be going out?" Lucy asked, somewhat eagerly.

I gazed to the rain outside and then to my wife, waiting for a smile to show it had been a joke. The smile never came. I said: "What, *really*…in this weather, are you serious?"

She twisted her lips in thought, gently biting on the lower as she looked out the window. For a moment, she seemed in a daze, her bright blue eyes dull and dreamy.

"Lucy, dear, are you okay?"

"I'm fine," she said, out of her trance in an instant.

"Is it about your French?" I asked, feeling bad; I really didn't want to get in her way, again thinking of the nuisance of someone, anyone, knocking on the door or bypassing the knock and haphazardly entering my study when I'm painting. Who am I kidding? Of course those distractions always came from sweet Lucy, but they were only ever for good reasons…nearly always, like the time she had seen a blackbird in the garden; she wanted me to see, thinking it might inspire my painting. Birds have very little interest to me…but I adored her eagerness to please.

I felt so keen to get out of her hair that I even flicked through the local paper for the cinema listings, though I loathe modern film and haven't been to the pictures in ten years. As I expected, there was nothing worth seeing and there was no point telling her I would go and see the latest Disney picture, because she would have known I was only going to give her some space. I thought she would have declined my offer.

"How about I stay in the bedroom?" I said. "I'll read that Fredrick Forsyth I bought…it's supposed to be a good book."

She ran fingers through her long auburn hair, and then tied it back in a ponytail. She didn't seem too pleased about the suggestion, though she would never say so.

"Okay, if you don't mind?" she said.

"No, of course not," I said and gave her a hug. I even went to the trouble of fixing myself a jug of juice and some sandwiches so I wouldn't have to come out of the bedroom at all until she had finished.

So I positioned pillows against the wall, sat in bed and started to read. I had read to the fifth page when I first noticed the whispering. I frowned and listened. The whispers were incomprehensible. I first guessed it was the TV turned on quietly—just a background sound, and only after I had read to page eight of Forsyth, did I decide the whisper came from Lucy's lips. She must have been quietly speaking in French. That was quite understandable—I doubt many would have the confidence to start speaking a foreign language aloud, especially when there were people at home. I smiled, feeling proud that she was spending her leisure time learning a language.

I listened a little longer to see if I could make out any words; I learnt French at school. Perhaps that was another reason for her keeping her voice down, probably worried I would hear her pronunciation and feared I'd correct her.

I flicked the page of my book and continued to read. My finger was below paragraph two on page eleven, when the tip halted its passage across the print. I placed the book down, frowning. I was sure I had heard a second whisper...a whisper over the top of the original? I started searching my brain, trying to decide whether it was possible to distinguish between whispers. I sat up, leaning forward in silence. Again I heard it; it was deeper and louder than the one I assumed belonged to my wife. She must just have the TV on, I thought; yes, that's what it is...that's what it sounded like—when you come out the bathroom or in from work and you can hear distant voices in the house; not so much whispers but far off voices, and you expect to turn into the living room and discover friends have popped round for a chat or relatives have dropped in with their holiday snaps—then it turns out it was just the television.

Well, my friend, there is one easy way to find out, I thought, and rose to my feet. I walked over to the door, stopping to yawn away some tiredness that had remained with me close to lunchtime. I came to the decision to have one of my foil wrapped tuna and cucumber sandwiches after investigating the voices.

As my hand came within a fraction of touching the handle, a vision of my wife talking to another man flashed before my eyes. I paused, waiting to see if my imagination's video player would show me more…it did: the tall dark stranger, topless, putting his arms around Lucy and kissing her neck, then her tilting her head back so they could meet lips.

I shook my head, wondering where that scene had come from. I put my hand on the door handle but for some reason I couldn't do it. Maybe due to the guilt after having promised Lucy I wouldn't distract her…and partly disturbed by the vision, I guess.

I took a few seconds to compose myself. What was I waiting for? Surely I really hadn't even considered, even deep in my subconscious, that Lucy was having an affair? An affair while I was in the house?

No, that *would be* stupid…but she didn't want you in the house, did she? She wanted you out yesterday…and told you to go to the pub though she disagrees strongly with intoxicating oneself during the day. And today, my friend, I thought looking out at the dark rain clouds; today she wanted you out in spite of the awful weather.

Oh my God, surely not?

But now I stared hard upon the white bedroom door, as if trying to penetrate it with my vision.

The phone. *Of course!* But whispering…to him?

She might be on the phone to him right now, that's the whispering—Lucy was trying to hide that she was using the phone. No, that made no sense…as then I wouldn't have heard the other voice.

This was ridiculous, I thought, cursing my own paranoia. But I still listened, and still I heard the whispering. *The keyhole*—I could look through the keyhole, and then I would know for sure. I was ninety-nine percent certain that I was thinking like a lunatic, but it couldn't hurt to look, right?

So I looked and the sight caused my heart to skip a beat, but then rather than anger I felt immense frustration, for though through the keyhole I could see my wife and I could see the pink fluffy pencil case, the water glass, and the French language book spread open, I couldn't see why my wife was looking away from the table, glancing slightly up as if somebody stood next to her just out of keyhole view. And she was talking…whispering.

There is someone in my home.

I now had to know. I opened the door fast...I don't know why—if someone were there, they wouldn't have had the chance to hide before I entered, regardless of how quickly I barged in.

My wife's head snapped down from the position it had been and her eyes locked with mine. I smiled at her. "Are you okay?" I asked, but I could hardly hear myself for my mind was screaming: *There's no one there! There's no one there!*

"Yes fine," she said and took a sip of water.

I had to say something for my sudden appearance so I said: "Toilet...is it okay if I just go?"

She smiled and laughed. "No, you have to go out the bedroom window," she said.

I smiled and tiptoed over to the bathroom in an exaggerated attempt to be quiet; as I flicked the bathroom light, I had the sudden idea that he might be hiding. He might be hidden somewhere in the bathroom.

"That's stupid," I muttered as I locked the door, but my hand was already moving towards the cupboard handle. I pulled it open and came face to face with some soft yellow towels—freshly ironed.

I forced what I could from my bladder then flushed. I then went back to the bedroom without a word, Lucy's eyes lost in her French book.

I shut the bedroom door and returned to my Forsyth.

"Come on, Forsyth, grip me and take my mind off Lucy!"

When the whispering started again, I sighed, brought my hands to my face and rubbed hard. I waited, listening, and then there it damn well was! The other bloody voice!

I also realized I had passed a page and a half, having no idea what I'd just read. I put the book down for the last time, not bothering to mark the page. I twiddled my thumbs, listening.

I couldn't figure it out. Why had she been looking away from the book like that, as if someone stood by the table? What was she saying? She was just practicing her French, the voice in my head said. But I responded with: Does she know enough French to recite without looking at the page? The voice had no answer for that...neither did I.

I even put my fingers in my ears to try to block the whispering...it was getting ridiculous. I would just have to ask her. Ask Lucy straight out: Are you having an affair? Okay, so he, the mystery person, wasn't here now, but maybe he had been yesterday. That would explain the smoothie and the good mood; she was sleeping around and making smoothies to deal with her guilt. Isn't it the cheating husband that buys his wife flowers and chocolates? Maybe the cheating wife operates in fruit drinks.

You might be thinking I'm crazy right now...I don't blame you and I won't go as far to say I wasn't, because I really don't know if I was—or if I still am.

Anyway, I got from my bed, peered through the keyhole, and watched my wife; again, she was talking to something, someone or nobody above her right shoulder. From the amount she was tilting her head back I guessed if it were a man, he was well over six feet tall and it wouldn't be a good idea to go out there fists blazing, for I would probably end up unconscious on the floor.

She was either talking to no one, and therefore maybe she was the crazy one and not me, or there was something there—just something that could...*vanish*. Then something in my brain—like the light bulb in cartoons—sparked. I don't know why, but I was suddenly convinced the whispering was some form of chanting and she was talking to what...Some kind of devil?

Then I gasped as a knock came on the door. I staggered back, holding my heart, sucking in through a gaping mouth.

"Yes," I said as steadily as I could.

Lucy came in and asked if I was okay, only she thought she heard me walking about. I thought she had a concerned look to her face...Perhaps the look she might've had if she thought I'd seen something through the keyhole I shouldn't have.

"No, I'm fine," I lied, but I had to get out of the house, get some air, cool off and think logically about the events.

"I think the rain has eased," I said weakly, then turned my head to the window and winced...it certainly didn't appear to have eased, but to my surprise—or what probably should have been the response I expected—she agreed and offered to fetch my coat.

So I left her to it, looking back as I began to shut the door.

"Is the French going well?"

"Yes, I think so."

"Well, au revoir," I said.

She smiled and shut the door.

I shoved my hands in my pockets and gazed up to the clouds, having to squint as the rain splashed on my face. I started out along the driveway, already feeling a little better for the fresh air, when my damn brain offered a suggestion.

I turned my head and glanced up at the balcony. *Oh, God, don't do it*, I thought.

I watched the rain pounding the road ahead; the road that I could walk down to reach the park or the lakes; in fact, even if my destination had been Australia that road would have been the route to take. But I knew there was only one way I could know for sure. Perhaps solve the puzzle. And that was to climb the drain and look through the window—see if Lucy really was involved in some kind of witchcraft or devil worship.

So I climbed, and I am no chimpanzee so it took awhile, but with the help of the balcony, I thought I had a firm foothold. I glanced inside but the curtain obscured my view. I leaned a little more, glancing down, aware how perilous my position was on a wet railing. However, I got far enough to see her, my wife, whispering to the thin air on her right. Now I didn't know what to think…but she stood so I leaned out of view and waited, listened. For a while nothing, so I chanced a look and then something happened that I have replayed over in my mind a thousand times, trying to recall *exactly what did happen*. But I think, I'm sure, I locked eyes with my wife for a split second before she shoved the window open and I plummeted, breaking an arm and dislocating four fingers.

Then I remember her standing over me, explaining to the medics that she hadn't known I was there—and when she opened the window, she'd accidentally knocked me down.

My next recollection was the whispering, oh, God, the damn whispering! I was aware that my eyes remained closed and I could hear the voices. One was clearly my wife's, the other…who knows?

I stopped myself from opening my eyes too quickly because I guessed he, or It, wouldn't be there if I did. On reflection, I wish I had opened them immediately as it would have saved me a lot of pain for the months to come. I heard my wife say, or should I change that to whisper: "I did do it…but I think he's going to be okay." She sounded disappointed. I have thought over that phrase a thousand times also, trying to decipher its meaning. *Yes, she did do it.* On purpose? Maybe.

I began to open my eyes, already accepting *It*, the other voice, wouldn't be there…*but he was.* I left my eyes at a squint and watched, stunned, at the sight of the man. He wasn't tall, he wasn't dark, and he wasn't particularly handsome, but he *was* there. *He did exist.* Only he also appeared to be slightly transparent, I should add.

I opened my eyes, but over the course of my eyes opening, he grew fainter and fainter until with my eyes fully open, he was no more. Vanished.

"You're awake," Lucy said.

"Yes."

"I'll go tell the nurse," she said. And walked away, without any apparent concern about how I felt. Just as the door was shutting, I heard her whispering in the corridor.

I pulled the sheets away and assessed my injuries—nothing life threatening I figured and climbed from my bed. I hobbled over to the door and looked out…And there he was. He was in the corridor, standing with my wife in his arms. I blinked and rubbed my eyes. He was ghostly, see-through, and yet somehow full of colour. He wore a red sweater, blue jeans and had fair hair.

I had to follow them as they walked along the corridor…I *had* to.

I lost them somewhere in the car park while waiting for an elderly woman in a Zimmer frame to get through a door. Her damn wheels were stuck! I was exasperated, resigned to defeat. But I had a final hope and that was if I could cut across the field I might be able to reach the main road before they did…assuming they had departed along the road. I limped and hopped as fast as possible, wincing as my injured ankle fired bursts of pain. It was a slight ascent up the grassy hill but above I would have a clear view. And it was Lucy's car that I saw. I tried hopping down but tripped and ended up rolling. If I hadn't things might have been different, because I don't think I would have gotten down quickly enough.

Battered and bruised, I hobbled out into the road, trying to stop my wife, confront her about this mystery man. But I had not gauged the distance well enough to realize she was too close to stop and in a second of recognition I saw my wife's eyes bulge and her mouth ready for a scream. In contrast, the fair-haired man in the passenger seat stayed quite calm. My wife wrenched the steering wheel and headed for the grassy bank—the car skidded sideways, and then rolled down the bank in a crash of shattered glass and thud of mangled metal. The car lay upside down with dust floating all around. The horn blared while a single wheel span round and round.

I stared, shocked, and then slowly walked over—my chest pounding as I tried to swallow my fear. Sweet Lucy's neck was broken. But of course the fair-haired man had vanished…as I knew he would have.

I thought that must be the end to it. I was wrong. And of all nights, it was the night after the funeral that I had the unwelcome guests in the house. I awoke, middle of the night, having had a nightmare about my dear wife running across a field of flowers with the Devil himself, when I noticed I was not alone in bed. Lucy was there and so was He, the fair-haired man, and they were…they were sleeping together—fucking—right beside me. I began to cry, not knowing what else to do. The shock spread through my body, making me completely numb.

"*Go away!*" I screamed. "*Go away!*" But they didn't, they just continued as if oblivious to my being there. I ran from the room and from the house with no intention of returning.

The house is up for sale and I have a court case hanging over my head, when I'm expected to give my side of the story about my wife's premature death. I haven't decided whether to tell the truth yet.

And as the weeks have passed, the thought of returning to the house has eaten away at me like a cancer. My appetite is non-existent and I know I must return if I want to confront my demons and start afresh with my life.

So now I stand outside the house with the key in my hand. I hold it to the keyhole and shiver. Then I realize there is no need to enter. I put the key away and crouch down to the letterbox. I raise the flap…and inside I can hear it—the whispering.

~The Hostage~

He had just gotten a call about the hostage situation. He jumped in his car, started the engine and shot off down the road. This would be his second hostage situation in the space of a day. That morning he had negotiated the release of an elderly lady taken hostage for the sake of her week's pension money. The world was full of sick bastards. The negotiations had been relatively simple. The man, Derek Pilgrim, handed himself in as soon as it was mentioned that a judge might go easy on him if he voluntarily gave up.

He changed gears, overtaking a slow moving bus and turned onto the motorway.

The negotiator's mother was English and his father Greek, and that's how he ended up with the name: Rupert Zagarokis. He had been teased on a daily basis at school. Now a thirty-five-year-old highly successful negotiator, he was having the last laugh. Most of those teasing kids at school were stuck in dead-end jobs, scraping up roadkill, working at the local petrol station, or doing time behind bars.

He exited at the junction, rounded the corner and saw the heavy congestion of police vehicles outside one particular house. He had arrived at the hostage scene. He pulled up along the curb and stepped out. He straightened his tie, flattened the creases on his jacket and used his fingers as a comb. He walked confidently toward the approaching cop. Ten years of successful negotiating added a swagger to one's stride.

"I'm Zagarokis," he said. "Rupert Zagarokis—the negotiator." They shook hands.

"Thank you for coming," the chubby cop said. They walked over so to be facing the house. Rupert examined its shape, size, and surroundings, so he was familiar with the hostage location. Rookie negotiators often overlook extensive observation. But Rupert thought it vitally important to know the hostage scene like the back of his hand before he even considered entering the danger zone.

"What's the deal then?" he asked, his eyes still scanning and recording information.

The cop nodded gravely. "The hostage is a seven-year-old girl."

"Jesus," Rupert said, blowing air from his cheeks.

"Blonde—her name's Poppy."

"Right."

"She had radio contact with us."

"Good."

"But her words were being monitored, we think, and now the radio's switched off."

"Okay. Where are her parents?"

"Unknown, haven't been able to contact them yet."

"They left a seven-year-old alone?"

"It would appear so."

"Christ. Is the suspect armed?" Rupert asked.

"We believe so."

"But you don't know. Fine. What are his or her demands?"

"Well...he doesn't have any."

"What?"

"That is...he hasn't demanded anything. He might be in it for the kicks, you know, psycho?"

"Mmm."

"There's one other thing I should probably show you before you enter the house," the fat cop said, gesturing for the negotiator to follow.

They walked along the pavement, passing the flashing lights of one of the police cars and reached the side gate. The cop swung it open. The sight caused Rupert's jaw to drop, his eyes to widen, and his forehead to give birth to grooves of bewilderment.

"*What the...?*"

"Bones," the cop said. "Yep...human bones."

The negotiator looked from the cop's grim face to the bones and back again.

"But...*Human bones?* I...*what the hell is going on?*"

The cop raised his eyebrows and released a lungful of air. "They were thrown out that window," he said, pointing to the small, frosted glass at the side of the house.

"I don't follow," Rupert said, shaking his head, trying to comprehend.

"Well...we believe them to be the bones of the negotiators we've been working with."

"Why?"

"Simple mathematics. None of those that have entered have come out again...so it's a valid assumption."

Rupert backed off a step. "Jesus Christ. How many have gone in?"

The cop shrugged. "We were working down the telephone directory," he said. "You're fortunate your surname starts with a Z," he said, forcing a smile.

"Lucky my name starts with a Z," Rupert parroted slowly, as he continued to back away, gaining in pace. The cop raised his arms. "*Wait!* You can't just leave."

"*The hell I can't!*" Rupert said as he spun round and marched towards his car.

"But the girl—Poppy, you can't just leave her in there!"

Rupert tried closing his ears, blocking out the cop's calls. It was hopeless. He began to see visions of the seven-year-old girl, crying, terribly scared, the psychopath holding a pistol to her head. Rupert stopped, looked up to the heavens and then shut his eyes. *Why me?*

He heard the cop's footsteps approaching.

"Please, Mr. Zagarokis, we need your help," he panted. "Poppy needs your help."

He turned and faced the cop, glancing to the dark house. "And if I don't?"

The cop shrugged. "Well...I guess we've lost. You're our last hope."

"Don't try and blackmail me—there's dozens of negotiators you could bring in."

"They're all dead...or unavailable. You're the last. Like I said...lucky

Zagarokis starts with a Z." The cop thought for a moment. "Of course, you would be a national hero if you pulled this off."

Rupert digested that information. He would be a national hero. He might even get on the Parkinson show. He liked Michael Parkinson. Hell, he might even make Jonathon Ross's show.

"Do you think I'll get on *Parkinson*?"

"Huh?"

"*Parkinson*—you know with that Michael Parkinson?"

The cop leaned back, staring at Rupert as if he were some weird alien species.

"Yeah, sure thing, you'll get to meet Michael Parkinson."

Rupert nodded stiffly. "I guess I could open negotiations. It is my job after all. And if I don't...I'll make all the newspapers for being the negotiator that left that little girl in the house with an extremely dangerous man, won't I?"

"You certainly will, sir."

Rupert strolled casually toward the house while the cop used the loudspeaker to inform the killer that another negotiator would be entering the house. Rupert Zagarokis pushed the door open.

"I'm entering the house," he called out. He stared into the house. The hall was enshrouded in shadow. He slowly stepped over the mat and walked along the hall.

"I'm walking along the hall...I have no weapons. Repeat, I have no weapons."

Rupert paused and gulped. His mouth was dry. This was different to how he usually felt before negotiating. His confidence was low—low because he was dealing with behaviour he had never before witnessed. Crazies that chopped up their hostages with axes were fine—he had dealt with them, he knew them, and he understood them; how they worked, how they thought, their logic. But this man...this thing was...was what? Was he devouring human flesh and tossing the unwanted bones out the window? Jesus, maybe he had one of those cremators. Burned the victims—his fellow negotiators—and then tossed their bones out. It made no sense; he could not identify with this man's actions.

"I'm approaching a door," he called. "I'm going to open the door. And

I repeat…I have no weapons. I am no threat to you…I just want to talk."

He opened the door. It led to another room, which was home to various stuffed animals that stood on perches, the mantelpiece, the table and a cupboard. A fox was attacking some invisible foe—its teeth bared in a snarl; an eagle lurked above his head, its sharp beak pointing down towards him. Rupert could hear the bird's squawks and imagined it soaring from its perch and pecking at his eyes, pulling them free and dragging the eyeballs away from the dark sockets.

He cringed, shivered and broke eye contact with the winged beast.

"Please help me!" called the girl.

Rupert swallowed what saliva he had in his mouth, and then gazed to another door. He held his hands out in front of him to see how much they shook. *Too much*, he thought. Sweat had begun to clot under his armpits; he could smell his own fear in the air.

"I'm coming," Rupert called in response to the girl. Then he directed his next comment to the killer: "Now, don't do anything stupid…I just want to talk with you."

He wondered if fear had been apparent in his voice. He was finding it difficult to breathe now. He reached the door. He paused and listened. At first there was nothing but then he heard the crying. A girl sobbing—Poppy's sobs.

And they were coming from behind the door.

He turned the handle and pushed it open. The door swung and he gasped as it revealed Poppy, standing with head slumped, tears spilling from her eyes. She had her arms crossed and she was shivering. Her blonde hair was sitting in golden curls on her shoulders and she wore a little blue dress.

"Poppy, I'm the negotiator. Where's the man?"

She continued to cry.

"Poppy, listen to me. Where is he?"

She slowly raised an arm and pointed. She was pointing across the room to the far side, which Rupert couldn't see due to the door's position. He swallowed. The psycho was probably in that very room.

He slowly crept in—his eyes adjusting to the dim light. He took a few more steps then saw what Poppy pointed to. A wardrobe.

"Poppy, are you hurt?"

She shook her head, still crying.

He walked over towards the wardrobe, turning to watch Poppy every few seconds. He didn't like this one bit. He had icy bursts shooting through his veins—his heart drummed painful tunes. He began to shiver as he touched the wardrobe door. He turned the knob...and the door, of its own accord, swung open. Inside was dense blackness. He could not see a thing—having to wait for his eyes to adjust as if waiting for a black fog to pass.

He heard the breaths behind him and turned slowly. Poppy stood before him, smiling wide. Her cheeks were flushed with colour and her eyes twinkling green. She lifted her hands and shoved Rupert—he tripped on the bottom of the wardrobe and fell inside. The door slammed shut....

...Darkness engulfed Rupert but he could see something materializing—it reminded him of when Alice saw the Cheshire cat appearing from thin air. And like the Cheshire cat's grin, this creature was all teeth—sharp teeth that encircled a monstrous mouth and pink tongue...

Out the front of the house, the chubby cop sat waiting for news. The flashing lights of the police vehicles lighting the night sky. Then they heard the screams.

The police officers gazed to the house. They held their heads, some turned away; cursing the fact that another negotiator had failed. The chubby cop stood and took enough steps forward so to be able to see the window from which the kidnapper hurled bones. He could hear Rupert's cries.

"*Oh, God...Christ almighty!...Please no! Bloody Hell!*"

Then the shrieks stopped. The frosted window opened and bones flew out, each thudding onto the grassy lawn.

A rookie cop came over. "What now, sir?"

The chubby cop removed his hat and wiped the sweat from his brow. "This clearly isn't working...let's go for a coffee and reassess."

The house stood in darkness. The girl was giggling. The monstrous mouth was grinning, using its tongue to dislodge the dead pieces of the negotiator from its razor teeth.

~Chess~

"And you're sure you want to play?"

"What choice do I have? I don't have your money."

Mr. Bernard gazed across the table, inhaling a long breath. "Very well." He waved for his servant to bring the board and playing pieces.

Mr. Bernard and Mr. Samson were sitting across a square pine table from one another in a small white room. There was a bright light above them, which illuminated the table. There were no shadows, no dark areas. There was nowhere to hide.

Mr. Bernard lit his pipe and sucked.

"Do you mind?" he asked, releasing smoke.

Mr. Samson shook his head, his hands in his lap clenched to stop them shaking. He took two low breaths; his foot jiggled beneath the table. Mr. Bernard stared upon him without blinking, his grey eyes analyzing beneath heavily grooved lids. His face was grey and aged; tufts of dark hair sprouted from his ears; his creased forehead rested below a high scalp line and hair that was combed neatly backwards. He sucked the pipe, released more smoke.

The servant returned and placed the chessboard on the table, wiping from it the dust with his white-gloved hand. He then slid one oval box of chess pieces to Mr. Bernard—the black box—bowed slightly and then passed the other to Mr. Samson. He then stood straight.

"That's all," Mr. Bernard said and the servant bowed, turned and left the room. The door clicked as it locked.

Mr. Bernard chewed on the end of his pipe, staring hard into Mr.

Samson's eyes—Mr. Samson wondered whether his thoughts were read, maybe Mr. Bernard delved to discover each and every move he intended to make during the game, searching for those hidden tactics.

"You're white," Mr. Bernard said. "You shall go first."

Mr. Samson fingered the white oval box then gently lifted the lid. Beneath the lid—in the holes—stood his chess pieces. Only the chess pieces were not simply pieces of wood but his family and friends. He had decided the pawns should be people he wasn't that close with. Uncle Frank for example—he had only exchanged a dozen words with him over the previous year. Frank waited expectantly; he had a grimace upon his face and wasn't too pleased at having gotten involved with this barbaric game. The small chessman lifted his knife and swiped it to show he was ready to be placed on the board. Mr. Samson lifted his uncle, careful not to smother his little face and placed him gently on the board. Once upon the chessboard, Uncle Frank looked around and got to grips with the surroundings. With his feet firmly placed on the painted wooden square, Uncle Frank bent down and touched his toes, and then swung his arms to warm his joints.

He had been terrified when woken the previous night and taken hostage by the black-cloaked man. The strangers explained that he had been one of the chosen pieces for the chess match, and that unless he accepted the invitation, they would kill him. As a pawn, however, he was equipped with merely a knife.

Mr. Samson took several more pawns from the set, all wearing the white robes. Among them, Auntie Natasha and Auntie Michelle as well as his school friends, Stuart and Melanie. Each equipped with a single knife. Then onto his close family and friends—the pieces that would be equipped with superior weapons and therefore have the best chance of survival.

The rooks were Mr. Samson's two children. Ben aged fourteen; Stephanie aged sixteen. They had been given axes and light armour. Ben raised his axe, vowing to try his best in his father's name. Mr. Samson kissed each of them then placed then on the board.

Playing the part of bishops were Mr. Samson's brother, Colin, and sister, Jacqui. They had spiked clubs as weapons. And the knights—his mother and father—were equipped with swords and shields. He placed them onto the board. He then collected the White Queen, his Queen, his beloved wife Christina. He gazed at her flowing locks of blonde hair, her blue eyes…and tears spilled down his cheeks.

"It's okay, darling," she said. "You had no choice. You knew the rules—you knew those not selected for the game would be executed," she said, thinking of those already murdered. Aunts, uncles, nieces, and nephews—all given lethal injections that very morning.

Mr. Samson kissed Christina and placed her on the board—then came the final piece, the White King. Wearing a helmet, fully armoured, equipped with both sword and dagger; the White King, the piece he himself would play, placed upon the board.

Whilst Mr. Samson had been setting up his pieces, Mr. Bernard had been doing the same. Each of his pieces wore black robes, many of their little faces badly scarred. One or two pawns were missing fingers and one an entire arm. His more powerful pieces also showed evidence of previous fierce battles—cuts and scrapes that had barely healed. Mr. Bernard's black set were stony faced, had murderous eyes, bodies that rippled with muscle—a gang of assassins, gangsters, thieves, and rapists.

The rules of the game were those of chess except one. And that was the pieces didn't simply take one another. Upon entering enemy territory, the invader would fight the defending piece in a duel to the death.

Mr. Bernard took several puffs then exhaled smoke—there was a dark twinkle in his eyes, and a smirk rose partially up into his weather worn cheeks.

Mr. Samson could feel the sweat beads escaping the pores in his skin, could feel the chill in his bones. The man across the table showed very little concern about the game, about the health of his pieces. Maybe that was because they were so well trained, because they had been in so many battles previous, or maybe he just didn't care. Wouldn't care should someone massacre his son, should one of Mr. Samson's white set impale his own mother through the heart, should his father's throat be slit.

But Mr. Samson did care, deeply, and his fingers trembled as they touched the tops of several pawns, trying to decide who to endanger first. To make things worse, the little pieces gazed at him, shaking their heads as his fingertips approached them…and Auntie Natasha broke into tears. Panic set in, its icy grip around his flesh, he began to hyperventilate, a headache cut deep into his brain.

Mr. Bernard smiled. "You must make your move," he said. "Otherwise all your pieces will be burned in the fire."

Mr. Samson nodded. He was very aware of that. He had signed the contract himself on New Year's Day. He wished he had never gotten involved with Mr. Bernard, but the opportunity was too good to turn down—so many thousands of dollars for the simple transportation of diamonds. But he had cheated Mr. Bernard, gambled the money he had stolen and lost it all. At least this way, by this game of chess, he had given some of his family and friends a fighting chance…better at least than receiving a lethal injection whilst they slept.

He lifted Uncle Frank and moved him forwards. Standing alone, Uncle Frank felt suddenly isolated. He raised his knife, waiting for the black pieces to approach.

Mr. Bernard seemed pleased the game had started and quickly made his move, his nimble fingers sweeping up one of his pawns. Uncle Frank was visibly trembling, muttering something beneath his breath.

Mr. Samson moved Melanie forward, apologizing to her in doing so. Mr. Bernard moved a pawn, Mr. Samson a pawn, Mr. Bernard a bishop, Mr. Samson a knight, Mr. Bernard a pawn, Mr. Samson a pawn, and then Mr. Bernard, sucking upon his pipe, moved a bishop across to attack Uncle Frank. Mr. Bernard leaned back in his chair, a relaxed spectator. Mr. Samson leaned forward, elbows on table, grinding his teeth, wiping sweat from his forehead.

The black piece, a man in his mid-thirties sporting a snake tattoo on his left bicep and a barbed-wire tattoo around the right, approached with a spiked club, a grin upon his face. Uncle Frank raised the knife and jabbed forward with it. The tattooed bishop easily dodged and lunged forward, swinging the spiked club, catching Frank around the head and knocking him down. Uncle Frank lay lifeless on the board. Mr. Samson thought he was already dead, but the black bishop wasn't going to take the chance and swung the spiked club once again, crushing Frank's skull in doing so. He raised his hand in victory. Mr. Bernard clapped lightly and the game continued…

The pieces now spread evenly over the board. Two apiece taken. Albeit only two pawns from Mr. Bernard's set. Mr. Samson's own son, Ben, had slain the black pawn with the missing arm. The pawn had attacked Ben, but Ben had dodged the assault and lashed the axe up into the one-armed man's throat, spilling his lifeblood and killing him instantly.

Mr. Samson's father had put up a courageous display against a young, hairy ruffian from the opposition. Being a knight, he had been able to deflect the axe blows with his shield and even managed to gash the hairy man's arm, but the man was immensely strong, got his hands around the throat of Mr. Samson's father, and strangled the life right out of him.

Mr. Samson was carefully laying more and more bodies back in the white box—so many friends and dear relatives. Each time he removed someone from the board, he would try to recall a few precious memories and say a few words of prayer.

He had also noticed Mr. Bernard was no longer smiling and a film of sweat had spread across his brow. He now sucked incessantly upon his pipe, his eyes fixed on the board, his brain ticking over. He was concentrating hard on the game and Mr. Samson thought he was worried, maybe he had never played somebody of his calibre before. It was true he hadn't played for many years, but Mr. Samson had once been the college chess captain. Though rusty, his memory served him well and he was now two pieces up. But Mr. Samson had to stay focused, the pain he felt each time one of his loved ones was killed had to be confronted and controlled. Unless he was at his best, concentrating fully, all of them would die. *Him* included.

Mr. Samson picked up the White Queen, his wife Christina, and held her for a moment—he could feel her heart's beat, her racing heart's beat. They locked eyes; in that moment they spoke more love for one another than they had ever before, and this was without words. She nodded. Mr. Samson could see the opening, could see the chance to win but he would have to put Christina in mortal danger first. He did...and waited...waited. To his relief, Mr. Bernard, his grey eyes now darting about the board, his hand shaking, his facial muscles tense, moved the knight back in defense rather than to attack the queen. But it was a flawed moved and it was checkmate. The game was up. Mr. Bernard had surely lost.

Mr. Samson checked and doubled checked and triple checked and then moved his son forward, accompanied by his wife they had the Black King at their mercy. The Black King, being in checkmate, was disarmed and his weapons vanished. He would have to defend himself with his bare hands. Mr. Samson watched as his chess pieces attacked; his son with axe and his wife with long sword and dagger. The Black King had no chance, though he did land a nasty blow to Ben's head, but a helmet protected him and he volleyed back. Then Christina's sword sliced through the weak spot under the Black King's ribs and he sagged to the ground, blood spilling.

Mr. Samson sighed, crying in joy, looking to the heavens. Then he looked to Mr. Bernard—but Mr. Bernard was smiling wide, no longer fear in his face, no longer trembling. Again, he was that emotionless pipe-smoking, mind-cutting thinker. Taking his pipe from his mouth, he leaned forward and removed the helmet from the dead king. But the face wasn't his own as it should have been—it wasn't the face of Mr. Bernard as the Black King was meant to be...but the face of Mr. Samson.

Mr. Samson's son and wife gasped across the chessboard. Christina began to sob. Mr. Samson tried to comprehend but couldn't. He looked to Mr. Bernard for the answers. Mr. Bernard took a long drag and released the smoke across the battlefield.

"I'm not particularly good at chess," he said and now removed the helmet from the White King. The face was also Mr. Samson's. Both the kings had been Mr. Samson; the game had been a cruel set-up and impossible for Mr. Samson to win.

Two Mr. Samson's upon the board—the White King alive and well, reflecting the shock on the face of the Mr. Samson that had been moving the pieces; the other, the Black King, lying on his back, hands clutching the fatal wound, surrounded by a spreading pool of blood.

"So it was safer to stack the odds in my favour," Mr. Bernard said, grinning like a demonic clown.

Mr. Samson watched as the Black King—He—breathed his last breath, his head slumping, and simultaneously the real Mr. Samson toppled from his chair, and fell dead upon the floor. The living chess pieces of his family and friends ran to the edge of the board, looking down to the dead Mr. Samson. They sobbed and cried their pain.

Mr. Bernard summoned the servant to the room, so he could remove Mr. Samson's body before the next game was due to commence.

Mr. Bernard sucked on his pipe and exhaled with a smirk.

~The Dead Man~

When his wife phoned to say he needed to come home, he assumed that she had a problem. He had been correct, but never imagined the problem would be murder.

"Sophie, what the hell happened here?" James asked, lighting a cigarette and gazing down to the body on his kitchen floor.

His wife stood shivering in shock. She had not taken her eyes from the dead man since James had arrived home, probably not since killing him.

"Sophie…"

"It—it was an accident, James—*I swear to you it was!*" she said unblinking, the colour having flushed from her face.

"*Who* is he?" James asked.

Sophie acted as if she had not heard the question, beginning to sway as if she may faint. James held her, supporting.

"I killed him," she said slowly. "I didn't mean to…but I did."

James dragged on his cigarette then exhaled with the words, "It's okay. I know it was an accident, sweetheart…but *who* is he?"

She took a deep breath. "He said…he said he was a salesman."

"Selling what? Did he have a bag?"

"I told him I wasn't interested and he burst in—grabbed me, pinned me down and told me not to make a sound otherwise he'd kill me!" Sophie began to sob as James held her, thinking things through.

"Darling, how long has he been here?"

"I don't know exactly…maybe three hours?"

"Three hours! You only called me half an hour ago."

She broke down in tears again, gasping between sobs. "I was scared—

I tried calling you but your phone was switched off. I didn't know what else to do!"

"It's okay, sweetheart. It's okay," he said, rubbing her back. He could see that blood had leaked through the man's dark brown hair and stained the kitchen floor.

"His wallet, James…it's by the breadbasket—and a key. I searched him…that's all there was."

"You checked all his pockets?"

"Yes…was that wrong?"

He shook his head, though her fingerprints would now be all over those items of course. James collected the belongings. The key had a tag on saying, *Salvation Army Hostel* and stated the address beneath. The wallet was brown leather and tatty. He opened the wallet as if it were an ancient artefact, feeling that if he were too careless, it might disintegrate in his hands. A strange odour rose from within—an odour of old age and mould. Inside he also found a driver's license. The dead man's name had been Ronald Hamilton. The photo ID bore little resemblance to the man on the kitchen floor; however, the photo was ten years old.

James slipped the card back inside and found an expired library card, an aged condom, and a train ticket from a week earlier. There was less than a pound of change in the zip compartment. James put the items away and sighed.

"What did you hit him with?" he asked, but as he finished the question, he saw the answer. The iron sat on the kitchen surface splattered with blood.

"The iron," she said, squeezing her husband tightly as he came to her side. She raised her head. "He wasn't breathing—there was no pulse…he's dead, James…*dead.*"

"Sophie, sweetheart, it's going to be okay, all right? I know what to do…just leave it to me."

She nodded, meeting eyes with her husband, as if pleading for him to save her from the repercussions of the man's premature death.

James stepped over to the carcass that he needed to move. That was all it was now, a piece of meat, albeit one with tattoos decorating the bare arms.

"Get me a wet cloth, darling," he said, rubbing his chin, plotting his evening's work. James accepted the cloth from his wife, exhaling smoke, holding the cigarette in his left hand. He started with the iron, carefully wiping. The blood resisted his efforts at first, having already partially dried.

"What else did he touch?" James asked. Sophie said the door, both the outside to push it open, and the inside handle to shut it…and the lock, the man had flicked across the lock. James took care of the aforementioned areas, careful first to make sure nobody was watching. They lived in a busy city street. That would probably be a blessing, for people were too busy minding their own business to notice minor details the police might check.

"Where else?" James asked, as he rinsed the cloth under the tap.

Sophie had her hand over her mouth, taking long thoughtful breaths, still understandably in shock. She tried her best not to look at the body, but her eyes insisted on wandering each time James asked her to speak.

"I don't know…I think that's all. We struggled in the kitchen before I hit him." The memory of this seemed to knock the wind from her. She staggered, leaning her weight against the kitchen surface, eyes closed.

James scanned the room for any further clues that the man had entered their house. He could see none—he would however have a more thorough search later, but first he must dispose of the body.

He walked into the unlit living room and peered out through the net curtain. It was dark outside—that was good news. Nevertheless, a busy street tends to be busy always, except perhaps in the middle of the night. James thought about that, perhaps he could wait until the early hours of the morning before disposing of the body, although, if he were seen doing so, how would he explain going out in the middle of the night…and, of course, having a corpse for company. Less people being about would mean he was more conspicuous. Disposing of a body in the dead of night was expected, to move it at 8 p.m. while a steady flow of traffic passed, was not.

He stubbed out the last of his cigarette in an ashtray then immediately lit another. He needed to be fully relaxed to make this work. He turned to see his wife covering the man's face with a towel. He would have to dispose of that too.

"Sophie, if anyone should ask, a salesman did come to the door, but you said you weren't interested. He then asked if he could use the toilet. You agreed and he did so, leaving no more than two minutes later."

Sophie had walked into the darkened living room, head slumped, arms crossed by her stomach, looking small and frail in the dim light. "You don't think we should call the police?" she asked, in almost a whisper.

James shook his head. "I fear we have left that too long. They might not believe your story now. Three hours is a long time to wait before contacting the police."

Sophie's eyes widened. *"But I'm innocent—I swear I've told you the truth, James!"*

James had other reasons for not informing the police. Five years earlier, two years before he had met Sophie, he had spent eighteen months in prison for assault. James made a living from smuggling jewellery from abroad, India in particular, and the man he employed to get the jewellery through customs, had tried blackmailing him in return for his continued silence. James had not meant the incident to go so far; it was supposed to be a warning. Things had gotten out of hand. In a struggle, the blackmailer whacked his head and slipped into a coma. If the police were to turn up at James's door now, and if they discovered this man in his kitchen had been dead for three hours, it would raise suspicions. The fact that he had nothing to do with the killing was irrelevant. They would check his criminal record and convince themselves he *had* killed the man and then asked his wife to cover for him. He was glad Sophie had not called the police. He was better off dealing with this himself.

James looked over to the dead man on his kitchen floor, towel covering the face. The man had carried a lot of weight in life; in death, he would be even heavier with the arrival of rigor mortis. This could be a tricky business indeed.

"James...what are we going to do?" Sophie asked, lighting a cigarette of her own, taking a long drag. She seemed to have calmed herself, but still she trembled.

"Don't you worry. I'll get rid of him. I just need you to remember the story about him coming here, using the bathroom, and then leaving."

"Who's going to ask?"

"Hopefully no one, but let's be ready for all eventualities." James collected a blanket from the airing cupboard and returned to the kitchen. He placed the blanket on the floor and then rolled the body inside.

Sophie watched. "What are you going to do with him?"

James had the body concealed in the blanket, and had dragged it across the tiled floor so he could mop up the blood that had leaked from the head.

"Don't you remember?" he asked, stubbing out his cigarette.

She frowned, running her fingers back through her hair, shaking her head.

James smiled. "Don't you remember we once had a conversation about whether we would commit a murder if we knew we could get away with it? Neither of us was sure, but you especially thought it through, having had a pretty awful day at work. You said you'd love to kill your boss."

"James, I didn't mean that!"

"Yes, I know, but we discussed how we would do it if we did. I gave you my theory on the best way of committing the perfect murder and then disposing of the body."

She nodded. "I remember now."

Sophie waited in the kitchen while her husband went out front and reversed the car into the driveway. He would have preferred to reverse it into the garage, but there was not the room with all the junk already in there, it would take too long to clear it all out. He returned with key in hand, smiled, and then went through the garage door. She could not help thinking he was almost enjoying himself. As if the undertaking of body disposal was a form of amusement, mental stimulation. He returned carrying a petrol canister.

"What's that for?" she asked. "You're going to *burn* him?"

James nodded. "I've changed my mind about the perfect crime. I think it's better to burn than bury...that way I can get rid of all traces hopefully."

Sophie looked at the bulky six-foot lump on the kitchen floor, wrapped in a blanket. "It seems so..." she said. "*Burning* someone."

"He won't feel a thing, sweetheart. He's dead."

"But won't someone see the flames?"

"I'll make sure I'm well away from civilization before I do it. Now, give me a hand with him…he's too heavy to carry alone."

She rested her cigarette carefully in one of the ashtray grooves and cautiously approached the dead man.

"Take his ankles and lift on three—go on, quickly," insisted James, as she bent down, shuddering as her fingers touched the skin around his ankles.

"Have you got a grip?"

She nodded.

"One—two—three—*lift*." Sophie exhaled as they lifted. They ambled over to the door, James heading backwards. He stopped and glanced out into the street, waiting for a woman walking a dog to pass. He took a step out onto the doormat, only to have to shift the dead man back through the doorway as a cyclist rode by. James waited another few seconds, scanning house windows for nosy people keeping an eye on the street. Satisfied they were safe, or at least as safe as they could be, James ushered them out to the car.

"Quickly now!"

The boot of the car was already open, the back seats down because he had made a delivery the previous day. There was plenty of space. They slid the body in and James slammed the boot. When he did remove the corpse from his car, he would be alone, and it would be easier to drag it from one of the back doors.

"Darling, now go inside and give the kitchen a proper clean. Oh, almost forgot," he said as he strode back into the house, returning with the man's wallet, key, and the petrol canister. "I'll be gone at least a couple of hours," he said, kissing her gently on the cheek. "It's going to be okay," he insisted again, then jumped into the driver's seat and started the engine.

Within fifteen minutes, James had left the city behind, heading along a road towards the countryside. He inhaled thoughtfully on his cigarette, doing a steady sixty miles per hour. The last thing he needed was for the police to pull him over—especially with his current load.

James blew the smoke ahead of him—it dispersed against the glass. He flicked his wipers on to remove dead bugs from the windshield, and then took another drag of the cigarette, gazing in his rearview mirror to the blanket-shrouded corpse. James smiled, almost laughed. Had this day really happened, or was he to awaken at any moment?

He thought things were going smoothly. The man, Ronald Hamilton, appeared to be a Mr. Nobody. He had lived at the *Salvation Army Hostel*, had less than a pound in his wallet, hadn't been carrying any cash cards or credit cards, and his library card had expired. James was confident that this Ronald Hamilton wouldn't be missed too badly. He would be surprised if anyone came looking for him. Most likely, when a man like this goes missing, people assume he has just wandered off to some new destination, or perhaps even killed himself, as he had nothing to live for. In fact, creating what looked like a suicide may have been a better idea. He could have thrown the body over a cliff for someone to find. He didn't think anyone would question it. Unfortunately, James had left his fingerprints all over the man. Now he had little choice but to burn or bury him—burning, he thought, the more conclusive.

As he flicked open the ashtray compartment and disposed of the dog-end of his cigarette, he noticed a police car pull out from a side road. It was directly behind him and closing. James released an exaggerated sigh, and took a deep gulp to replace it.

"Stay calm now, James, keep your nerve." The words did little to comfort him, his eyes darting between the road ahead and the police car in his mirrors. It had closed to within striking distance. In fact, if he suddenly broke, say for example if a deer ran across the road, he thought the police car would ram into his rear end.

James was convinced that at any moment the blue lights would flash on and the siren would blare into the night. He was not doing anything wrong as a driver, but if the cops were bored, they might pull him over for a routine check.

James continued ahead, both hands on the steering wheel, constantly checking his speed, his position in the road, and anything else that could result in them stopping him. He desperately wanted another cigarette but dared not release the steering wheel. Trees bordered the road as he travelled further away from the city—trees that seemed to squeeze the life right out of him, causing claustrophobia.

The sight of an approaching roundabout gave him something new to concentrate on. He wanted to take a left, but thought he would take a right then double back if the police car didn't follow. He had to hope the police went straight over. *They did.* James gasped in relief, laughed, and then lit a cigarette. After a mile, he turned on a farm track and returned to the roundabout, first making sure the police car was nowhere in sight, before continuing.

Twenty minutes later James turned off along a narrow road, then took another left and headed along a track, which at this hour he assumed nobody else would be using.

He stopped the car and thought things through one last time. It would be silly to make a careless error at this stage.

James climbed out from the car, taking the petrol canister with him into the trees. He stood in silence for a minute just to make sure nobody was about. Apart from an owl, he appeared to be alone.

He found a clearing in the trees and allocated it to be the fire site. He began to collect sticks. Finding that there were not enough, he headed back towards the car where he had seen some dead wood scattered about. When James heard whispers, he was sure his ears deceived him. A trick of the wind perhaps? He gingery walked toward the car, starting to fear someone might actually be in the forest with him, perhaps taking the dog for a walk. The time was only 9 p.m. It was far from improbable that somebody might be there, even in this remote woodland.

The rear of his car faced him as he listened. There it was again...definite talking. James's heart was in his mouth. Then he saw something that shocked him to the core. Through the car's rear window, he saw a head rise, then lower again. He blinked stupidly, stunned. As the head lifted again, James ducked. A gust of wind passed, and then he could hear the voice. But it was not comprehensible, so he edged nearer to his car, keeping low. When he reached the back bumper he stopped, listened.

"It's going to plan," said the voice of the dead man. "He's gone to collect firewood...listen, I have to go—he could be back any minute."

Silence followed a slight shifting inside the car. James remained crouched, running the information through his head. Who the hell did this son of a bitch think he was? James saw no option now but to go through with the plan anyway. Crouching, he carefully walked from the car, until concealed by trees. From there he was able to release the breath he had been saving. His eyes fixed on the car but there was no movement now. He had better return soon though, otherwise the dead man might get suspicious.

James finished collecting the wood, forming an admirable pile. He soaked the wood in half a canister of petrol, took a deep breath, and then approached the car.

He opened the back door, hesitating only a second before taking hold of the ankles that poked out of the blanket. James dragged the man from the car—as he did, the man's head hit the woodland soil with a thump.

James pulled the weight to the petrol-doused wood, and then paused, gazing down to the blanket-hidden body. He watched, expecting any moment for the man to shift, to make *his* move, whatever that might be.

Then he did so. He couldn't tell what the man was doing, but noticed movement under the blanket. James grabbed for the petrol canister, pouring the contents over the man. Then as quickly as he could, he found his matches and struck one—at that moment, the man in the blankets coughed and groaned.

"*Jesus fucking Christ!*" James yelled in mock surprise.

"Where am I?" came the muffled reply.

"*I thought you were dead!*" James claimed as a gust of wind killed the flame of his match.

"*No! No, get me out of here!*"

James smiled, positioning a second match, ready to light. The man apparently realised James was one-step ahead in the game of death. He struggled amongst the blanket, trying to free himself. James struck the match, but applied too much pressure and it snapped—he fumbled for another, panicking himself now, dropping the box and spilling its contents on the ground.

Ronald was free of the blanket, brandishing a knife—it glinted in the light of the moon. James lunged for the metallic petrol canister and before the dead man could slice his throat, James had cracked the canister over the man's head. Ronald dropped onto his back, dazed but still conscious. James repeatedly smashed the canister over his head until something popped. Panting, James admired his handiwork. The dead man was now most certainly dead, and there would be no encore of the first miraculous resurrection.

Having regained his breath, James yanked the body up onto his pile of wood. He searched the man's pockets and found his mobile phone. He had no other belongings, other than the knife that lay on a bed of fallen leaves.

James collected the knife and pressed the blade back inside so it was easier to handle. He then selected the *Phone Book* option on the dead man's phone, scrolling through the *A's* and *B's* and *C's* until reaching the letter *S*. He found the name Sophie. He checked the number. It was the number for his wife's mobile phone. It was a bitter pill to swallow for James, but he did so. He sent his wife a text message from Ronald's phone.

I've done it. All went to plan. But need your help. Follow the Pilbury road for 1 mile, then take track on right. You will see the car. Bring a shovel. I need help digging the grave.

He selected send.

Message sent.

James recalled his wife's face an hour earlier, when he had mentioned their previous discussion about disposing of a body. She, of course, pretended it had slipped her mind. She had known that he wouldn't contact the police, not with his previous conviction, and she knew how he would get rid of the body, having already told her in that earlier conversation—his blueprint on murder, corpse disposal, and escaping detection. She must have planned *his* murder with this Ronald Hamilton. She had sent her husband off with the man who was merely the stand-in corpse, playing James's role until the final Act. In that closing scene, it would be *he*, and not Ronald, she envisaged roasting on the fire.

He remembered his wife's astonishment at the news that he would be *burning* and not *burying*. Presumably, Sophie had based her plans with Ronald around the idea of a burial. It would have been much easier for Ronald to climb from a partially filled grave and to cut James's throat, than it would be to rise from a blazing fire.

James lit a cigarette, tossing the match onto his bonfire. Flames ignited instantly, engulfing the body in orange heat. He sucked at his cigarette, and then exhaled. Ronald's phone bleeped. James checked. It was a new message. It was from his wife.

I'm on my way.

James slipped the phone into his pocket. He took another drag on his cigarette, smiled grimly, and then went to hide behind the nearest tree.

Sophie headed up the lane, stopping the car behind James's car. She stepped out, shut the door and slowly walked towards the fire. Her eyes transfixed by its glow as she neared.

"Where are you?" she asked, watching the body in the fire burn. "I have the shovel."

There was no response so she walked closer, turning her head away as the night breeze brought the smoke into her face. She closed her eyes to prevent the ash getting in them. When she opened her eyes again, she saw the figure step out from behind a tree.

James smiled, shook his head and then sighed. He pressed the button on the knife and the blade shot out. "Nice try," he said, walking over so to be between the fire and his wife. She took a step away, as he asked, "Why?"

Sophie swallowed.

"Tell me why and I might spare your worthless life."

She shrugged, looking beyond her husband to Ronald, whose corpse sizzled in the flames, now unrecognisable.

"Money," she said. "Do you need more?"

James didn't. He looked from the sharp blade to his wife and then back to the blade. He could see the reflection of the flames in its shine. "Get the shovel," he said.

Sophie nodded, turned, then suddenly whipped round as she pulled the gun from her belt. She smiled. "No...I think you should get the shovel, darling."

James stared upon the gun in her hand. "How did you know?"

Sophie walked forwards, gesturing for her husband to drop the knife. He did so.

"It was simple," she said. "Ronald is...I mean *was* illiterate. He can neither read nor write, so how could he have written me a text message?"

James sighed, looking to the burning corpse, and then to Sophie. "You chose him over me?" he asked.

"I chose his life over yours, yes. It didn't have to be this way, darling, but you never were fair with your money. I would have thought as your beloved wife I'd deserve at least half of what you earned."

"I do give you half of all the money," he lied.

Sophie smiled, holding off a laugh as she removed a folded piece of paper from her pocket. "Need I open it?" she asked. "This is a letter from a certain Mr. Mukesh of Jaipur, India, promising you the sum of one million pounds on the successful smuggling of gems into London. I know only too well that you did get the gems to London, as I helped you. You told me you were to be paid fifty thousand…that's a fair bit short of a million, isn't it?"

"You can have your half," James said. "But I suppose you'd prefer the whole lot with me dead?"

Sophie chose not to respond. She told James to collect the shovel and then to start digging a hole. James got to work, shovelling soil to one side, his sweat from the exertion glistening in the light of the now dying fire.

"I'll give you the million anyway…there's no need to kill me," James said, as he continued to dig. "How deep do you want the hole?" he asked.

"Just keep digging until I tell you to stop," she said. "I'd feel safer having the money *and you dead*…it eliminates the possibility of revenge, don't you think?"

James chose not to respond on this occasion. "Who are you involved with?" he asked. "I don't believe you just happened to bump into Ronald on the street and came up with the plan to murder me." James wiped his brow and waited for Sophie to speak.

"*Keep digging!*" she yelled, aiming the gun at his forehead.

"Okay," he said casually. He continued until his intended grave was a couple of feet deep. He climbed out, leaned upon the vertical shovel and lit a cigarette. He exhaled. "You realise you've left yourself with somewhat of a dilemma?"

"What's that?" she said with her finger ready to pull the trigger.

"Well, if you had read my will, you would know that you only get my money when I die."

"So?"

He smiled, taking a drag on the cigarette. "If you bury me, how will you prove that I'm dead and not merely missing? My will clearly states that only after an absence of ten years will I be presumed dead, and only then will you get my money. If you bury me and can't prove I'm dead, you've got ten long years to wait until you get your hands on my riches."

Sophie tried to conceal her horror, but she could feel herself shaking with anger. "An anonymous phone call ought to do it," she said. "I'll say I was tipped off that you'd been killed and buried out here."

James grinned, shaking his head. "What about the trail you've left?" he asked.

"What trail?"

"Car tracks, fingerprints, hairs that have fallen from your head…do I need to go on?"

Sophie stared wild-eyed towards her husband, hating him even more than she had previously for that smirk on his face. He thought he was so damn smart! But he might be right—what the hell did she know about the world of forensic science? This was not supposed to be her role in this operation; she paid Ronald to take care of her husband. She glanced to the burning remains of the man she felt had failed her.

"The only way either of us is going to get out of this mess, is if we work together…hide the evidence and move on," he said, still leaning on the shovel. "Let's scrape up Ronald's remains and bury them. I'll give you your half of the money and we can go our separate ways. What do you think?"

Sophie shook her head; not as a response to her husband's proposal but because her thoughts were so tangled and she wanted to unravel them. She just could not think clearly. She nodded. "Okay, but I'll keep hold of the gun."

James nodded and began pounding the fire with the shovel, trying to extinguish those last flames. Having done that, he raked Ronald's bones into the hole, and started covering it over with soil. Within half an hour, he had finished.

They returned to the cars. Sophie kept the gun pointed at him throughout.

"Are you ever going to put the gun down?" James asked.

"I haven't decided yet," she said.

James started his engine first, watching Sophie in his rearview mirror. He slowly pulled away while glancing over to where he had buried his would-be killer. Sophie followed close behind in her car—still she held the gun aloft.

They headed out onto the main road, the only two cars on the road. James smiled as he lit a cigarette, gazing at his wife in the mirror. Who could have guessed things would have turned out as they had? He shook his head as his foot pressed down on the accelerator. As he expected, Sophie copied his every move, presumably afraid he would shoot off in the distance and leave her behind. She was near enough to shoot him in the back of the head. In fact, she was too close—far too close. This would be easier than James had anticipated.

He waited for a bend in the road, taking a final look at his wife, before slamming his foot on the brake. The car skidded, but he had the driving skill to fight the car's attempts to fly off the road. His wife, he knew, would not be so competent. Her car slid across the tarmac as she tried to avoid a collision, clipping the back of James' car in the process and giving him a nasty jolt. He had only just recovered from the impact as his wife's car sailed from the road and into the woodland. The noise of crushed metal and the engine roaring might have woken the dead.

James undid his seatbelt and went to observe the wreckage. His wife's car was upright but looked as though it had been to the crushers. He climbed down the slope to the trees and went to the mangled car. Sophie's face rested on the steering wheel, but she looked anything but peaceful with blood flowing from her head.

James checked her pulse. She had one, though only faint. She was alive, but he needn't be a qualified doctor to know she wouldn't be for much longer—not with the amount of blood she was losing.

James sighed, noticing the shovel on the back seat. He had little choice now but to dig a second hole. He took hold of the shovel and walked over to the trees, searching for suitable spot for a shallow grave.

END

Printed in the United States
56131LVS00009B/3